DISTANT
MEMORY

MAUREEN A. MILLER

DISTANT MEMORY

memory:
something remembered from the past; a recollection

reincarnation:
the rebirth of a soul in a new body

PROLOGUE

The car jostled over the rutted dirt lane, where not even a pearl of sunlight could squeeze through the dense canopy of trees. Ahead, a ghostly mist marked an exit to the shady funnel.

Emerging into sunshine was painful at first. A blink or two to acclimate revealed a lush clearing carved out of a stockade of pine trees. The rectangular plot was flanked by a split-rail fence, and at the end of the unpaved lane sat a two-story farmhouse.

Approaching on foot, the scrape of shoes against flagstone amplified in the crisp forsythia-scented air.

The front door towered just steps away.

So tall.

So very tall.

Dark knots speckled the wooden surface.

A hand reached up and curled into a fist, preparing to knock…

CHAPTER ONE

Hollie Musgrave woke with a start, her hand still fisted. A quick glance at the clock on the nightstand read 2:17 AM. Seven minutes had passed since the last dream, and about eight minutes before that.

All the same dream.

All ending at that door.

Swinging her feet off the bed, she moved on auto-pilot to the medicine cabinet. Over-the-counter pills were not going to make the dreams go away, though.

Why now?

Why had they returned?

It had been over two decades since the same dream had assaulted her with such frequency. Back then, she could crawl into bed with her parents—into a sanctuary that would temper the visions.

There wasn't anything particularly scary about them. A tree-canopied road. A large fenced-in yard. A rustic house. There were no monsters.

Still, she always woke with the same apprehension.

"You're too old to be spooked," she chided the image in the mirror.

The garish glare of the bathroom light revealed smudges of fatigue beneath charcoal brown eyes, and any traces of Florida sunshine had waned from her cheeks. Of course, the mirror was rarely flattering at 2:30 in the morning.

Hollie swept dark bangs away from her face and massaged her temples to ease the pounding.

One flick of the light switch and her reflection disappeared.

"Trouble sleeping again?"

Hollie stared at the black grounds speckling the surface of her Styrofoam coffee cup.

"A little," she shrugged.

"I worry about you," Maryann Baumann nagged.

Hollie smiled at the silver-haired woman sitting opposite her in the lobby of their condominium building. Maryann Baumann was her best friend. Maryann was eighty-one-years-old. If that said something about Hollie's social life, so be it.

The only affordable waterfront rental she could find in the Tampa area was this building predominantly occupied by senior citizens. The limited view of the Clearwater intracoastal waterway was an indulgence she couldn't resist.

Maryann Baumann had been her next-door neighbor for the past three years. They lived in back-to-back corner units on the third floor with views of the causeway bridge and the Clearwater Beach lights in the distance.

"Florence!" Maryann called with a slight German accent. A thin wrist wrapped in pearls waved in exaggeration. "Come over here. Hollie is having the dreams again."

Shrinking back into the plastic upholstered chair, Hollie sought to hide behind the potted yucca plant.

Florence bustled over from the laundry room and plopped down on the loveseat next to Maryann. Her unnaturally red hair was scored with a white skunk line along the roots.

"The farmhouse?"

Nodding, Hollie ducked her head. There were no secrets in the Harbor Breeze building. At times it was a curse, but more often it was comforting. Hollie's mother had passed away when she was just eleven, and her father was now enjoying retirement in Arizona, leaving her with no family but the curious and delightful Harbor Breeze community.

"You should see someone," Florence echoed Maryann's declaration.

"See someone?" Hollie raised her eyebrows. "For *dreams*?"

Not waiting for their response, she flipped her phone up to check the time. It was only 7:30. "I'm late for work."

"No, you're not," Maryann scolded. "And yes, you *should* see someone for dreams. A counselor. A psycho-somezing."

Hollie clutched the phone between her knees, staring at her jeans. There was no need for her to dress up today. She was heading to the stadium for a publicity shoot with the NFL team and a group of special-needs athletes. At her feet was her camera case, ready to go. She stooped to retrieve it, but her hand wavered at Florence's next decree.

"Reincarnation."

Hollie's gaze shot up.

"That's a tad excessive, don't you think?" She forced a chuckle.

Maryann's coral lips sucked in and she looked like she might make the sign of the cross.

"Really, Flo. That was certainly not my first thought."

Florence flicked slightly jaundiced eyes back and forth between them and then her head jerked at the sound of a sliding glass door opening in the foyer. If it was the Meals on Wheels delivery, this conversation would be history and Florence would latch onto the volunteer.

Unfortunately, it was just a delivery of newspapers secured by twine.

"Oh, here comes Frank." Florence looked past the deliveryman toward a woman who was rolling her walker through the entryway.

Frank was actually Francine Lentine—a robust figure with a bag of donuts cradled between the legs of the buggy.

"Frank!" Florence called out loud enough to guide a ship in from a storm. "Hollie's having those dreams again."

Francine's head snapped like a dog hearing the word *treat*. One wheel squeaked as she changed trajectory of the walker and ambled over to them.

"It's those late dinners," Francine chastised as she plopped down into a seat. "If I eat after five, I'm plagued with dreams. Of course, mine usually include a pool boy, not a farmhouse." She winked a lid caked in blue eyeshadow.

"She had the same dreams when she was a child," Florence recited from previous powwows such as this. "And then they just stopped. I think she is recalling a past life."

Hollie closed her eyes and squeezed her fingers at the top of her nose. A whopper of a headache was brewing.

A memory of her mother sitting at the kitchen table with the sleeves of her robe spilling across the surface replaced the engrossed voices around her.

"*We've lived in Florida since you were born, Hermey.*"

Hermey was a nickname her parents had coined for her when she was a toddler. It came from the *independent* dentist elf in Rudolph the Red-nosed Reindeer. Hollie was just as independent. If her mother tried to cut her food up for her, Hollie's face would turn beet red and her little fists would pump in frustration. She never wanted help. She always wanted to do it herself.

"What you're describing doesn't sound like the Gulf coast. Maybe you saw it in a movie—at school?"

"No," Hollie would shake her head and frown. *"This is different. I can—"* she hesitated, *"—smell it."*

A gleam of collusion sparked in Ginger Musgrave's brown eyes.

"Maybe it's reincarnation."

"What's reen-carashon?"

"They say when you're real young you can remember your former life. But then you grow up and forget about it."

Indeed, a year or two later the dreams had stopped and any memory of them had lapsed.

"Look ladies," Hollie grabbed the handle of her case, "I really have to be going. I've got some staging for the event to get started on."

"Maybe you'll bring home a football player tonight." Maryann raised thinning eyebrows.

"Oh!" Francine clapped. "Bring us all one."

Maryann's eyebrows fell. "Stop being selfish," she scolded. "Hollie is zee one who needs za boyfriend."

Francine clamped her lips tight and then nodded. "True. True. I don't know how they don't go crazy over you. You know, I had a hot body like yours once upon a time. What are those jeans, a size 6?"

Usually they would have been a size 6, but she wasn't eating well. Today she had on a leftover pair of size 4's. And regardless of whether or not she had a boyfriend, this intent group would then decree that the boyfriend wasn't good enough and that she needed a *different* boyfriend.

Basically, in the eyes of these lovely ladies, Hollie always needed something.

In the eyes of this family, she deserved the best.

Feeling a touch of moisture creep into her gaze, she climbed to her feet and stooped over to hug each woman in turn.

"Okay ladies, I'm off."

"What time will you be back?" Maryann asked.

The invasion of privacy should have aggravated her, but it didn't. The women fawned over her. They would literally stage a vigil for her return, and if she was five minutes late they would call the police.

"I've got a dinner function with the crew so probably not until nine or so."

"A *dinner* function." Flo's eyes widened. The ladies exchanged knowing glances.

Hollie snorted and left through the sliding glass doors with a smile on her face.

CHAPTER TWO

Cold air blew across her bare shoulders. Hollie delved deeper under the sheets to escape the air conditioning. It had been a long day. The shoot went well, with the athletes and children interacting in a way that tugged at her heart.

One athlete in particular, the kicker, paid close attention to her to the point that he received several elbow-jabs from his teammates. Hollie was flattered, but, truth-be-told, she was a justified introvert—even at the ripe old age of thirty-two. It was the reason she was *behind* the camera and not in front of it. Granted, there had been dates over the years, even an eight-month-long relationship. But, that guy finally decided he wanted something more flamboyant. *Flamboyant* came in the guise of a cheerleading coach.

Hollie drifted into a fitful sleep defending the fact that she wasn't *flamboyant*.

The door loomed ahead.

A pocket of gnats flitted before her face. She swatted at them and hesitated, looking up at the flat face of the house. Brown. The house was brown. There wasn't much else she noticed because she was walking toward the door.

That tall door.

She climbed the first step and felt the coarse iron rail under her fingertips—

—fingertips that curled up into a fist.

The air conditioning still churned, but the sheets had been tossed aside, one tangled around her leg like a python. Hollie kicked herself loose and sat up, reaching for her cell phone on the nightstand. Snatching it up, she sat cross-legged, her back stiff against the headboard.

She typed one word in the search bar.

HYPNOSIS.

There were several online self-hypnosis videos that claimed to aid in memory recall. After the third video of spinning wheels and creepy voices, Hollie set the phone aside.

A quick glimpse at the clock had her reaching for her jeans.

6:18 AM

Another night had passed with very little sleep.

"So, there are a few people in Tampa that offer memory retrieval through hypnotherapy," Hollie mentioned.

Maryann sat in a quilted bathrobe, her white anklet socks visible beneath the kitchen table. She frowned mid-sip over her porcelain tea cup.

"Hollie." With her accent it sounded more like *Hole-lay*. "If it's really bothering you that much, do what you have to, but—" she set the cup down. "Just be careful."

"I want to see if there is more to this dream. A street name. A house number. Something I can investigate."

Hollie swept a hand through her tousled hair, taking a moment to rub her fingers over the pain behind her forehead.

Fool! Dreams were stories. Illusory movie reels. They didn't contain specific street names and house numbers.

Maryann primly adjusted the gap in her robe. "I'd just be worried about one of zose hypnotists having control of my mind. Zey might ask for your bank account number or somezing wizout you even knowing it."

Hollie concealed a grin behind a lock of hair.

"That's a myth," she said. "As I have read, you're actually in full control under hypnosis. You will only answer the questions you want to." Reading Maryann's skepticism, she continued. "A hypnotherapist is just a guide, helping you dig deeper into your mind—ummm, like a navigator."

Unconvinced, Maryann shoved a plate full of cookies across the table. It didn't matter what time of day or night Hollie came over. That plate of Vienna Fingers would be there.

"I can go wiz you," Maryann offered.

Glancing across the doily-covered table at the woman with bobby pins securing white curls for the night, Hollie marveled at the glowing skin. A regimen of cold cream and sunscreen voided many of the wrinkles on Maryann's face. Shrewd blue eyes stared back at Hollie as pale lips pressed over the edge of her cup.

"You don't have to do that," Hollie answered automatically.

A gray eyebrow arched in retort.

"Well, let's see if I even find someone," Hollie added hastily. "You know I'll change my mind a thousand times before I schedule anything."

"Zat much is true." Maryann set her cup down, a puddle of tea pooling in the saucer. Gnarled fingers smoothed out the doily. "You know, if your mind was preoccupied zese dreams might go away."

Tucking her head, Hollie knew where the subject was heading.

"It's been a long time since—Mark."

And *bam*, the M-word.

Usually Maryann preceded the name with such harsh adjectives as *louse*—or even the dreaded, *foul ball*.

"Yes, Mark was a mistake," Hollie admitted.

A big mistake.

"But I'm not ready to jump back into the dating pool. One day I'll dip my toes back into the shallow end."

Reaching for the remote, Maryann turned on the early morning news.

"You've been saying zat for over a year now. Wouldn't a husband take your mind off some pesky dreams?"

A husband was an outlandish and impractical notion. Not after Mark decided that the cheerleading coach had more to offer him. But, Mark aside, it was the pesky dreams that no one seemed to understand. Innocuous as they were, their frequency and veracity were destroying her sleep and chipping away at everyday functionality. Even now, the television screen in the living room was blurry until she ground her palms into her eyes.

"One day," she answered.

It was an evasive defense she used religiously. So frequently that Maryann pursed her lips into a crooked smile.

It was tempting to counter with, *what about you?* But Maryann's husband, Henry, had died when they were both still young. That left Maryann with no children of her own and no incentive to find another man. To her, there would never be another Henry.

A nephew took care of some of Maryann's affairs, but he was married with children—children she only received pictures of. Hollie and Maryann were orphans together in this coastal establishment.

"Well zen, while you're off to work I will start making some calls to local counsellors."

Eeek! That was a scary notion. Hollie could imagine Maryann discussing and enhancing every gritty detail of her situation.

"For heaven's sake, I'm not that bad."

Maryann reached for another cookie. "Drink more coffee." She waved her hand at the cup. "*Lots* more."

"Give me a big smile, Benny."

A cute boy with choppy brown bangs and a few missing teeth beamed up at Hollie. He wore the distinctive red and pewter jersey of the Tampa Bay football team. One arm was circled around a football, while the other sleeve hung empty.

Around her were other children with similar disabilities. From their enthusiastic interaction with the NFL players, you'd never suspect they were challenged.

This was Hollie's favorite part of the job. Working on events with children of all walks of life, getting to experience a day with their favorite sports hero. Benny was staring up at Colton Brooks, a hulk of a man busily signing autographs.

"Do you think Colton will sign my football?"

Hollie's smile faltered ever so slightly. Colton had an ego larger than his 300-pound physique. She'd had run-ins with him in the past. Evidently hating the PR aspect of his career, he was never very cooperative. She glanced up and met the eye of Benny's mother who was locked in conversation with a group of mothers, all tapping fingers on their cellphone cameras. The woman nodded her consent.

"I don't know," Hollie replied, "but let's go ask him."

She wanted to place herself there to soothe any sort of rejection.

"Mr. Brooks?" she addressed on behalf of Benny. "Benny here wondered if you'd sign his football."

Gray eyes under bulky eyebrows stared at her a little longer than necessary before the gaze passed her shoulder to the lineup of pom-pom wielding young women posing with a group of kids.

Jerking his eyes from them down to the young boy, his lip curled up in some semblance of a smile.

"I usually charge $600 for an autograph."

Benny's face fell. He tucked the football under his armpit and looked up at Hollie with sad eyes. "I don't have $600," he whispered.

If she could, she would give Colton Brooks an uppercut into that square jaw and send him flying into the cardboard likeness of himself three feet away. Almost all of the players she'd ever worked with were actually very sweet. Particularly the ones who attended these charity events—they usually had big hearts.

"Just kidding, kid," Colton laughed, but it was a sound you might shrink from.

Benny gave Hollie a quick look. She nodded encouragingly, vigilant of Colton's actions—her fist at the ready. But the beefy man carefully extracted the football from under Benny's arm, scratched across it with a pen and handed it back over. Benny grabbed the ball and tucked it back into his armpit.

"Thank you, Mr. Brooks!" he shouted. Then, with a beam cast at Hollie he scurried back to his mother's awaiting arms.

"Cute kid," Colton mused at her side. "If you like kids."

Hollie sighed and stepped away from him with a mumbled excuse. Maryann had visions of Hollie hooking up with a professional athlete, but working with them was her *job*, not her life. Actually, she had no idea what type of man she wanted to hook up with, but someone in the spotlight—that just wasn't for her.

Her wrist vibrated.

Hollie glanced down at the message on her watch. *Found doctor.*

One thing she had been diligent to do was to teach Maryann how to text from her phone. Sometimes the texts were tough to decipher, but if there should ever be an emergency, Hollie felt better knowing that Maryann could call or text her. Maryann's nephew had also rigged her up with some sort of Life Alert necklace, but he lived too far away to react in time. He was aware of how much Hollie helped out, and linked her as a contact to that system.

Smirking at this text, she could only imagine what doctor Maryann had located. Images of an elderly man with thick bifocals came to mind as she packed up her equipment.

It was worth a try, though.

Anything was worth a try for a solid night's sleep.

CHAPTER THREE

A young blonde woman with glasses and a ponytail sat with her hands folded over her lap. She was a certified clinical hypnotherapist, not a licensed medical doctor as Maryann had presumed. It didn't matter to Hollie one way or another. At the moment, she was locked in an internal debate on whether she wanted to bolt out of this office or not.

"I can see you're anxious," the woman cooed.

Hollie almost snorted. The result was a quick inhale of vanilla and coconut. She searched for the source and found two candles near the window. Candles were one of her weaknesses. Anytime she saw them out in a store she had to stop and sniff each one—usually resulting in an impulsive purchase.

The scent soothed her more than the woman's calm demeanor.

"Tell me what it is you hope to achieve with hypnotherapy?"

"Sleep," she joked with forced mirth.

Patience clamped the therapist's lips tight until Hollie was forced to elaborate.

"Details," Hollie dragged the word from her defenses. "I have a dream—a recurring dream—of a house I've never been to."

"You know for a fact that you've never been there?"

Hollie nodded. "I had this dream as a young child. Neither my mother or father recognized the description, and I'd never been away from them on my own, so my mother found it quite odd that I kept having the dream."

"And the dream went away?" the young therapist prompted.

"Yes. I don't know when exactly. I'd say when I was eight or nine."

"And you're here today because—"

"They're back." Hollie's shoulders slumped.

Was this woman judging her?

A brief glimpse assured that was not the case. In fact, her look of understanding eased some of Hollie's angst.

"Why are they back?"

Fair enough question. One she had mulled over without a profound revelation.

"As silly as it sounds—I was sitting on the couch, eating a bowl of ice cream, and watching one of those fixer-upper shows…and I fell asleep. That was the first night I recall having the dream. I mean, since I was a child."

"All right," the woman said. "What details are you hoping to obtain?"

"I don't know. Something that might tell me the house is real. A street name. A mailbox. Any small fact."

"Okay." The therapist used the heels of her shoes to inch her wheeled chair closer.

"For the record, people come to me to recall forgotten passwords, forgotten names. Some forget where they put their keys. It's all in here." She tapped the side of her head. "Sometimes we just try too hard and that pressure only makes the resistance all the stronger."

Maryann's warning reared its sinister head. "Will you ply my bank account password out of me?"

The therapist, whose name was Samantha, chuckled.

"All I ask of you is that when you leave here today, please try to dispel concerns like that to anyone else seeking hypnotherapy." She smiled patiently. "You are not going to be put into a trance. You and I are just going to sit here and have a relaxed conversation. You will be in total control at all times. You answer only what you want to. The keyword here is *relax*. Relaxation is the only way to open up your mind."

Relax.

Hollie nodded and tried to breathe. She occupied one of two comfortable guest chairs seated before a glass and chrome desk. It wasn't as if she was reclined on a couch or anything cliché such as that. There were no spinning wheels taped to the wall. No swinging watches. Only a framed degree, plus a lovely sunset painting.

Samantha had rolled her office chair out from behind the desk and sat facing her.

"Do you want to try?" she asked with a conspiratorial smile.

Curiosity made Hollie's head bob in assent.

"What do I have to do?"

"Unclench your hands. Snap them to get some of the tension out, and then lay them flat on your lap."

Okay. I can do this. I want this to work.

Snapping her hands, Hollie let them fall flat on her thighs.

"Start at the top of your head and feel all your muscles go south."

"I'm thirty-two, my muscles are already heading that way."

"No joking," Samantha chastised with a smile. "Close your eyes and feel your muscles drain one by one."

Hollie concentrated and forced herself to imagine each muscle turning to putty. Melting. Unwinding.

"Deep breath, and now watch my fingers."

Opening her eyes, Hollie stared at Samantha's pointer and middle fingers clenched together. Was she going to *Baby Shark* her into a trance?

"Follow them," the therapist instructed in a calm voice as she moved the fingers in the sign of a cross, and then a circle, and then an X, and back to a circle.

Hollie never blinked as she followed the rhythmic motion of those fingers.

"Close your eyes," Samantha commanded softly.

Hollie obeyed.

"Feel your eyelids relax. They're heavy."

Indeed they were. So desperate for sleep lately, Hollie could feel that temptress beckon. She could so easily fall asleep sitting here in this unfamiliar office.

"Breathe deeply."

She inhaled.

"Now tell me about your dream," the voice was so soft.

On the cusp of dozing, Hollie easily slipped back into the dream. Recognizing that she was awake and could open her eyes at any time, it was still so simple to slide into that tunnel of trees.

"Tell me," the wispy voice instructed. "Tell me what you see."

"I'm in a car, I think. I'm being jostled around. The ground is uneven. But I'm looking up. I'm going through a tunnel. A tunnel of trees."

"Can you look to your left?"

Hollie's head remained straight, but her eyes shifted beneath her eyelids.

"Trees."

"Right."

"More trees. But—" she hesitated, frowning as she concentrated.

"Relax, Hollie. Relax your muscles."

Her forehead smoothed.

"I can see glimpses of light. There are some gaps in the trees on this side."

"Can you see anything between those gaps?"

"No. But I'm looking ahead. The tunnel is so dark. I want to get to the light."

"Okay," Samantha assured. "You are approaching the light now, and what do you see?"

Tempted to raise her hand to ward off the brightness she heard Samantha's soft mantra.

Breathe.

"The sun is so bright. It's hard to tell."

"That's okay. Let your eyes adjust. You have all the time in the world to take it in."

Breathe.

The sharp tang of forsythia filled her nose. There were no forsythia bushes at her parent's house so it was curious how she could identify the scent.

"The road—or driveway—it takes a turn now and runs down the length of a long, fenced-in yard. It seems to stop at the end of the property. The whole clearing is barricaded by a wall of trees as far as I can see."

"What is in front of you?"

Hollie's eyes slid beneath her eyelids.

"A house."

"What else? Is there a mailbox? Any lawn ornaments?"

"Ummm, no?" She frowned with effort.

"Relax."

Relax.

She took a step forward in the dream.

"There is a rock path to the porch. Flagstones."

"Good. Are you walking on them?"

"Yes. I hear feet—shoes scraping against them."

"Your own, or is there someone with you?"

"I—I don't know."

"It's okay," Samantha assured in a voice that blended with the rustle of the leaves and the chirp of crickets. "Tell me about the house."

Hollie tipped her head up slightly. "It's brown."

"Brown," the therapist repeated. "All right. Can you tell me more? If it's brown, is it a log cabin?"

Another step. Another flagstone.

"No, no. It's big. It looks like an old farmhouse maybe. There are windows upstairs. The whole front of the house is flat...and brown."

"What else?" Samantha prompted.

"There's a short staircase up to the front door." Hollie paused as she moved toward the stairs. "A black railing with some sort of fancy patterns in it."

She felt the chipped black paint scrape against her fingertips. Those fingers curled up into a fist as she raised her hand.

"What else?"

The question stopped her from knocking. Every time she tried to knock on that door she woke up. Now the moment was suspended. Hollie looked up. The door was so tall.

"Out loud," Samantha urged softly. "Tell me what you see."

"The door—it's so tall."

"You want to find something to identify this house, Hollie," she reminded. "Is there anything on the door? A number?"

"I don't see anything," she replied, growing frustrated.

"Easy, Hollie. Listen to me. Put your hands in your lap. Unclench your fingers. Feel your arms grow heavy. So heavy. Feel the muscles in your face relax. Feel the muscles under your eyes relax. Breathe in deeply."

All the triggers were working. That rumble of agitation died down as Hollie's body felt like it was sinking into the chair. The relaxation opened her mind and she searched the door again.

Dark, rustic, and knotted, it had a black knob, but no windows—no peephole. The momentum of the memory propelled her forward, raising her hand. Before her knuckles could connect with the wood she hauled her eyes up.

Damn.

No wonder she had missed it. The doorframe was dark wood. The house was painted brown. It was almost impossible to distinguish the black stenciled numbers above the door. Especially under the glare of the sun. But, there it was.

1649

"1649," she repeated out loud.

With little time to process the number, her hand curled into a fist and reached up.

"Hollie?"

The voice stopped her.

"It's time to take a break. You've accomplished a lot this session. I am going to count backwards from three to one and you will be fully alert, and these dreams will no longer torment you. You will be a casual observer from now on, and simply fall right back to sleep."

Fall right back to sleep.
Fall right back to sleep.
"Three. Two. One."

CHAPTER FOUR

1649

Hollie pecked the numbers on the keyboard.

A slew of historical references from that year appeared in the search results.

How old was the farmhouse? It seemed rustic enough to have been built in colonial days.

The stenciled number revealed little about its logistics, though. House numbers could be arranged consecutively on a street. Some were marked from a crossroad, and some represented a physical distance to a starting point.

1649 Florida

And so her vague search for street addresses began.

If she had to research every county in every state, so be it. Hopefully her quest would yield a workable list—no matter how long it took.

A knock on her balcony door drew her eyes up. For anyone else, a knock on a third-floor window might be startling, but Hollie slid out from her kitchen table and approached the sliding glass door with a smile. A waft of salty air filled her kitchen as she slid the panel open.

"Where did this come from?" Maryann asked, stooping over to sniff at the potted yellow bush.

Hollie crossed her arms and grinned.

"I found it at a nursery on Dale Mabry."

Maryann's hair-sprayed curls nearly ruffled in the wind. "Forsythia?" Her bloodhound nose surmised.

"Yes!" Hollie beamed. "How did you know?"

A cocked eyebrow and a *seriously?* expression made Hollie giggle.

"You're in good spirits," Maryann observed as she stepped in from their shared balcony.

At three stories high, no one could scale the wall beneath, and they felt safe leaving their sliding glass doors open for access by each other in case of emergency.

"Does that mean it went well?"

Hollie grabbed a bottle of iced tea out of the refrigerator and held it up in invitation. Maryann nodded.

"Better than I would have expected."

Sitting at the kitchen table, interest flashed in the elder woman's eyes. "Tell. Tell."

The details seemed much more vivid now—not the shadowy recollection of a dream. Hollie explained how she was systematically trying to build a list of 1649 addresses.

"But za therapist shed no light on your childhood? Zat zis was a memory from then?"

"No," Hollie was not discouraged. "I feel happy to have even gained this knowledge."

True.

As the sun set over the bay, she had a feeling it would be the first time she had a good night's sleep in over a month.

A shrill sound woke Hollie.

Sitting up in bed, she blinked away the fatigue. Her laptop rested at an angle across her feet, close to tumbling off the mattress. Sun inched across the floor from a crack in the drapes.

Turning toward the source of the noise, she nearly smiled. How long had it been since the alarm had woken her?

Immersed in her search last night, she had finally drifted off to sleep. The dream had been there. She was certain of it. But she had slept through it. She no longer woke with this angst to decipher it. Angst, instead, turned to curiosity. And the deciphering took place on her laptop and the pad next to it with the growing list of potential addresses.

The scenery of the dream evoked impressions of the eastern region of the country. That narrowed down her days-long search. *Street View* assisted even further. In most cases she was able to see images of the houses and rule them out. It was the images omitted by *Street View* that left her with a very workable list of possibilities.

It was Friday morning. Generally, she worked on the weekend and had off Monday and Tuesday. Snagging the laptop, Hollie pulled up the airline schedule. Flights to Newark, New Jersey from Tampa weren't too bad in price. Looking at the short list on her pad, she could easily attack the New York and Pennsylvania addresses in that limited time.

Hollie padded on bare feet to the balcony window, sliding the drapes aside to view the sultry pink of daybreak. A crescent of lights still dotted the bridge arching across the causeway.

Was she crazy?

Was chasing after a list of 1649 addresses in states she had never visited the act of a rational woman?

How she longed for her mother at moments like this. Ginger Musgrave would have been on the plane right beside her, enthusiastic about the adventure.

In her peripheral vision, Hollie caught a glimpse of the framed photo atop her dresser. A six-year-old version of herself with two missing front teeth and brown pigtails sat on the knee of her father who was caught in mid-laugh. Her mother stooped over behind them with her arms looped around her father's neck. Virginia Musgrave was beautiful with long tawny hair slipping down her shoulders and framing the tousled dark hair of her father.

Where in that blissful childhood did the mysterious farmhouse fit in?

Crazy or not, she was going to do this. The hypnotherapy session had aided in her sleep. Now, hopefully, this search would take care of her manic curiosity.

They were all there early Monday morning as Hollie wheeled her overnight bag through the Harbor Breeze lobby. Florence, Francine, and Maryann, each still in bathrobes sat on two loveseats, hoisting themselves up upon her approach.

Hollie drew to a halt.

"How come I don't get this sort of send-off when I travel for work?"

Even at the ghastly hour of 5:15am, Frank's blue eyeshadow was plastered on.

"We know what you're doing when you fly off for work," she huffed. "We know you're with people you've worked with before."

"We wish we could go with you," Maryann inserted, nervously patting at flat white curls.

Moisture gathered behind Hollie's eyes as she reached out and hugged Maryann, and then took turns with the others.

"Two days, guys," she chided in a hoarse voice. "I'll be back Wednesday night—most likely unsuccessful."

Flo blinked a few times and raised her hand.

"You'll tell us everything when you return, right? Take pictures."

Hollie nodded.

Francine fished in the basket hanging from the front of her walker and retrieved a white paper bag.

"For the plane."

Hollie recognized the logo of Francine's favorite donuts.

"You don't give me donuts when I fly for work," she joked.

The ladies' soulful eyes gave Hollie a brief moment of trepidation. She shook it off. This was nothing more than a fruitless waste of money and time. She would have been better off spending the money on a trip to Arizona to visit her father.

But she had to find that door…

A quick glance down at the GPS confirmed that it was another twenty miles on Route 202 to reach her destination outside of Doylestown, Pennsylvania. With a quick stop in Flemington for gas and a cup of coffee, she resumed her trek through the rural New Jersey countryside. Before this trip, all she had heard of New Jersey was the Turnpike and the various sporting complexes some of her teams had traveled to. She had no idea how peaceful this western portion of the state was with farms as far as the eye could see, and cows dotting green pastures.

Yesterday's address in New York had proven lame. This was the last 1649 location to check before she headed back home.

She was an idiot.

Only an idiot would fly here based on a cryptic dream.

Who is to say that the number she witnessed in hypnotherapy was even legit? It could have been implanted in her subconscious from something she had witnessed earlier in the day. Maybe she dialed someone's phone number at work that ended in those four numbers.

"Turn left onto Narraganset Street in one mile," the crisp British accent instructed.

No sense in turning back now. Her flight wasn't until tomorrow morning. If this was a bust, as she imagined it would be, she'd try to catch a flight tonight.

Turning onto Narraganset Street, she noticed new construction pressing toward the highway. Another mile, though, and there was nothing but farmland interrupted by wedges of dense forestry. Tension crept up her spine as she watched the mailbox numbers flash by. Several of them had no accompanying houses— only long drives disappearing into the woodland.

Occasionally she caught glimpses of structures through the foliage. Little snippets of secret lives. In contrast, her street growing up contained very few trees, and the neighbors were close enough to touch.

A group of mailboxes were congregated together at the head of a dirt trail.

1637.

1639.

Another mile passed before she saw 1641.

Hollie's fingers fisted around the steering wheel.

A tractor rolled by on her left, the pungent scent of fresh-cut grass permeating the car vents.

1647.

Squinting against the sun glare, she chewed her bottom lip for another half mile before the next mailbox on the right appeared. Overgrown weeds circled its foundation.

1649.

She tapped the brake and then hiked her eyes up to the rearview mirror. No one was behind her so she stopped in the middle of the road.

A rutted driveway carved through a blend of crab grass and gravel disappeared into the trees about a hundred feet away. Hollie stared hard into that shadowed barrier until a horn jarred her. She threw on the blinker and hauled the steering wheel to the right. With a jarring thump, her rental car bounced down the incline and leveled out onto the driveway.

Again she hit the brake and rested her fists on top of the wheel. Her heart thumped heavy in her chest. Perspiration crept across her forehead. Kneading the steering wheel, she drew in a deep breath and tapped the gas pedal. The car lumbered forward, swallowed by the canopy of trees. Adhering to the grooves in the dirt, her hips swayed with the rocking of the car as she crept toward the finish line.

Emerging into the sun, she raised her hand over her eyes. Squinting, she noticed the driveway branch down the length of a split-rail fence, bordering a field flanked with tall pines. A quick sweep of her eyes brought her back to the farmhouse before her.

Thump. Thump. Thump.

Her heart lumbered.

The farmhouse was navy blue. It had black shutters around the windows. Those were the only two features that didn't resonate from her dreams. Everything else might as well have been plucked from the recesses of her mind.

Shaky hands put the car in park and cracked open the door. She slipped out, leaving her purse on the seat, while stalking zombie-like toward the house.

A warm late summer breeze carried the scent of forsythia as her sandaled feet negotiated the flagstone sidewalk leading up to the front door. Four cement stairs were all that separated her from a portal that looked so familiar. Perhaps the house had been painted—the shutters—the wrought iron railing—but the door hadn't changed. It was such a solid barrier there was no need for upgrading. Her eyes skimmed the frame above it and found the stenciled numbers 1649. The 6 was slightly askew, resting against the 1.

Hollie climbed those steps, her hand curling into a fist before she even had time to develop a plan.

For the first time ever, her knuckles met wood without her waking up.

CHAPTER FIVE

Todd Hewitt cursed the knock at the front door.

He nearly didn't hear it over the exhaust fan. It was enough of a disruption to make his steady hand jerk, leaving a silver streak from the soldering iron across his circuit board.

"Bah."

He switched off the rod and set it down on a hotplate.

Angling around a table full of circuitry, he peered out the kitchen window. From this perspective he could not see the front door, but the rental car sticker on the front of the sedan parked outside renewed his anger. He was tempted to ignore the interruption altogether, but another knock fueled him into action.

Hauling open the front door, he was startled by the woman with her knuckles raised in midair. She gaped at him and then chocolate eyes slid past his, curiously staring inside.

That plaintive gaze stole some of his zeal, but he cleared his throat and muttered, "If you're from the press, I'm not giving interviews."

Puzzled by her silence, he added, "I *mean* it. I have nothing to say to you."

Dark lashes fluttered as if the woman was waking from a trance. Her hand fell to her side, but her fingers were still curled tight.

"Interview?" she sounded perplexed. Clarity gradually returned to those soulful eyes. "Are you someone famous?"

It might have been comical if not for the bewilderment on her face.

"No. I am not someone famous."

She nodded and licked her lips nervously. As much as he didn't want to, he studied those full lips and the heart-shaped face around them. A healthy tan infused high cheekbones hugged by wisps of dark brown hair.

"I'm sorry to bother you," she began, but floundered after that. "It's just that—I—I think I may have been in this house. When I was a child."

Well, that was a new tactic. One that wouldn't work, but certainly unique. His cynicism returned, not about to be dissuaded by this wayward waif.

"Look, I've lived here for three years now, and I would hope people like you would respect my privacy. And, what are you—" he searched the earnest face, and swept down the lithe figure in jeans and a t-shirt, "—less than thirty? The owners prior to me had lived here much longer than thirty years, and had no children. So, your spiel doesn't quite jive."

The realtor had been vehement about that fact, as if any potential juvenile damage might forfeit the contract.

"I'm thirty-two," the woman responded, distracted with the view behind him.

There wasn't much to see back there. Just the foyer with a staircase directly behind it.

For a reporter, she wasn't very tenacious. Most would try to pack questions in even as he was shooing them off his doorstep.

There was an awkward moment where her curious gaze left his as she tipped her head back and scanned the face of the house, her head angling down to the overgrown bushes that hugged the cement foundation.

Todd crossed his arms in dismissal, but the gesture went unnoticed by her roving eyes. In fact, she was so engrossed he found himself following her exploration. Maybe she was part of a tag team. Maybe she was the distraction, and someone was sneaking around the back. Looking for—what?

No, the reporters just wanted to harass *him*. They didn't care about his house.

But, this one...she was definitely peculiar.

He coughed, and her head jerked at the sound.

Cocking his eyebrow, he nudged his chin toward her car in a not-so-subtle suggestion.

A sigh hefted her chest, drawing his attention there.

Well, hell—he was human. He didn't get to see many attractive women tucked away in this haven. No matter her purpose for being here, she was refreshing to look at.

Attractive or not, what he noticed now was pure fatigue—a woman who must have been running on adrenaline that drained with that one simple sigh. Slim shoulders caved and she looked lost.

"I'm sorry to have bothered you," she murmured.

Distracted, she searched through the doorway again. "It sounds ridiculous. I mean, I know it must sound ridiculous to you, but even to me it sounds ridiculous. I'm not deranged. I'm very levelheaded, but lately—the dreams—I was hoping I could see something—*anything* that could make me remember. I mean, how can it be that I remember this house?"

The dialogue was introspective, but she did keep casting plaintive looks behind him as if she desperately wanted to be invited in.

At least there was some civility to this reporter in that she corralled herself from outright asking. In fact, her submission as she turned to leave startled him.

"That's it? You're really not here to question me?"

Oh, yeah, Todd. It's all about you.

Okay, he sounded like an ass, but he was hardened to these invasions.

She turned her head back to look at him and he was struck by the conflux of emotion there. She looked sad, but those full lips were clamped in resolve.

"Maybe you can answer a question for me," she muttered.

A-hah.

"Can you tell me the name of the couple that owned this house? I tried to search online and couldn't really find any records of ownership of this property."

That would be his doing. He had corresponded with most of the major online realtor sites to have the metadata removed in those first few weeks when the reporters were relentless.

But this woman was asking about the *previous* owners. Not him. It was all very curious, but not curious enough to crack his armor.

"A rather brazen question. If it's not public knowledge, then it's probably not right for me to share it."

The woman's head snapped as if she had been slapped. Rummaging inside her purse with a trembling hand, she extracted a business card.

"Again, I'm sorry to have troubled you," she murmured, not quite reaching his eyes. "I'm not usually like this. I've just had such problems sleeping lately— and I have this wonderful group of ladies pushing me to get help—" Realizing that she was rambling, her lips closed.

Staring at her business card for an awkward moment, she finally thrust it at him. "If you—I don't know—if you can think of anything about the history of this house that you might be willing to share—"

Ending the discomfort, she hastened down the steps, pausing at the bottom to gaze down the path that continued alongside the fenced-in field. A slight breeze ruffled her hair revealing the profile of a narrow chin and the soft curve of her neck. Without another word she walked to her car, careful to step on each flagstone along the way.

Todd watched the sedan disappear into the arcade of trees. He stood there for several moments listening to the crunch of tires against dirt and rock before he turned back into the house.

Her curious brown-eyed stare made him reevaluate the interior as he closed the door. This house was built a little over a hundred years ago when the notion of *open concept* was not so fashionable. The living room was enclosed with a small arched door into the narrow dining room, which had another tight doorway leading into the cloistered kitchen.

Inside the foyer, an ultra-narrow staircase led up to three small bedrooms upstairs. The compartmentalized layout suited his personality. But all the tiny rooms added up to a pretty sizeable farmhouse—large enough that he was tinkering with the idea of visiting the local pound. The only reason he had not done so was the inevitability that he'd come home with five dogs.

Todd glanced down at the business card in his hand.

Hollie Musgrave
Athletics Marketing Manager

"Huh?" he said aloud. "Athletics Marketing Manager. What the hell is that?"

It didn't sound like the title of an intrusive reporter, but it could be a ruse. Or, maybe she thought some famous sports star previously lived here.

Whatever the case, she piqued his curiosity enough to turn away from the kitchen toward the thin wooden door that led down to the cellar. The pungent musty smell assaulted him the moment he opened it. In a farmhouse that dated back over a century, this cellar evoked all childhood fears with its backless staircase and stone floors that were permanently mud-stained from recessing floods.

Three years ago he'd brought little with him, so now there was only a box or two of his possessions sitting directly at the bottom of the stairs.

You would think at the mature age of thirty-six he wouldn't harbor juvenile qualms of basements, but some impressions surpassed adulthood.

Light from the single bulb at the top of the stairs revealed tarnished pipes along the walls. A concrete twin laundry tub sat in the corner. It was such a solid piece he doubted even an earthquake could destroy it. He had used it to clean paint brushes, but that was the extent of his time spent down here.

Switching on the phone flashlight, Todd cautiously crossed the floor, certain that nature's slithery finest would deem this den a perfect escape from the heat.

In his first few weeks here he had considered converting the basement to his workspace. That was the last time he had crossed the floor and peered into the nooks that ran the length of the farmhouse.

There was a cinderblock wall that dissected the basement with a tight doorway carved out of it. Poking his head into that half of the basement, all he found was a stack of cardboard boxes that looked weathered enough to crumble at his touch.

No, this area wasn't suitable for work. This area could host a ghost gala, and he avoided it at all costs.

Now, Todd directed his flashlight through that doorway, raking his hand at a thick cobweb that hung across it like a crime scene tape. The thought of touching those boxes was unappealing on so many levels. First, there was the apparent decades-old layer of grime on top. Then there was the obvious intrusion. But he had lived here for three years and no one returned to claim them. From what the real estate agent told him, an elderly couple had spent the past few decades here until they finally required assisted living. They had no children or pets, so he was assured there was little damage to the house. Based on the description of their age, they might not even be alive today—or certainly in no condition to retrieve these non-essentials.

Well, *he* owned the house now.

His property.

It wasn't absurd to peek at something that was sitting on *his* property.

Todd used the cell phone to flip open the topmost box. Training the flashlight inside, he snorted.

That was anticlimactic.

It contained a stack of pots and pans, the one on top charred black at its center.

Feeling foolish, he flicked the lid closed and shined the flashlight into the recesses of the room. Aside from this stack of boxes, the cellar was empty. Returning his sullen glance to the cardboard tower before him, he didn't even want to imagine what the bottom container looked like. Too many floods from the nearby river had passed through here.

I think I may have been in this house when I was a child.

So what? Maybe she had. Or maybe Hollie Musgrave, the sports publicist, or whatever the hell she was, was just full of crap and fishing for a story. He had nothing to say. He had nothing to say to the press back then, and he certainly had nothing to share now.

But, he was down here. He was already covered in grit. Why not complete the task? Maybe there was something in these boxes that was worth contacting the previous owners about.

An hour and fifty sneezes later, he confirmed that was not the case. There was some broken china, a bound stack of newspapers, some old photos, a box of toys—*toys?*—and a box of record albums. He deliberated over the albums for a few moments, smiling at the *Kenny Rogers and the First Edition* LP. His father had this same album. It had been passed down from *his* father.

Todd inspected the box of toys again. Stuffed animals and dolls that had seen a child's wear and tear.

They had no children. No pets.

It was hard to date the toys. Some stuffed animals were timeless. Perhaps they came from a previous family. But that would place these toys over forty years old at the least.

The intrusive woman on his doorstep was not over forty.

Hauling the stack of newspapers out, he read headlines that were mostly plucked from the early to mid-eighties. Some headlines he recognized.

Sally Ride becomes the first American woman in space.

The Chernobyl nuclear reactor explodes in the USSR.

Todd set the stack aside and reached deep into the box for the pile of photos. Some were in small frames yet. He scooped them into his free arm and decided to look at them upstairs, in a much less creepy environment…and after a shower.

An early evening rain beat steadily against the kitchen window as Todd took a swig of coffee that had been sitting on the table for hours. He dusted off the framed picture with a paper towel and studied the couple. A woman with gray hair cut into a bob sat on an upholstered chair. Standing behind her was a man with salt and pepper hair, his chin tipped up in confrontation. Neither smiled. Todd studied the background to determine if the picture was taken here in the farmhouse, but the couple was the primary focus, filling the frame.

Setting that aside, he continued through the pile. Most of the photos were of two men, most likely brothers. If they weren't twins, they were certainly close in age and appearance. They looked to be in their twenties or thirties in the picture he held, but as he shuffled through the pile he found more of them at various stages of youth. A small photo slipped out of his hand and fluttered onto the floor. Staring down at it lying on the polished oak, he frowned. One of the brothers stood there in adulthood, but his hands were clasping the shoulders of a young girl. She was maybe four or five years old.

Todd stooped over and picked up the picture by its white border. The image was tarnished from the conditions it had been stored in, but the girl's long dark hair and dark eyes were still visible.

I think I may have been in this house when I was a child.

Staring at the young girl's face, he tried to mature it. Hair that hung down to the girl's slim hips receded in his mind to just below her shoulders. Youthful round eyes transitioned into a womanly slant, framed with long dark lashes. Plump cheeks elevated and the jawline narrowed.

When his conceptual transformation was complete, he was left with an image of Hollie Musgrave.

Oh, get over it. She was just here fishing for a story.

Rushing through the rest of the stack he located one more photograph of the young girl. This time she stood alone, and she was definitely at this house, crouched down on the front steps with one small hand wrapped around the wrought iron railing. Long bangs draped over one eye and her lips were thinned into a straight line.

Just put it all back in the cellar, Todd's logical inner voice commanded.

The trouble with logic was that it hadn't lived here alone for three years. Logic wasn't lonely. Logic hadn't searched the woman's face to see what angle she was playing, only to discover disillusionment. Logic didn't notice that the stranger hadn't looked *at* him. She looked *through* him in an attempt to see what lingered behind.

As best he could tell, Hollie Musgrave didn't give a damn about him.

Tapping his cellphone to life he did a quick search of the company listed on the business card.

There she was.

Our senior publicist, Hollie Musgrave, handles media relations and is the director of communications for the Tampa Bay NFL and MLB teams.

It went on, but he could see no angle that would motivate her to write about him.

The same phone number that was listed on the website was on the card. Before he acknowledged what he was doing, his thumb pressed on the number and the phone switched into dial mode.

"Hello?"

Damn. Should he hang up?

She would see the caller ID and just call back.

"Umm, Miss Musgrave. You stopped by my house a while ago—" He withheld his name.

"*Yes?*"

The earnest response made him plunder forward.

"Well, it's just that I found some old photographs. There's some of a young girl. You mentioned you thought you might have lived here as a child. This girl kind of looks like you. Perhaps—well—maybe the photographs belong to your family."

There was a long pause—a pause in which he berated himself every way imaginable.

"Can I come see it?"

"Well," he fumbled, "I'm sure you're far away by now. I can scan it and email it to you."

"I can be back there in less than an hour. I'd much rather see it in person." She hesitated. "Please."

Todd looked at the porcelain plate clock on the kitchen wall—another piece left behind by the previous owners.

6:30 PM

An hour placed her estimated arrival still under some form of daylight.

"Okay," he sighed. "But just take the picture and go."

That sounded rude, but too bad.

"Great, I'm on my way."

Glancing at the melee on his kitchen table, he uttered, "Fine," and hung up.

Testing the tip of the soldering iron, he found it to be cool enough to stow away. A glimpse at the cold coffee made him consider putting on a fresh pot.

Instead, he opened up the refrigerator and hauled out a beer.

CHAPTER SIX

Despite the fact that rain had kicked in, Hollie made it back to Bucks County in record time. A steady downpour drilled the roof of the rental car until she pulled off the road and benefitted from the ceiling of trees. In this tunnel the steady *thwap* of the wipers was unnaturally loud. Switching them off, she emerged blindly to a sheet of water until a manual swipe of the blades revealed a slice of the farmhouse.

For a moment she sat in the idling car, waiting to see if the rain tapered. Through the driver's side window she noticed several lights on inside.

She had no idea what the man's name was. He didn't seem very friendly, but she didn't seem very sane. To say that she was surprised by his call would be an understatement. It wouldn't be hard to imagine him muttering, "good riddance" as soon as she pulled away earlier.

Personalities and opinions aside, he said he had a photograph. That was all that concerned her.

Too impatient to wait for a break, Hollie climbed out of the car, slammed the door behind her and jogged up the steps to the front door. There was no roof over this tight landing so she stood under the wet assault as her knuckles rapped on the wood.

The barrier flew open to reveal a brief glimpse of the man before he stepped back and commanded, "Come in."

Hollie stumbled inside, grateful to be out of the rain. Swiping damp hair back from her eyes the realization struck her.

She had crossed the threshold.

Her dream always terminated at the door.

Sweeping a curious gaze around the rustic foyer, she found it softly lit from lamps turned on in the bordering rooms. A jacket hung from a wooden coat hanger nailed to the wall. Next to that was a wood-framed mirror with her shadowy reflection in it. Her head tipped back to see the raised ceiling with a lantern chandelier hanging above. Directly before her was a narrow wooden staircase with a white wood banister. She glanced up it, but the landing was obscured in darkness.

It was all quite quaint.

It was all foreign.

"Do you need a towel?"

The voice startled her. Her head snapped toward the wide back of the man as he nudged the front door shut. When he turned around, his face was cast in shadows and hard to read. He was taller than her by at least five inches, but not inhumanly tall like some of the athletes she worked with.

"No. It actually felt refreshing."

She read his body language. That, combined with her earlier reception hinted that she was going to have limited time here.

"Thank you for calling me, and for letting me come see the picture."

His head was cocked as he studied her with shuttered eyes.

"I promise—I'll only take a moment of your time," she rushed to add.

The man crooked his fingers, beckoning her to the adjoining room. Passing through a tight dining room with lace valances, and crossing a creaking floor, she expected something to trigger a memory.

There was nothing.

A warm kitchen with yellow paint and blue glass vases perched on the windowsill seemed like an oasis. A butcherblock table was halfway littered with paraphernalia. Most looked like electronics and computer boards.

"Your work?" she asked.

He glanced at the pile and shrugged. "Work. Hobby. Thin line."

Hollie's eyes latched onto another, more intriguing pile. Even from here she could see the wear and tear the photos had been through. Digital photography was essential to her job, but this pile had withstood the test of time. Digital photos were only as good as the technology that hosted them.

"I guess you can have a seat." The man hesitated, debating. "I have coffee or beer."

Beer sounded so tempting, but she still had to drive back to Newark Airport tonight.

"Coffee. Thanks." She looked up at him. "You all but kicked my butt off your property before. Why the sudden change in demeanor?"

When he crossed his arms muscles bunched up under his black t-shirt.

In the kitchen light she could finally study his features. Tawny hair—maybe slightly more brown than blonde was cut short, framing a tanned face with a strong jawline and wide lips. If there was such a thing as blue hazel eyes, that was what he had. They were like autumn trees with flashes of cerulean sky peeking through.

"Trust me, the butt kicking is now self-inflicted. I'll try to remain civil for a few minutes. As long as you don't start asking me questions."

"You thought I was a reporter. I'm not here for you. I don't even know who you are."

It was true. He had one of those faces that if she had seen it before she would definitely remember it.

Unlike this house.

Another glance around the kitchen and there wasn't even the teeniest nugget of familiarity here. How could she remember the outside so vividly?

"Did you do a lot of renovating in here?"

Even as she asked the question, she knew the answer. The house looked old. The cabinets were painted over to try and give them an extended life. White Formica countertops peeled up at the corners.

"Not exactly." He glanced around, self-conscious. "I have been too busy."

Grabbing a mug out of a cabinet, he poured the coffee and set it down on the table. Then he wrapped his fingers around a half-filled bottle of beer and brought it over to the table before sliding into one of the seats. A tear in his worn jeans revealed a glimpse of flesh.

"Go ahead." He prompted with a nod. "Sit down. Have a look."

Dropping into the seat in haste, Hollie shoveled up the first picture with greedy fingers. A distinguished-looking man in a suit stood with his hands gripping the slight shoulders of a young girl standing before him. That was the extent of attention Hollie bestowed on the man. Avarice eyes feasted on the little girl. The sepia hue washed out any true colors, but long dark hair, void of barrettes or bows fell down the front of a denim jumper. Solemn brown eyes stared back at her.

With a lump forming in her throat, Hollie reached for the next picture, the one with the girl sitting on the front steps. White fingers were wrapped around the black railing. Closing her eyes, Hollie could feel that coarse surface against her own palm. She opened them again and stared at the girl.

Same hair.

Same eyes.

Same house.

"This isn't me," she croaked.

Perhaps her raw response elicited some form of empathy from the man. Under the hanging lamp his gaze lingered on her for a moment.

"Were you expecting it to be you?" he asked, rifling through the rest of the pile.

"I—I don't know what I was expecting."

Yes. Yes, I was expecting it to be me.

Anything to explain the dreams.

"Maybe you visited here once."

"Maybe." She was unconvinced. "It's just so strange to remember this house so vividly from the outside, but—" her head swung around, "—have no recollection of the inside."

The porcelain clock ticked loudly now that the beating rain had stopped.

"You said you were young," he pondered with a slow sip from his bottle. "Memory is tricky in a young mind."

Hollie stared at her fingers resting only six inches away from the pile of photos. She glanced up at the clock again.

"I thank you for letting me come back here. I thank you for digging out these pictures. If—if—" she fumbled before dropping the subject and instead grabbing her purse and slinging it over her shoulder as she rose.

"If what?" he prompted.

"Never mind. I understand that you don't want to share the name of the couple you bought this house from. That is private information." The tangy scent of forsythia floated through the open windows. It blended with the post-rain humidity. "I really better head back now. I have an early flight."

The man rose, his head cocked in contemplation.

"So you really weren't here to grill me?"

The guy needed to get over himself.

"I don't think there's anything to grill you about. I don't know those people." She nodded at the photographs, finding it hard to swallow. "And I don't know you."

Nudging the chair under the table with her hip, she decided it was time to flee this embarrassment. Not just embarrassment. Humiliation. The utter sense of failure. All the efforts to get here—to find a memory—and the discouraging hollowness of the aftermath.

Aware that he followed her to the front door, Hollie rushed to pull open the panel and felt the assault of muggy air. Outside, her rental car was the only item out of place in a tableau she relived nightly.

"Thank you for your time—"

"Todd."

Hollie frowned. "Your name, or the people who lived here?"

A disarming grin had her reassessing the man. He definitely was attractive, but aside from that brief physical acknowledgement, she was too depressed to care.

"My name," he confirmed. "The last name of the previous owners was Johnson. I don't think that's giving away much."

Johnson.

The surname rolled around in her head, bouncing off the walls with hollow echoes that developed into a throbbing headache.

"No, I guess that's not much to go on. But, I do appreciate it."

Slipping her fingers around the railing, she stepped down the stairs.

Slowly.

Methodically.

Each clash of sole against flagstone resonated from her dreams. She reached the car and opened the door, standing just inside it as she cast one last glance around the familiar property.

Inevitably, her gaze was drawn toward the front door—that ominous barrier from her dreams. Only now, it was open and a man stood with his shoulder hitched against the doorjamb. Outwardly, he seemed relaxed in his black t-shirt and jeans, but there was a tension in his frame. Half man, half taut rubber band—just waiting to be released.

Hollie averted her gaze.

She didn't need any more enigmas.

With a curt nod, she ducked into the rental car and slowly rumbled under the tree canopy, searching the rearview mirror until the farmhouse was reduced to a pinpoint of light that finally disappeared.

CHAPTER SEVEN

Lingering on the doorstep, Todd turned back into the house. The soldering iron tip needed to be cleaned before he could use it again.

He paused inside the kitchen doorway.

A coffee cup sat on the table.

A coffee cup that someone else drank from.

That had not happened in three years.

He stared at it, tempted to leave it there for a while longer.

The distant screech of brakes cut through the open windows, followed by the dull thud of impact. The driveway was less than a quarter mile long and he often could hear sirens or drag racers on the main road, but the enclave of trees sheltered him from external chaos.

Stepping up to the window, he listened for any fallout. Distant shouts. Distant sirens.

Distance.

But not distant enough. As cloistered as this farmhouse was, it wasn't distant enough from the rest of the world.

How long had he stood on the front doorstep? Seconds? Minutes? Just the amount of time it would have taken the woman to reach the street. Surely she was fine. What were the odds that the remote impact had been her car?

Ignore it.

Not your problem.

Get back to work.

Only a chorus of crickets singing their ode to the end of summer could be heard outside now.

Grabbing the circuit board, he tried to focus.

Dammit.

Todd set the board down and trudged to the front door. A few more steps and he was marching through the tunnel of trees.

I'll just go to the end.

Just to check it out.

It's probably nothing.

The length of the tree canopy seemed extraordinarily long today. Darker with the onset of night.

He picked up the pace.

Reaching his mailbox, Todd saw the slight curl of smoke from the embankment down the street and his stomach clenched. Breaking into a jog, he crossed the road and felt his heart lumber as he recognized the rental car. Cautiously approaching the vehicle, he found that the back end of the driver's side had been crushed. The damage was extensive and perilously close to the gas tank. Slipping down the ridge to the driver's door, he called out, "Are you okay?"

Hunched awkwardly, he peered inside to discover the car was empty. Jerking his head up, he searched over the roof into the field behind it.

Also empty.

An angry voice sounded in the distance. It echoed from down the street.

With the sun already settled behind the tall trees, the approaching figure was nothing more than a lithe silhouette marching down the shoulder of the road. Her hand stabbed in sync with her agitated dialogue.

Jabbing the phone into the back pocket of her jeans he watched Hollie stalk toward him.

"Nice neighbors you have around here." The angry outburst clashed with the trace of shock in her eyes.

"What happened?" he asked, climbing out of the ditch.

"I just pulled onto the road and someone must have been sitting in the next driveway down." She pointed at it.

"Bam! They plowed right into me. I mean they *gunned* it and smacked the side of the car. They knocked me into the ditch and then *kept going*." Her hands shook. "Seriously, what the hell?"

Todd looked at the gravel driveway across from the damaged sedan. Just like his lot, this house was not visible from the street. He had only seen his neighbors a handful of times in the past three years. Nothing more than cordial waves were ever exchanged, but they didn't strike him as malicious.

"I think they have a son out of school. You sometimes have to gun it because the driveway is much lower than the road. He might have lost control."

"And not stopped to check on me?" She steamed.

Gone was that dazed soul on his doorstep. This woman was a hot mess of resentment and spunk.

"Afraid of the insurance," Todd suggested. "Did you call 9-1-1? Are you injured?"

Even as he asked the question, sirens could be heard in the distance. He searched her body but saw no sign of trauma—just an infusion of heat in her cheeks that was fading with the sun.

"They're on their way, and I'm fine. Just—" she hauled shaky fingers through her hair. "—just ticked off more than anything. I mean, the rental car company doesn't have a replacement available until the morning. By the time the police arrive and all that," she looked up at the amethyst sky, "it's going to be dark. Is there a hotel nearby?"

"It's not the hicks," Todd defended. "There is an interstate only seven miles away."

Some of her antagonism was fading as a mild dose of shock settled in. She hugged her arms about herself despite the thick humidity that now curled into steam atop the wet pavement.

A fire engine crested the top of the hill, immediately trailed by a patrol car. Garish lights pulsed across the road.

Todd remained through the entire process, mostly because the woman's feisty bout had waned and she looked disoriented. Only when the police announced that they were going to question the neighbors did her bravado return.

The neighbors were alarmed and surprised by the intrusion, but their near-adult son was sprawled across the couch, and his blue Sentra sat parked under a tree, clearly not the white pickup truck that Hollie had described.

What shocked Todd the most was their troubled expressions when they looked at *him*. In the few instances that their paths had crossed, he labeled the Steins as reclusive, which suited him just fine. It seemed though, that it was *him* they had an issue with. They avoided eye contact, but were effusive with the officer and Hollie.

"There are deer hunters in this area," the husband, a reedy man in his fifties or sixties, explained. "We have a pretty substantial piece of acreage and we always catch them hunting on the perimeter. I don't want to get sued if they accidentally shoot each other."

"Or our son," the dour-faced Mrs. Stein added.

"Anyway," Mr. Stein continued, "if they were the ones that hit you, I imagine they don't want to stick around and get caught."

That summation seemed to satisfy the police officer who snapped his pad shut. He turned his shoulder for privacy as he called in his report.

Todd noticed Mrs. Stein watching him again. Ogling, with very little tact.

"Is there something you want to add?" He couldn't resist glaring back at her. What was her problem?

To his surprise, Hollie interrupted.

"Have you lived here long?"

Edgy, but finding Hollie less intimidating, the woman replied with a cautious, "yes."

"Did you know the Johnsons well?" Hollie asked.

"The Johnsons?" Mrs. Stein seemed startled. "You mean the Marianis?"

"Phyllis," her husband growled, crowding in against her shoulder.

"Yeah, we knew the Johnsons," he murmured, casting a guarded look at Todd and then the cop. "They were a quiet couple."

"Did they have a daughter?" Hollie persisted.

The wife's eyes widened, and her head twitched. Whether that was a negative or positive response was up for interpretation.

"Alright." The police officer finished his call and turned back toward the group. "We have everything we need. A copy of the report will be emailed to you." He nodded at Hollie. "If you think of anything else, just call the number on the report. Likewise, we'll be in touch."

He tipped his hat at the middle-aged couple standing shoulder to shoulder in the doorway. "Thank you for your time. And, please, if you have any more illegal hunters on the premises, let us know."

The officer shifted his attention between Todd and Hollie, settling on the latter. "You declined an ambulance, are you going to be okay?"

"Yes." She nodded hastily, her cheeks pale under the porch light.

As the officer started toward his car, the neighbors pressed their front door closed with Todd and Hollie barely off the first step. Glancing over his shoulder, he caught them watching him through the window before a curtain fell back in place.

"Is the rental car company coming to pick you up?" he asked Hollie once they reached the road.

Night had descended.

There were no streetlights along this sparsely-populated road. A deep violet band of sky clung to the top of the trees, not yet ready to surrender to the inky black of night.

"No. I'm not traveling on business, so of course I went cheap." She shook her head in disgust. "Their closest location is either Philly airport or Allentown. They said they could have a replacement waiting there for me, but I'll just change my flight to one of those two airports. They're closer, and maybe I can get an Uber or something to one of them."

Hollie grabbed her phone out of her purse.

"I can drive you. But why don't you come in and sit down for a minute? You're shaking."

Flinching as the words poured out before he could check them, Todd witnessed Hollie's eyes flare in disbelief.

"Oh, no. I've already troubled you."

"You're trembling. I mean, seriously, you should even consider going to an Urgent Care."

An impatient wave of her hand dismissed that notion.

Todd read her indecision. Why should she accept his offer? He was a stranger. Basically, he'd been an ass.

"I'll be okay."

As the officer pulled away, the trees were swathed in red and blue until the overhead lights were switched off. Left in darkness, Todd could barely see Hollie's face, but he did notice her cross her arms and heard her soft exhale.

"Well, if I could just stay at your house until I can get a ride—" The profile of a narrow chin clipped the waning light. "I don't want to stand out here in the dark. Apparently it's not safe." She snorted at her own joke.

Todd smiled, but he doubted she saw it.

"Fair enough," he agreed. "Let's get back before the mosquitos attack."

In the dark, the echo of footsteps at his side proved bewildering. Unsure of what to say, his thoughts returned to the alarmed looks of his neighbors—all directed at him. What the hell was that about? Maybe they *were* responsible for Hollie's accident.

Lost in thought he barely noticed that the accompanying steps had ceased. He paused and glanced curiously behind him.

A ghostly silhouette was profiled by the mounting moonlight. As still as a deer, all that was animated was the flash of her eyes when they shifted straight ahead.

"What?" he asked.

"I get chills standing here," she whispered.

Her haunted voice almost elicited the same reaction on his arms.

"Why didn't you come back to this farmhouse years ago?"

She tucked the tips of her fingers into the front pockets of her jeans as if at a loss for something to do with them. For a moment he thought she wouldn't answer.

"It's a long story," she hedged.

"Well, you can wait outside for an Uber from a complete stranger, or you can go into the house that seems to fascinate you so much and accept a ride from me whenever you want. If you want to leave in five minutes I can take you. If you want to leave in an hour and see if you can find anything familiar inside, I'll still take you, or I'll screen your Uber driver and make sure he or she seems credible."

Hollie stepped closer and he could see her frown in the scope of the front porch lantern.

"Why are you being nice? From the moment I got here your sole aim was to get me off your property."

Maybe I'm curious.

Maybe I'm lonely.

Maybe I'm a fool.

"You were almost seriously injured outside my property. Maybe I feel guilty."

"Maybe you're preying on my curiosity."

"Maybe you're still a reporter, and this has all just been an elaborate ruse to interview me."

"Maybe—" Hollie lost the next challenge and began to laugh.

A smile tugged at the corners of his lips. The muscles cramped from atrophy.

"Well, then I'm an ingenious and masochistic reporter," she recovered. "And I deserve an interview for my efforts. The only problem is that I have no idea who the hell you are. Off the top of my head, I can't think of any entertainers or athletes named Todd."

"Maybe I'm a politician."

"You're a politician?" she sounded surprised.

"No." He smirked. "Come on. Let's get you something to drink. You really are still shaking."

Extending her arms for a quick examination, she quickly tucked them back against her sides.

"I need to make a phone call first."

"Of course." He bowed his head. "I'll leave the front door unlocked if you want privacy."

A mosquito landed in her hair. She swatted at it after it made its way to her forehead.

"If it's okay, I'll do it inside."

Todd nodded, suddenly uncertain about his hospitality. It was too late, though. He heard her footsteps trailing his up the front porch and then she was lingering in the foyer, pecking at her phone before a soft dialing sounded.

"Hi. Hi. Yes, everything is going great. I found the house."

It was impossible not to eavesdrop on her side of the conversation—even from the kitchen. Acoustics in the vaulted foyer resonated throughout the house.

"I promise," she asserted. "I slept last night. I don't know what time I'm flying back tomorrow, though. I have some last-minute tasks."

Interesting.

No mention of the accident.

"What? Okay, put Frank on the phone."

Frank?

Not my business.

"No. It hasn't really helped. I guess we'll see tonight. It didn't answer too much. Look, I really have to go. I'll talk to you all tomorrow."

Frank pretty much sucked if Hollie couldn't share the accident with him.

"Good bye." Hollie finished.

At that, he heard her steps approach through the dining room.

"Everything okay?" he asked, noticing her troubled expression.

"Yeah, I just—" Lost for words she flailed her hand helplessly.

"I understand." *Not really.* "Look, do you need an icepack? Some ibuprofen?"

She shook her head musingly, back to that inquisitive survey of her surroundings.

"I'd offer you that beer again, but if you hit your head—maybe coffee is more in order."

The wandering eyes settled on him, their gaze like the brush of ethereal fingertips.

Everything about her reeked of determination, down to the clenched fists resting on his kitchen table. But it was in the depths of those brown eyes that he witnessed vulnerability—as if what she sought was intangible.

"I'll try some coffee, but if my hands start shaking blame the caffeine, not the accident."

Todd set about making a new pot, feeling her eyes on his back. It was unnerving, and oddly stimulating.

"So, do you have a last name I should recognize?" she asked. "I mean, considering you are a world famous politician/celebrity that has reporters scaling the walls of his farmhouse."

Todd snorted, but kept his back to her.

"Hewitt," he finally said, turning around.

"Todd Hewitt."

He could see the name rolling around in her head.

"I've got nothing," she remarked. "So why are you so paranoid about reporters?"

His shrug didn't come easily. "I was in the news once. The proverbial 15 minutes. Some reporters feel like beating a dead horse." He winced at the analogy.

Before she could respond he switched the subject. "But what about you? Your business card states you're from Tampa. So what brings you up here? Did you live in Pennsylvania as a child? Is that how you recognize this place?"

With her level stare, she saw right through the segue but let it slide.

"No."

"Family here?"

"No."

Now who was being evasive?

"Well, I had grandparents in New York," she admitted.

"What were you trying to do over there?" He tilted his head in the direction of the neighbors. "Grilling them and all."

"I—" She cracked. Voice and body. The night was taking its toll on her. "Look, I better check into that Uber ride."

Unsteady hands fumbled with the phone. He felt the impulse to hold them. How many times had his own shook like that?

Reading the screen, she announced, "It says that someone can be here in a half hour."

"Let's see the profile." Todd rounded the table to lean in over her shoulder.

If the driver looked like some sort of shmuck, he was definitely going to state it.

The citrus scent of her shampoo mixed with the sultry sheen of humidity in her hair.

"Greg," she read. "4.8 rating. Drives a Prius."

"I don't trust his face."

"What's wrong with his face?" She tweaked her fingers so the image increased. "Looks like a school teacher. Glasses. Cleanshaven." She leaned back and her eyes fell on Todd's jaw.

"Yeah, I didn't shave yet today," he muttered. "I wasn't expecting guests."

That glance lingered long enough for him to feel it coil around his stomach, but then she turned back to the phone.

"It's a Prius," she declared as if that was eligible for sainthood. "I'm putting in the order."

Fine.

"You'd rather this guy over me?" he challenged.

Wait, that didn't sound right.

"I mean," he cleared his throat, "you'd trust a ride from this Uber driver over a ride from me?"

The eyes again.

"You're a stranger too," she pointed out.

Right. Fine. He wanted this woman out of his house. He wanted his privacy back. He wanted to get back to his work.

The hiss of the coffeemaker dragged his attention away. On autopilot, he poured a cup of coffee and set it down before her. As she shoved her phone back into her purse, he caught a glimpse of the green notification confirming her ride.

"I really do appreciate you letting me stay here until the driver comes," she said, wrapping slim fingers minus a wedding ring around the mug. "Really, I just came to this house to see if it triggered any memories. I know I probably sound like a flake, but I'm not."

"I never said you were a flake." He chose to stand, leaning back against the kitchen counter so he could look through the window for the driver's approach.

"I was intrigued," he continued. "Intrigued enough to brave the cellar on your behalf."

Hollie's eyes followed his gaze to the narrow door just outside the kitchen. A chill rippled down her bare limbs.

"What is it about cellars?" she whispered with a forced smirk. "I'm surprised someone like you is afraid."

"Someone like me?" His eyebrow inched up.

"Well, I mean—" Her eyes traced his shoulders. "—you look like a strong man, not someone who is afraid of a few cobwebs."

Embarrassment blazed in her cheeks. The sight tugged at his lips.

"You want to go down there and look?" he challenged. "Be my guest."

Hollie's eyes flared with interest.

"I'm *joking*," he added.

Slender shoulders deflated against the stiff-backed chair.

"Are you sure you're not a reporter? You are certainly as tenacious as one."

"No. Dammit, I'm not a reporter. I'm just curious about this place. If I were to tell you the truth you would definitely be convinced that I'm a flake." She frowned. "But what does it really matter?" Glancing down at her phone, she added, "My ride will be here in 12 minutes. You'll be rid of me then."

It was a flash of bravado, but the soulful eyes clashed with the delivery.

"Well, then you have 12 minutes to convince me that you're not a flake."

Ignoring the challenge, she twitched her nose and reached for the mug. Taking a shallow sip, she seemed lost in uncertainty, contemplating him over the rim of the mug.

"It will sound silly," she said softly, "but I've dreamt of this house. Since I was a young girl. When I was—I don't know—five, six, seven, I used to dream of this exact house every night. I would describe it to my parents, but neither recognized it by my description."

Todd set down his cup.

"The dreams went away by the time I was ten, but recently, out of nowhere, they returned. Every night, sometimes as frequently as every ten minutes. The same images." Her delivery gained some strength. "I'm coming through the canopy of trees. I walk across the flagstone path. I climb the front porch stairs. My hand is on the very same railing that is still here. I reach up to knock on this very front door—"

Todd's hands settled beside his hips, gripping the edge of the counter. He was more engrossed with the expression on her face than the tale itself.

"What happened?"

When Hollie looked up at him, he no longer believed she was a reporter. The desolation in those eyes could not be feigned.

"Nothing," she whispered. "It always ends there. I always wake up."

Tick. Tick. Tick.

Unnaturally loud, the porcelain clock ticked away.

"How did you know where this house was if your parents say you've never been to Pennsylvania?"

Hollie blinked. She clutched the mug with white knuckles.

"I have a persistent group of friends who convinced me to go to a hypnotist."

"Wow. Whoa."

"Yeah." Her quick grin was a welcome change. "*That's* how desperate I had become. I wasn't getting much sleep."

"So you went?" he asked, fascinated. "What happened?"

"It's really not all that you see in the movies. I mean, basically you just relax enough that you can concentrate more. It helped me to pick out more details of the front door. This time I noticed the black stenciled numbers on top. 1649."

"So you had a house number, but hell, that's still the proverbial needle without knowing a street name."

"Oh, it is." She rolled her eyes. "Trust me. I had to break down internet searches by every state, sometimes even counties. I would write down any viable address and then do a street view or satellite view to see if it matched the layout with the long tree-covered driveway. I was able to eliminate 90% of the addresses that way. And I also just had a gut-feeling that it was on the east coast, so that narrowed it down to a couple addresses that I could handle in one trip up north."

"Damn," he murmured.

A flash of light appeared in his periphery. Outside, headlights were creeping up his driveway.

"It looks like your ride is here." Leaning over the sink he could see the Prius pull up beneath the front porch light.

"Perfect timing." She jumped up, grabbing her purse. "Because I just shared way too much information, and I'm pretty mortified."

"You shouldn't be," he called after her hastily retreating form.

A car horn sounded outside. A few seconds later a quick hammering on the front door announced the driver's arrival.

Hollie stopped with her hand on the doorknob. Her head turned toward him and he swallowed in reflex.

"I am really sorry for invading your privacy. Thank you for tolerating me. If—"

"Yes," he agreed softly. "If I find anything else, I'll let you know."

Relief shined in those dark eyes.

Hollie pulled the door open to find the man who looked like a school teacher. It should come as some relief to Todd that he matched the Uber profile picture, but he still didn't like the guy or her choice of transportation.

"Hollie Musgrave?" the driver asked.

"Yes," she replied, hiking her purse strap over her shoulder and giving Todd one more lengthy look.

"Hey," the driver said. "This just fell off your front door."

He strategically thrust the envelope forward in the space between them, not knowing who it was intended for.

Todd reached for the unmarked envelope and opened it, pulling out the single sheet of paper.

"Where did you find this?"

"It was lying on the doormat," he defended, reading Todd's dark expression.

"Did you see anyone leave it here? Did you see anyone walking along the driveway, or out on the road?"

Todd felt Hollie's curious gaze. He avoided it.

"No, man. I just walked up the steps and it was there." He pointed down at the concrete. "I was just trying to be courteous."

"Thanks," Todd replied harshly. He reached into his back pocket for his wallet and pulled out a twenty dollar bill. "Sorry for the inconvenience, but we're not going to need you."

"What the hell?" Hollie injected.

"You paid for the ride already online," the driver huffed as he snagged the proffered bill. "No refunds."

"Yeah, got it. Thanks." Todd shut the door, locking the man out.

In a few seconds he saw red taillights pull away and fade into a rosy mist inside the tree tunnel.

"Dammit, what are you doing? That was my ride."

Todd finally looked at her. She was frowning and reaching for her phone as if to call the driver back.

"I didn't trust him."

"What? *4.8 stars*!" She thrust the phone in his face.

"Want to explain this?" He held the piece of paper up.

STAY AWAY FROM THIS HOUSE, HOLLIE.

CHAPTER EIGHT

Hollie grabbed the note with trembling fingers. The penmanship was hasty—a series of ballpoint slashes.

Her eyes slid to the man handling the envelope. He caught her suspicious glance and frowned.

"Don't even," he uttered in reproach.

"Then who?"

"You may not remember everything about this house, but someone remembers *you*," Todd remarked, inspecting the blank envelope.

"Whoever wrote this note wants me to leave, and that's just what I was about to do." She stared at the closed door. "But you stopped me. Why?"

Mr. Stoic lost some of his composure. He looked a bit rattled.

"I don't know. I mean, in all respects it would be best if you were gone from here, but—" he set the envelope down on an antique console. "The last time you left, it didn't go so well."

A near bout of vertigo had Hollie reaching for the wall. She saw Todd make a move toward her but impatiently waved him off.

"No. That's just—just paranoia."

Even as she denied it, the possibility bloomed like a red hot rash on her brain.

"Regardless of the ambiguity of the accident, this note isn't innocent. Who wants to keep you away from here, Hollie?"

"Besides you?"

"Get past that."

Hollie drew in a shaky breath. There were countless opportunities for this man to get rid of her. Honest concern seemed to draw creases around the corners of his eyes. She truly doubted he left the note.

"Your neighbors."

Todd seemed to mull that over and nodded.

"Yesterday I would have said that's ridiculous. I don't even know them. Today—"

She saw his throat bob as he appeared to look through the walls to the property next door.

"They just seemed awfully edgy to me," he concluded.

"Should I go confront them?"

"Ah, no. I think you need to be a little more cautious than that."

"Should I show this to the police?"

Todd shrugged and nodded simultaneously, an unproductive gesture.

"That's probably the right thing to do. I doubt they'll do anything about it."

"They can join me in interrogating the neighbors. That'll intimidate them."

"True. But you saw how tight-lipped the Steins were even with the police there. If you go over with threats, they'll just burrow deeper under their turtle shell."

Frustration, fear, and a few cramped muscles from the accident started to take their toll. She wanted to punch something, but instead reached behind her neck to massage the tension.

"Come on, you better sit back down," Todd urged.

Staring at him until he shifted uncomfortably, she dissected this stranger—this unwitting aid. He was tall and lean in jeans that hung low on his hips, and a black t-shirt that clung to his shoulders and biceps. A splotch of oil tarnished the front of the shirt. His chin and jaw were shadowed with dark bristles, but the short hair on his head was a shade lighter. Those keen eyes were watching her. She tried to gauge if they held any malice. Earlier, she witnessed impatience there. Now, the blend of autumn and sky just looked curious, and maybe even a tad concerned.

Feeling unsteady, she drew in a deep that calmed her slightly.

"Okay," she conceded, following him back to the kitchen.

This time there was no decorum on her part. She dropped into the chair, stretching her legs out before her and swung her elbows atop the table.

She was tired.

So tired.

What would it be like to fall asleep in this house?

Would it prove a catharsis?

Would her dream unravel under the symmetry?

"I've got plenty of rooms here."

Todd's deep voice invaded her thoughts.

"You look too beat to tackle anything right now. We can go to the airport first thing in the morning."

What was the alternative?

Drive with him to the airport?

There weren't any flights at this hour

Get to an airport motel and sleep? She'd pass out in the car along the way.

The invitation was tempting.

"Look," he said. "I know you have no reason to trust me. But you'll be fine here. If you don't feel that way, I promise I won't turn away the next Uber driver you call. I was just—that note—well, if it was me, that wouldn't sit well with me. And I don't want anyone getting hurt on my property."

As if fatigue besieged him as well, his head dropped forward.

"I don't want that," he repeated in barely a whisper.

Unsure of how to respond, Hollie clutched the coffee mug again.

Crossing his arms and peering out the kitchen window, Todd cleared his throat.

"Let me go do a nose check on the guest room. It's clean—" his shoulders hefted, "—but it's a room that never gets used. If it's too dusty I've got some clean sheets."

"It'll be fine," she assured. "I'm not going to care about some dust."

Todd rubbed his wrist. "Okay then. I'll be right back."

As she watched his wide shoulders disappear through the arched doorway, her voice overruled her senses.

"Todd?"

That long back shuddered and he grabbed the doorframe, turning to look at her over his shoulder.

Now that she had his attention she wished she'd kept her mouth shut.

Aside from the kitchen light, and the diffused glow from the foyer, the house was dark. He stood on the threshold of a dining room cloistered in shadow.

Could she admit to him that she was afraid to go to sleep?

"Yeah?"

Gulp.

Her throat narrowed to the size of a pinhole.

"Could I—" she swallowed, "—could I maybe take you up on that offer of a beer? It might help me sleep."

The tension around his mouth faded.

"Sounds like a great idea."

With the cold sweat of the bottle against her palm, Hollie felt her stress ebb. Heck, she hadn't even taken a sip. The bottle was like an ice pack to reduce her swelling fear.

"Thanks," she said, watching Todd as she took the first tentative sip.

Back in his station against the counter he held his bottle up in a brief salute before taking a swig.

"So this dream—you're afraid of it?" he concluded after a spell of mutual silence.

What point was there in denying it? By tomorrow she would be long gone and never have to face this man again.

"I'm afraid of having the dream inside this house. A convergence of sorts." Trying to shrug it off, she added, "I warned you that you would think I'm a headcase."

"That you did."

In an unexpected motion, he straightened from his slouch against the counter and settled onto the chair opposite her. He grabbed one of the circuit boards that he'd set aside and held it up to the light.

"I'm sorry to interrupt your work. What is it that you do?"

"Nothing terribly exciting. I do custom circuit board printing."

Hollie frowned at the green plate in his hands. "What exactly does that entail?"

"Well, depending on the specs of the customer, I will laminate copper onto this, or solder components based on a CAD drawing that is emailed to me. I work for a company in Boston, but they let me work remotely. I used to—" he hesitated, "—I used to travel too much. Now I can stay put."

Hollie took a sip of beer and then saluted him with the bottle. "I am a travel warrior as well, and it's grueling. The majority of my work is in Florida, but I have to do road work too."

"Is it what you want to do for the rest of your life?" he asked.

"No." She looked down at the table. "But freelance photography doesn't pay the mortgage. At least, not yet. I'm working on it."

Todd clinked the rim of his beer bottle to hers in salutation.

"Good. I was an electrical engineer. Now I'm working freelance as well. I mean, yeah, my primary customer is in Boston, but I'm easy. I'll build boards for anyone with legitimate ideas. There are a lot of entrepreneurs out there who just need a little help."

"That's nice that you're helping people."

She stared at the rim of her bottle, realizing that it had come in contact with something touched by his mouth. The notion made her stomach tumble and she stole a glimpse of his lips set firmly in thought. Maybe it was just the effect of a few sips of alcohol on an empty stomach.

"But it doesn't explain why you get reporters lurking on your doorstep. Am I missing something?"

Okay, maybe that was a bit forward, but she did deserve to know if he was a serial killer just recently released from prison. It was too late to escape to the bathroom and do a quick internet search on TODD HEWITT.

Another discreet glimpse at the hulk of a man across the table revealed that the question unsettled him.

"Fair enough question. But, no, you're not missing anything. I'm nobody special. I just had an event in my life a few years ago that the media seemed obsessed with. Some still seek me out to see what I'm doing now."

Push it, or not?

The beer said push it.

"What type of event?"

In the ensuing silence she decided it was the wrong tactic. Todd tapped his pointer finger against the bottle. His bicep bunched up when he lifted the bottle, but he set it back down, untouched.

"My house blew up."

Hollie swallowed. It nearly went down the wrong way.

"Oh, my." She tried to read his expression, but it was stark. Nothing was revealed in the fixed set of his lips or the gaze trained at a spot on the corner of the table.

"That's terrible," she murmured.

Terrible, but did it warrant reporters stalking him for years?

Compelled to know what was behind the self-imposed confinement, she pushed further.

"What happened?"

Tap. Tap. Tap.

His finger caused trails of perspiration to run down the side of the bottle. A hasty tilt of his head and his neck cracked.

"High pressure in the gas lines on my street. Seven houses blew up that day. All within a two-block span."

Despite her will, her jaw slipped open.

"A Boston suburb? I think I remember hearing about that."

"Yeah." He smirked. "The press was pretty determined to keep it in the news."

"And they still harass you?"

Dark eyebrows hiked cynically. "Sometimes they follow up on it. The old, *let's see what happened to the victims* piece."

"But why?"

She sounded like a two-year-old with her relentless *whys*, but she could see the harassment clearly bothered this man.

"They always had questions. There was a settlement with the gas company. The press wanted to know how much. They weren't getting anything from the gas company so they harassed the victims."

Swallowing down any more questions, Hollie sat in silence.

The chair scraped as he nudged it back in order to lean his elbows on his spread knees.

"My turn."

Whoa.

Being the focus of that male scrutiny elicited a new bout of goosebumps. Men looked her over every now and then, but it was always a surface perusal. This absorbed scrutiny made her feel vulnerable and desirable in a way she was unaccustomed to. Topping it off was his evocative semblance of a grin, which increased her heart rate.

Chill, Musgrave.

"Hollie," he tested the name.

"Yes?"

"You don't look like a Hollie. You're too intense. You look more like a Sloane, or a Lauren." Flinching at her frown he added, "Don't get me wrong. I like Hollie. It counters that intensity. It makes you more real."

"I'm not intense," she retorted.

"Oh really? Tell a joke."

Hollie struggled to think of something funny to say. Her face lit up in recollection.

"I know one."

Todd leaned back in his chair and crossed his arms. "Please, *do* share."

Resisting the impulse to scrunch her nose at the challenge, she sat straighter and lifted her head in pride.

"How much does corn cost in Tampa?"

Across the table, Todd's lips curled up into a wry, but attractive grin. "I have no idea."

"A buccaneer!" She caved over, letting loose a belly laugh.

After a minute she realized that she was the only one laughing. Her curious glance collided with simmering eyes that studied her with amusement.

"Don't you get it? A *buck an ear*?"

After an interminable moment, he nodded. "Not bad, but stick to your day job."

Hollie flattened her hand on the table. "That was just a touch of my stand-up routine. I am practically a comic in the making. Even my name is the epitome of joy. Do you know why I'm named Hollie?"

"Can't even imagine," he remarked.

She pursed her lips at his amusement.

"I was born on Christmas Eve."

The laugh he had been struggling to suppress finally leaked out—like air from a tire.

"Okay." Wide hands rose in defense. "That seals it. You look completely like a Hollie to me."

Unsure if she'd just been mocked, Hollie sipped on her beer, gauging his expression.

"You know I'm just teasing you?"

Mulling that for a second, she had the sudden unexpected feeling that he might be trying to flirt.

Another glimpse over her bottle at the severe planes of his face and she decided that was absurd.

"Why?"

"You need to relax. You've had one hell of a day."

The joviality deflated. She stared at the folded piece of paper on the far end of the table.

"Someone left a note telling me to stay away from here."

Todd sobered as well.

"I know," he said, hesitating. "And it's not cool. Is it some kind of cruel prank? Some sort of sick joke?"

Hollie pinched at the pain between her eyes. "Maybe. But who would do it? I don't know anyone up here."

"Well, it pissed me off. I'm not going to let anyone threaten someone on my property." He stood abruptly abruptly to look out the window. His arms were crossed and a muscle pumped along his jaw. "You're safe in here. They'll have to get by me first."

Stranger that he may be, she believed him. For as much as he had portrayed himself as hostile when she first arrived, there was a certain trace of poignancy embedded in his gaze. And a rugged sense of decency that contradicted the facade he tried to show the world.

Still and all, as pleasant as it was that this man felt compelled to protect her, it didn't curb her anxiety.

She followed his gaze out into the night. Was there someone out there right now? Watching?

"You must be hungry." He interrupted her frenzied thoughts. "I've got—" Crossing over to open the refrigerator, he chronicled, "—hot dogs or leftover frozen pizza."

Despite the trauma of the day her stomach let loose a loud growl that made him glance over his shoulder with a quick smile.

"Leftover pizza sounds fantastic, if it's no trouble."

"As if that sounds like trouble." He retrieved the tray and slapped a few slices on paper plates, sticking them in the microwave.

"Tell me more about your dreams," he prompted as they sat and ate. "There must be some link."

Dubious, Hollie used chewing as a delay tactic. With a prolonged swallow, she cleared her throat and started to share the details leading up to her trip to the hypnotherapist.

Whether it was liquid inhibition, or the ease of anonymity with a stranger, or simply the encouragement in his eyes—she began to open up.

"It sounds strange, but as much as the dreams make me anxious, they also make me feel closer to my mom. When I was a little girl she would pour me a tiny cup of coffee to make me feel like an adult—and we would sit at the kitchen table and try to figure out where I could possibly know the house from. My mother loved mysteries," she explained. "She was an Agatha Christie junkie—and she took my dream as a mystery she needed to solve."

"Sounds as focused as her daughter," he mused, dropping a crust onto his plate. "So what does she say about the dreams returning?"

The pizza felt like a softball rolling down her throat.

"She passed away when I was eleven."

Todd winced. "Oh damn." He fisted his hands together. "I'm sorry to hear that."

The spontaneity of his response soothed her. For as much time had passed, she still missed her mother—a free soul who always traveled to a different beat. Quirky. That would have been the best way to describe her mother, and wholly in a good way.

"It was an accident. A work party near Howard Frankenstein Bridge— I mean, Howard Frankland. Too many cocktails. Too much sun. She drowned. It was tough on my dad. I think it's why he eventually moved to Arizona. He couldn't stand looking at the water anymore."

"Loss like that is hard to get over." he considered.

Adrift in her memories she pushed the paper plate back and folded her napkin atop the leftover crust. Fatigue, more so than beer, stimulated her to share more.

"You know, back when I was little, my mom thought that my dreams could mean that I was remembering a former life and that as I grew older I would start to forget it."

Todd's beer bottle came down with a thud. "Reincarnation?"

Hollie shook her head. "At least you don't cross yourself when you say the word like my friends do."

"Well," he hedged. "It's not a suggestion you hear every day. What are your thoughts?"

No judgement.

No disbelief.

Just a glint of interest in those magnetic eyes.

"I don't know." She shrugged. "She was right. The dreams did go away before I turned ten."

"But they came back." Sinewy muscles shifted as he sat up from his reclined position. "Why do you suppose that is?"

"That's why I'm here. I'm trying to figure out why."

"Wow." His head shook. "*So* not what I expected on my doorstep today."

Stifling a yawn, Hollie clasped her hand over her mouth.

"I live to impress," she joked, wearily.

"You really should try to get some sleep." He stood and took the plates to the trash.

In that corner of the kitchen he was half in shadow. Half man. Half creature of the night.

Maybe he was right. Every aspect of her body screamed for rest. Except for her mind.

"Can I just stay up a little longer?" *Hah.* She sounded like a little girl.

The depiction didn't go unnoticed. She was awarded with half a grin visible from the shadows.

"Of course. But the concerned citizen in me thinks that sleep is in your best interest right now." He stepped back under the light. "The sympathetic man in me understands, however."

"Sympathetic?" She raised an eyebrow. "You certainly have calmed down in a few hours."

Todd snorted. "Don't underestimate me. I'm still an ornery son of a bitch."

Hollie laughed.

"What about you?" He slid back into his chair, stretching out and hooking his ankles. "You hang around sports stars all day." He glanced at her left hand. "And you're not married?"

"Why do you say it like that?"

"Well, I mean, you're very attractive. I can't imagine the guys wouldn't have scooped you up."

If it was an offhand compliment, she'd take it any way she could get it. Her ego was sorely in need of a boost.

"I mean, I heard you talking to Frank," he added. "Isn't Frank concerned that you're here? Here in this house? With your dreams and all, I would think he should be concerned."

A giggle mixed with a swallow of beer created a fizz in her throat.

Todd rubbed at the back of his neck in discomfort.

"*Frank* is Francine," she corrected with a grin. "And she is eighty-four-years-old."

It was stimulating to see *Mr. Sexy and in Charge* at a loss for words. All he could do was take a long chug on his beer as she watched his throat flex and bob on each swallow.

"A relative?" he finally managed.

"A neighbor."

A glimpse at the black window, and she added, "Speaking of neighbors. Did you hear yours today? The woman mentioned the name—" she paused in recollection, "—Mariani?"

"You mean before her husband nearly muzzled her?"

"Yeah, odd huh?"

"I heard her," he said. "And I found several things odd with them. It might be worth dropping by for a neighborly visit tomorrow."

"Can I come?" she rushed.

Okay, two-year-old again.

"We'll see. But seriously you need to get some rest."

Hollie glanced at the clock. 10 PM. It seemed much later. One beer and two slices of pizza were like over-the-counter sedatives.

Beyond the warm span of the kitchen light, darkness loomed. It set her on edge and she began to rethink her decision to stay in this house. But if there was a chance she had been here before, this was complete immersion. Perhaps the cold, hard shock would inspire recollection.

"Are you going to be okay?" he asked quietly.

Within the arc of the doorway he was a virile silhouette that unsettled and beguiled her.

Would it be absurd to ask to sleep in the kitchen—to just bask under the safety of the hanging metal lamp—maybe even curl under the kitchen table, or tuck herself into the window nook?

Two-year-old.

The brawny outline shifted, the motion capturing her attention.

"Your room is across the hall from mine. If you need something, just holler. I'll hear you."

Translation. If I freak out, he'll know it.

"I'll be fine. I really appreciate this."

Hollie followed, grateful as he flipped on light switches along the way. Their feet strummed an awkward cadence across the hardwood floor, muted temporarily by the throw rug in the foyer. At the bottom of the stairs he switched the downstairs lights off.

Focus forward. Don't look back into the dark.

The only problem with that was that it fixed her eyes directly on a pair of worn jeans that hugged firm hips intimately. Muscular hamstrings pumped up each step. And the curve of—

Oh, look at the floral wallpaper.

Wrenching her gaze away she studied the accent strip that paralleled yellowed crown molding.

At the top landing, Todd switched on a tarnished hood lamp. It cast an amber glow down a long hallway with closed doors on each side. At the end, the glass pane of a window reflected a murky impression of them. Behind his solid profile she looked small. A quick breath and she drew her shoulders back to straighten her posture.

"Here you go," Todd said, opening the second door to her right. "That's the bathroom." He pointed at the first door.

Reaching into the bedroom, he turned on the light switch. She couldn't see much until he stepped aside. It was a quaint room with a twin bed covered with a patchwork quilt. A secretary desk with tons of little drawers sat between two lace-framed windows. The musty scent trapped under the low ceiling was oddly comforting. In the corner, a thin layer of dust fixed on a child-sized rocking chair.

"I'll be honest. I haven't been in this room much since I moved in."

"And how long ago was that?"

"Three years." He tucked his head in chagrin.

Hollie studied it again, but not for dust or size—for recollection. A frayed rug sprawled atop the lusterless wooden floor. The desk intrigued her, but it was not familiar.

"It will be fine. I'm sure I'll be up early. Do you want me to put the coffee on?"

The survey of the room was abandoned in favor of the beguiling curl of his lip. It took away some of the severity of his chiseled face. Curves replaced straight lines. It was a genuine smile and it looked like he battled against it.

Clashing with the musty scent of the room was the piney aroma of soap coming from his skin. They stood close together in the doorway—close enough that she could feel the heat of summer emanating off of him. There was an air conditioner in the window, but it was not on, making perspiration dot the back of her neck.

"You can turn that on." He nodded toward the air conditioner. "No reason for me to keep it on up here. I spend most of my time downstairs."

Hollie swallowed. "Of course."

"I'll be up early, too," he said. "I usually am. But if you need anything—"

"Just holler."

Her fingers delved into the front pockets of her jeans, at a loss for what to do with them.

Todd backed off the doorjamb, his arm inadvertently grazing hers—a brush of hair across flesh. Transfixed by that brief touch, it wasn't until she heard the click of his bedroom door that she realized he was gone.

Hollie stood still, trying to ebb the pounding of her heart. It wasn't necessarily from that brief connection with Todd. The farmhouse was now so still. So dark. The room before her, so foreign. She stared at the miniature rocking chair and approached it, wincing at an obnoxious creak in the floorboard. Reaching down she pushed the dusty wood until it rolled back on its heel, and then released it, watching it lumber into a soft rhythm for a few seconds.

What am I doing here?

Had she expected revelations? Well, there were none. Instead, she had a new set of demands. Who had left the note? Who didn't want her here…and why? It was to the point that she almost pounded her fists against her head, hoping to shake some sense into an all-too-cloudy mind.

Setting her purse down on the desk, she sat on the bed and finally reclined back, not even bothering to get under the covers.

Leaving the light on and the door open, she crept back into the kingdom of dreams.

CHAPTER NINE

Atop the pillow, Todd's fingers were laced behind his head. Moonlight poked through the clouds and drew slashes of light across his bedroom door. He had nodded off a few times, but for the most part he remained like this.

Listening.

There was a stranger in his house. *A woman.*

It shouldn't sit well with him, yet he was the one to invite her here.

Her.

Hollie.

The woman with doe eyes that switched to those of a cunning lioness in a blink. The woman with glossy hair, a thousand shades of dark, always escaping their latch behind her ear. The woman who remembered this farmhouse from childhood. The woman who casually tossed out the word, *reincarnation.*

Red flags all over the place.

All of them under his roof.

And yet, she intrigued him.

It probably wasn't hard for a woman to look sexy to a man who had been abstinent for three years, but she was more than just a sexy package. Beneath the exterior wrapping was an engaging mind, a sense of humor, and an adventurous soul, all tempting him to peel back the cover.

It took a long time for her to fall asleep. In this house he could hear every shift of the old mattress—

any variation in her breathing pattern—they were as loud as cymbal crashes behind these thin walls. After about an hour he heard the rhythm even out as he closed his eyes, hoping to do the same.

His sleep lasted eight minutes. That was confirmed by a quick glance at the bedside clock.

Motion sounded from across the hall.

Fitful motion.

Thump.

Her feet had hit the floor.

Creak.

Her door opened and a soft tread pattered out into the hall.

It's probably just a bathroom trip.

Footfalls continued well beyond the bathroom.

Todd sat up. As soon as he heard the squeak of the staircase, he swung his legs off the edge of the bed and crossed the floorboards. Certain she was out of sight, he drew open his door and peered out into the hall. A wedge of light from her room illuminated a portion of the landing. He crept toward it and then leaned over the bannister, searching the empty stairwell. To his surprise he heard the front door open and close.

I'll be damned. She called for a ride.

Except as he peered back into the open doorway of her room he saw her purse sitting on the desk.

Moving with less discretion, he descended the stairs and crossed over to the dining room window to peer out into the night. The porch light was off, but the moon was about to break free from the clouds. It slipped past its confines to illuminate the patch of dirt and rock before the front porch.

Empty.

No. Wait.

A figure stood just on the cusp of shadow and light. Had he not been focusing so intently, the figment might not even have materialized. A late summer breeze pushed the clouds along, capturing the profile in a cerulean haze. Hair as dark as the night itself fell over her shoulders. Slim arms crossed over her chest in a bolstering self-hug. An angular chin hinted that her head was tipped back, possibly studying the house.

Todd moved to the front door and stood inside it with his hand on the doorknob for several seconds.

Go out there.
Stay in here.
Go out there.
Stay in here.

He pressed his ear close to the wood and heard the crunch of foot against flagstone. Voyeurism wasn't his style, so he deliberately opened the door to confront the specter. A ghostly blue hand reached up to it just as he swung the panel open.

Hollie gasped and yanked back her hand as if it had been stung.

"It opened."

Her whisper barely registered over the chirps of a thousand crickets.

A breeze ruffled his hair, but the chill he felt stemmed from her vacant stare. Shadowed eyes gaped right through him, her lips parted in wonder.

Sleepwalking?

You were supposed to tread lightly with sleepwalkers, right? Don't agitate them?

What the hell did he know? He knew nothing about sleepwalking.

Before he could act, that vacuous gaze fixed on him in the moonlight. Even more surprising was when that light flashed against her teeth. She was smiling.

"Did you think I was sleepwalking?"

Todd stepped back as she shouldered past him into the house.

"Well, now that you mention it—"

Ready to go off on her, and remind her that someone left a warning on the very doorstep she ventured out onto in the middle of the night—the reprimand died on his lips.

Hollie's arms wrapped tight around herself. The waif stood in the middle of the foyer and began to shiver. Catching his concerned look she added a shrug to the rest of the shakes.

"I'm fine. I couldn't sleep—"

"I gathered that." He rubbed at his jaw.

"It's not often that I have the dream and then actually have the option to go outside and reenact it."

He nodded, unsure what to say.

"This time—" even her words were slurred by her trembles, "—this time when my hand reached for the door—" her eyes met his, "—for the first time, it opened."

Todd felt the wooden floor melt and congeal into cement around his bare feet. Those dark eyes paralyzed him. They pleaded with him and challenged the world at the same time.

"Please don't look at me that way," she whispered. "I'm just a person with a memory she's trying to unlock."

With that, the challenge faded and her chin dropped.

Nearly shaking as well with conflict, Todd managed a cautious step toward her. One more and he was able to reach for her. An awkward attempt to fold her into his arms resulted in a consolatory pat on her back. In that inept embrace, Hollie was equally as rigid.

Then she changed.

Everything that had been inflexible relaxed under his touch. Her forehead dropped against his collarbone, the soft wisps of her breath dusting the bare skin at the gap in his collar. In response, his hands settled over the dip in her spine, and after a second's hesitation his chin came to rest atop her head. He had to squeeze his eyes shut against the sensory assault.

Unsure what to do, or what to say, he remained that way, waiting for her to withdraw—waiting for her to protest. When she made no such move he allowed himself to absorb the sensations.

Just beneath the cotton barrier the warmth of her flesh splayed across his palms. Sultry summer air clung to her hair, and soft breasts pressed against his chest. Most enticing of all was her surrender to trust. It filled him with a virile need to protect.

At the first trace of tentative fingertips settling on his chest he swallowed hard.

What the hell am I doing?

Hollie just needs consoling. Loosen your grip, man.

Todd tried to pull back, but she burrowed in closer. A tiny sound of protest bubbled against his chest. It was enough to enfold her in his embrace. He did nothing more. He just held her like that, the two of them locked in the dark with crickets chirping loud enough to obscure the beating of their hearts.

Murmuring incoherent assurances into that glossy hair that smelled of summer and citrus, he struggled not to press his lips to her temple.

Enough, Hewitt!

That was it. He finally withdrew, placing distance between them, but still gripping her upper arms as she swayed slightly.

Maureen A. Miller

Hollie grabbed his arms and then finger-walked down them until she was standing on her own.

"Oh, God, I'm sorry about that," she stammered. "One beer and I am a mess. Note to self, Hol. You can't handle your liquor."

Evidently, neither can I.

"What were you doing out there, Hollie? One beer doesn't send someone outside in the middle of the night?"

In the ambient light he could see the profile of her jawline as she turned her head toward the front door.

"The dream," she replied softly. "I had it again, and this time I had the opportunity to recreate it."

Insecure, she wrapped her hands around her arms. "It didn't help."

"Can you go back to sleep or do you want to talk?"

Her head snapped up.

"You'd stay up and talk with me?"

Reaching in the dark for the foyer light switch, he flicked it on. They both flinched at the contrast, and then stared as if seeing each other for the first time.

"Yeah." He shrugged away the effect. "I don't think I'd get much sleep tonight anyway."

Hollie nodded, backing up a step. "Not used to strangers in your house. I'm surprised—"

She searched the walls.

"Surprised that I'm not used to strangers?"

A few startled blinks and she looked at him again. "No. I'm surprised you're here alone."

Todd cleared his throat. "Yeah, well, you saw the reception I gave you. Do I strike you as being overly hospitable?"

A tiny snort preceded her open-mouthed smile.

"Not particularly. But, you're not going to like what I have in mind to do right now."

93

Whoa.

Down boy.

"What's that?" His voice was hoarse.

"Well, I couldn't sleep, so I was just lying there running through the events of the afternoon—and your neighbors—"

"Yeah, what about them?"

His neighbors did not fit into the sultry images he had just rifled through.

"They mentioned the name, Mariani, remember? The name Johnson didn't seem to register with them. But *you* claim this house was owned by the Johnsons. Maybe Mariani was the previous owner."

"Yeah, but like I said, the Johnsons supposedly had owned this property for more than thirty years. Or that is what the realtor and lawyer's paperwork stated."

"All right," she conceded. "But I'd still like to find out about the Marianis, whoever they are. Maybe that picture of the little girl belonged to them. Maybe she—"

"Let's go into the kitchen. I'll get my laptop."

Hollie didn't budge. "Actually, I had another idea— umm—the one that you're not going to like too much."

Todd crossed his arms and raised an eyebrow. "Do share," he prompted drolly.

Nervously hooking her fingers in the back pockets of her jeans awarded him a pleasurable view. He yanked his eyes from the tight stretch of cotton.

"I thought," she waited until he looked at her again, "that maybe—I mean, if it was okay with you—that maybe we could go look in your cellar and see if there are any more photos." Reading the denial in his eyes she plodded forward. "You did say that you've never checked out the whole space."

"Right. Because it's a *basement*," he enunciated the word. "A basement in a really old house. You go in it only when you absolutely have to, and then you make your trip as short as possible."

One hand returned from its enviable spot against her rear to smother a giggle.

"You're really afraid of it?" Awe filled rims of caramel around wide pupils.

"Yeah, so what?" He frowned. "Spend a few minutes down there and it'll swipe that smug look off your face."

Hollie tried to flatten her smile, but she just started to giggle again. The mirth was infectious. It was a sound he hadn't heard in a long time and he felt a tickle inside his chest that threatened to bubble into a downright chuckle. He forced a sober expression, but that just made her laugh all the more.

"Don't worry, Mr. Hewitt. I will hold your hand and protect you."

To fully conceal his smile, Todd turned around and headed into the kitchen, calling over his shoulder. "Don't you even tell me you want to do this right now."

"I'm up. I can't sleep."

He heard her steps directly behind him, but didn't turn around. Instead he opened the refrigerator and stuck his head in. Maybe it looked like he was getting something to drink, but really the cool air was just what he needed.

"It's the middle of the night." He rose and looked at her over the open fridge door.

"So?" Her hands fell to her hips. "It's always dark in the basement. Night or day has no bearing down there."

"Oh, you're just making this sound better by the second."

"I can go down myself. I mean. I would rather not invade your privacy like that. It would be best if you were with me to supervise what I'm going through. But if you're afraid—"

"I am *not* afraid." Todd slammed the refrigerator door shut. "It's just—musty, and there are spiders. You'll get dirty."

If that notion didn't deter the woman, he didn't know what would. She studied him with an irritatingly sexy smile—more of a provocative smirk.

Fine. Let her consider him a coward. After tomorrow he would never see her again and his phobia of cellars would remain a private matter.

"Well, I have a confession."

His head snapped up. "Oh?"

"I've never actually been in a basement." Glancing back at the unmarked door with curiosity, she added, "We don't really have basements in Florida."

Todd frowned. "How old are you?"

Her chin jutted up. "Thirty-two."

"And you've never been in a cellar? How about a wine cellar?"

"My mom's restaurant had a wine cellar, but I was never down there. She said if I accidentally broke a bottle, we'd be in debt for life."

"Your mom owned a rather fancy restaurant then."

Hollie's smile fell. "She didn't own it. She was a manager. And yes, it was very fancy."

His beer bottle was on the counter where he left it earlier, with a ring of liquid still in it. Todd picked it up and dragged down that last sip.

"All right." He hauled open a drawer and pulled out a flashlight. "Let's get this done with then."

Well damn, she could at least manage some indecision for decorum's sake. Reveal some sign of fatigue after so little sleep.

But, no.

Instead, she all but bounced with the enthusiasm of a child at Christmas. Damn woman.

As he went to open the cellar door she crowded in behind him, trying to peek between his arm and the doorframe. Her nose wrinkled at the musty smell.

"Wow," she remarked. "If I had ever been in this house I'm sure I would remember that smell."

Todd switched the light on and started down the stairs. Once they reached the bottom, the glow from that upstairs bulb only extended as far as the giant basin. Hollie stood one step up from the cement floor and gazed as far as the scope of light would allow.

"Okay," she conceded with her hand on the railing. "Maybe it's a little creepy."

Flicking on the flashlight, he muttered, "We haven't even gotten to the creepy part yet. Follow me."

Her sandals grated against the floor as they crossed over to the cinderblock wall where he raised his flashlight at the black opening. To his dismay the productive little spiders had already begun closing it off again.

Holding the flashlight like a gun, he prepared to jab at the web, but heard her soft gasp behind him.

"We're going in there?"

"Yeah. What's the matter? Not so big on adventure anymore?"

An inarticulate sound that could have been anything from *yes, no,* or *go to hell* gurgled out of her throat.

"Okay." She coughed. "I'll admit that cellars live up to the hype. But you said that there were boxes back here."

"There are." He jabbed at the cobwebs, inching forward. "Someone else's property, mind you."

"How long have you been here?"

"Three years."

He felt her fingers curl around his arm as they passed through the doorway.

Maybe this wasn't so bad.

"And they haven't been back to claim it?"

"I used the same argument when I found those pictures I showed you."

The spherical beam reached the dismantled stack of cardboard boxes. Hollie moved forward to stand beside him, but her palm still rested on his forearm.

"Only one of these boxes had pictures?" she asked.

"Yeah. There are ceramics, toys, and newspapers." He swung the beam to the stack of papers.

"Toys?"

Her hand fell off. She crouched down to the box he indicated.

Todd concentrated the flashlight on that box so she could inspect it. Careless of the dirt, Hollie thrust her bare arms into the container. A disturbed spider scurried out and onto the floor. She didn't even flinch.

"I'm impressed. The spider didn't scare you?"

Hollie squinted up against the flashlight.

"That little thing? In Florida we have bugs that make the car shudder if you hit one while driving."

Impressed by her comfort with arachnids, he leaned in closer, joining in on her curiosity.

Sitting back on her heels, Hollie held up a stuffed bear that was missing one eye.

"Hello, Todd," she mimicked a deep voice as she wiggled the bear at him.

In the dark his smile went undetected.

"What makes you think it's a male bear?"

"I don't know. No eyelashes maybe?"

He shook his head and snickered. "What else you got?"

Hollie hunched over and extracted a red frame. "Wow, look at this relic."

"What is it?"

"An Etch a Sketch." She held it up over her head for him to see.

Todd grabbed it with his free hand. One knob was missing and the screen looked like it had lost its magic drawing abilities.

"Whoa, look!"

Surprised by Hollie's outburst, he stabbed the beam into the black void beyond her. A moistened cinderblock wall with a large crack in it had him envisioning an infestation of nightcrawlers.

"What?"

"There's a name on the back of the Etch a Sketch."

His shoulders slumped in relief. No infestation from the hellmouth.

Hollie pulled the device back down to her eye level, her fingers skimming over a peeling strip of masking tape.

"Nina. Right? It says Nina."

Todd took the frame and flipped it over.

"Yeah. Nina. So maybe that's the girl."

Rising to her feet, Hollie looked around. "Let's keep going. Is there more in the back corner?"

There were no windows down here. Nothing to expose that it was two in the morning. The darkness and the rank air were stifling. In the midst of the gloom, the woman coated in dust with a slash of grime across an enthusiastic smile diminished those effects.

"In the past I have just poked the flashlight through this door. These boxes were right inside the doorway. I haven't really searched any further back," he admitted. "I didn't need the space, so I just left it."

"Can we take a peek?" Hopeful eyes stared up at him.

Dammit.

There was no way in hell he wanted to do this task.

"A quick scan," he hedged.

She grinned and grabbed his arm, raising it to aim the flashlight into the void. He allowed her touch for a moment before he moved the beam on his own. Following the cellar wall, crossing over a blend of cement, mud, and grease, they located a potbelly stove laying on its side.

"Oh, if you restored this it would make a great decorative piece in the foyer."

Todd shook his head. "Umm, just what I was thinking."

The flashlight caught a glimpse of her grin as she resumed her exploration. A stifling fifteen minutes transpired, revealing little more than a heap of soiled rags and an empty wooden bin.

"I guess there's nothing more." Hollie stood silhouetted in the beam, like a Broadway star in the spotlight.

"Thank you for letting me come down here," she said, wiping her hands against her hips. "I'll try and investigate this Nina."

"Okay." Todd plucked a clump of cobwebs off his forearm. "Let's get back upstairs."

Did that sound too eager?

Regardless, he reached for her elbow and used the flashlight to guide her across any crevasses in their path. Only when they were climbing the cellar stairs and basking in the glow of the lightbulb did he begin to relax.

Hollie still clutched the red plastic frame, reciting the name, *Nina, Nina, Nina.*

"It doesn't ring any bells," she admitted, following him into the kitchen.

Thrusting his hands under the sink faucet he washed away some of the grime, and nodded at her to join him. Hollie pumped the soap bottle and lathered her hands in suds as he pulled his out of the stream. When she was through he handed her a towel.

Looking down at her arms in dismay, she declared, "I'm pretty filthy right now, huh?"

Todd's lip hiked up at the corner.

"Pretty much," he agreed. "You can use the shower upstairs if you want. I have some clothes you can borrow while you throw yours in the washing machine."

She nodded, but looked forlorn. "God, I'm like a whirlwind of disruption. You should be asleep right now."

Disruption would be putting it mildly, he thought. Whirlwind? More like a maelstrom.

And yet somehow, this was the best he felt in a long time.

He had a routine. Wake up. Make coffee. Work. Contemplate getting a dog. Work. Eat. And go back to sleep.

Hollie Musgrave had just annihilated that routine.

"I'll go put some clothes in the bathroom," he muttered.

"Okay, but then go back to sleep. You're really making me feel bad."

"And what are you going to do?"

"I'm going to shower and then do some research on Nina Johnson or Nina Mariani."

Todd swiped a hand across his eyes, pinching the area at the top of his nose.

Of course you are.

"Let me get those clothes." He turned away.

Get away.

Salvage your routine.

Return to solitude.

Blissful solitude.

CHAPTER TEN

Cold water beat down on his forehead.

Well, that's interesting.

There had never been an occasion to have two showers running simultaneously in this house. Evidently the guest bathroom was consuming his hot water.

Not the guest bathroom.

Hollie.

There was a naked woman taking a shower just down the hall. From the way the jeans had molded her lithe figure, and the t-shirt had hugged a curvaceous chest, he could just imagine what a feast his guest bathroom was having right now.

Cold water.

After a few more moments he turned the faucet and reached for the towel. Grabbing clean jeans and the only fresh shirt readily available, he padded down the hallway on bare feet. Light poured out from under the guest bathroom door along with the sound of running water and a feminine sneeze.

Pausing at the sound, he forced his feet into motion and continued downstairs. The porcelain clock read 2:55 AM. Reheating the old coffee, he sat down with a mug in front of his laptop and started searching for Nina Johnson. Several minutes later he heard the sound of footsteps on the stairs. He smelled her before he saw her. A fresh damp scent of soap and shampoo blossomed in the kitchen just before she entered in an oversized t-shirt and sweatpants with the bottom hems rolled up. Seeing her in his clothes stifled his breathing. He cleared his throat and forced on an unaffected smirk.

"Feel better?" he asked.

"Much." She hugged her arms self-consciously. "I saw the light downstairs so I came down to check on you. What are you still doing up?"

Todd shrugged and waved at the laptop.

"I started searching for Nina."

Hollie slid onto the chair opposite him. Damp tendrils of hair hugged a healthy face, void of makeup.

"You didn't have to do that," she recited out of obligation, but her enthusiasm took over and she leaned forward on her elbows. "Did you find anything?"

"Well, of course there are a million Nina Johnsons." Before she could form the question, he added, "There's almost a million Nina Marianis too."

With a slump of the shoulders, she turned on her phone and began typing. "I'll just start to narrow it down until I have a workable list like I did with this place."

Todd sat back. "Are you sure you're a publicist and not a private detective?"

Ready to retort, she looked up, but her eyes dropped to his chest and she hefted a hand over her mouth to smother her snort.

"What?"

"Your shirt." She tipped her head at it and smiled.

Todd glanced down, not even sure what he had thrown on. All he saw was a black t-shirt. His typical work uniform.

TELL THAT TO KANJIKLUB.

Oh, it was *that* one.

"Yeah, yeah. So, I like STAR WARS. They gave me this shirt at work the day I left."

Hollie dropped her hand. "Do you miss it? Them?"

"Kinda."

"I can't imagine what you've been through with the explosion and the press. Maybe one day you won't have to worry about people showing up on your doorstep."

"So far I'm surviving this day and this person."

Hollie wrinkled her nose in that funny precursor to a smile. Dipping her head back over her phone they both searched the internet in silence for a little girl named *Nina*.

"Well," Todd spoke up after a while. "I'm striking out."

"Me too," Hollie replied sullenly.

She stifled a yawn.

"What time do we have to leave to make your flight?"

"If we leave here by eight we should be fine. My flight isn't until eleven."

"We have four hours," he said, looking at the clock. "Any chance I can convince you to take a nap?"

As soon as he uttered the words he realized it could have been misconstrued as a joint invitation. Hollie's slight hesitation confirmed that. She was a trooper though. She passed by the unwilling innuendo and managed another jaw-dropping yawn.

"Yeah. The words are all blurring together at this point. Hopefully I'm exhausted enough now to stay asleep."

"If not—" Todd rose, "—please let me know before you scare the hell out of me by going outside."

"Sorry about that."

"Seriously, Hollie. Someone left that note. You should really consider letting the police know about it."

"I would, if I wasn't leaving the state. Whoever left the note…they're getting what they want."

It still didn't sit well with him, but once she was on that plane she would become someone else's problem.

"Look at that. They still haven't picked up the car," Hollie remarked as they pulled out of Todd's driveway.

"Whoa!" she cried out, grabbing the dashboard.

Slamming on the brakes, Todd saw the source of her outburst. His next door neighbor was about to pull onto the road as well.

"Oh gosh. Sorry," Hollie collapsed back in her seat. "A case of Déjà vu. I thought they were going to rush us."

Todd eyed the blue Sentra and smacked the blinker, pulling his Jeep off the road, purposely blocking the vehicle. Through the windshield he saw the startled teenager glare at him.

"What are you doing?" Hollie cried.

"Just stopping to say good morning to my neighbor." He put the vehicle in park, ignoring the blaring horn from the Sentra. "I realize that I have to start being more social."

Wide brown eyes flared as a smile slowly crept across her face.

Todd approached the Sentra with an amiable grin on his face as he leaned over, planting his hands on the open window frame.

"Good morning," he greeted.

Long red bangs concealed one eye of the teenager. The other watched him guardedly.

"You're in my way."

"Oh, sorry about that. I just wanted to say hi. I realize your parents didn't introduce us yesterday."

The teen Stein looked beyond Todd at Hollie leaning against the hood of the car. Todd couldn't blame the kid. She was definitely something worth staring at.

"Hi," the kid replied. "Look, I have to get to work."

"Work? Oh wow. So you're out of high school?"

Todd swore he heard one of Hollie's mirthful snorts.

"Yeah. I've been out for two years now."

"Cool. Cool. Hey, I'm Todd. Todd Hewitt." He thrust his hand through the opening and received a grudging return shake.

"Cooper." Was the curt reply.

"Cooper. Look, we were doing some cleaning in the cellar and ran across this picture of a little girl. It was an old picture. I mean, you probably don't even know her. She'd have to be—oh—maybe Hollie's age here." He swept a hand in Hollie's direction and she dipped her head in acknowledgement.

"What about her?" Cooper gripped the steering wheel and glanced back over his shoulder.

"Was she the Johnson's daughter?"

"No." Cooper flinched. "I mean, I really don't know."

"Well, some of the stuff we found is personal. I'd like to get it back to her. I'm sure she'd like to have it."

"Yeah, well, good luck with that," Cooper grunted. "She's dead."

Todd heard Hollie's swift inhale behind him.

"Oh damn. That's a shame," he said.

The crunch of tires sounded just before a white car rolled down the driveway behind Todd. It stopped and Mrs. Stein jumped out, glaring at him.

"What are you doing?" she cried.

Standing upright Todd flashed a smile. "Mornin'. Just wanted to stop by and apologize for the intrusion yesterday." He applied a heavy dose of charm. "It was a surprise to us all—particularly Miss Musgrave here."

Sharp green eyes shifted toward Hollie and then swung back again.

"I was just mentioning to your son here," he nodded at the teen behind the wheel, "who I thought for sure was younger because you look so young."

In fact, she looked well past the sixty mark. Tepid brown hair infused with gray combined with wrinkles that looked like shattered glass across her face. Regardless, his forced charisma seemed to ease some of those creases.

"We were cleaning up in the cellar yesterday," he continued, "and found a few old photographs and such."

The guarded look returned and she grabbed the doorframe.

"There's a picture of a young girl, and upstairs there's a small rocking chair," Todd explained. "I was just wondering if we could get in touch with her to return the items. But—" he hesitated, "—Cooper here just told me that the girl passed away."

Mrs. Stein shot her son a harsh glare.

"Well, yes, but that was a long time ago."

"A long time ago?" Hollie stepped up alongside Todd. "She was a child?"

A quick nod confirmed the fact, but the neighbor's lips remained clamped.

"Did you know her?" Hollie asked. "Nina?"

Taken aback by hearing the name, Mrs. Stein shaded her eyes from the sun creeping up over the treetops.

"No. I didn't know her. I saw her a few times. We had just moved in."

"She was the Marianis' daughter." Todd stated.

If he posed it as a fact and dropped the last name he might catch her in agreement.

Instead, she shook her head to the negative. "Their granddaughter." She swallowed and glanced over her shoulder.

"So the Johnsons were their children? The little girl was Nina Johnson?" He pushed.

Cooper propped his elbow inside the window frame and cupped the side of his head, sighing heavily. Mrs. Stein, however, grew more agitated.

"It's nice of you to stop by and all," she said, "but will you please let my son get to work?"

"Oh, oh, of course." Todd patted his chest in typical *my bad* fashion. "It's just that we found something that the Johnsons may *really* want to have."

Hook. Line. Sinker.

Mrs. Stein cleared her throat. "I see them upon occasion. Whatever it is—if you want to leave it with me, I'll see that they get it."

Todd smiled and nodded. "That's very gracious of you, but I imagine they don't want something so personal being eyed by so many people."

Hollie chimed in beside him with an empathetic plea. "I believe I knew Nina when I was a child. I'd really like to meet up with her parents."

Mrs. Stein snorted. "I doubt that."

"Why do you doubt that?" Irritation seeped into Todd's polished demeanor.

Her deep-set eyes ran up and down the length of Hollie. "I'm not one to guess a woman's age, but we moved here in 1983. Nina passed away the end of that year."

Todd sensed Hollie sway and resisted the urge to reach for her.

"What are you?" Mrs. Stein continued. "Twenty-five?"

Hollie held her tongue.

"*Mom*," Cooper growled. "I have to go."

The woman's head snapped and her eyes widened. "I can't help you. Now please move out of the way." She ducked back down into the car.

Cooper wrapped his hands around the steering wheel and glared at Todd.

Todd raised his hands and shrugged. He nodded at Hollie to get back in the car as he slowly rolled the vehicle into reverse. Cooper revved the gas to climb out of the driveway, loose rock pelting the grill of his mother's car. She then pulled out, glaring at them the whole way. She went so far as to tap on the brakes to make sure that Todd didn't linger.

"They're lucky you have a flight to catch," Todd muttered, "or I would have kept pressing."

"Why?"

He turned to look at his passenger, who was watching him with curiosity.

"Why would you press them? They're your neighbors. I don't want you messing up a relationship with the people next door just because of my crazy notions."

His angry foot let up on the gas and he twisted the air conditioning vent to shoot cold air at his throat.

"I have no relationship with these people. And it seems that was wise on my part. I'm still not convinced they weren't the ones to run you off the road, and that's certainly not someone I want to cultivate a relationship with. And besides—" He pulled his gaze away from her to look for the next turn. "—I'm curious about this Nina. She lived in my house. I saw her face. I'd like to know what happened to her. And—"

Todd tapped the steering wheel. The air conditioning couldn't produce cool air fast enough for him.

"And?" the soft voice prompted.

"And—" He turned to catch her gaze. Sun pierced the windshield, scalding her chocolate eyes with rays of honey. "And, I'd like to see you get a decent night's sleep."

He caught the furtive corner of her smile before she dipped her head to focus on her phone.

"I'm going to keep searching while you're driving if that's okay," she said quietly, her thumbs already plucking away.

Climbing up the ramp to get onto I-95, Todd let his mind drift back to the early morning hours. They huddled together over the table, struggling to stay awake before climbing the stairs together and breaking off to venture to separate rooms. When he woke four hours later, he realized how eager he was to see her again.

None of that mattered, though. This was a fluke encounter, and Hollie was on her way to the airport to board a plane and fly out of his life.

Privacy.

That's what I want.

Isolation.

That's what I want.

Managing a discreet glance at his passenger he saw glossy chestnut hair, fresh from his shower, cascading across her cheek as she stared down at her phone. Sunlight glinted off of long eyelashes and soft lips parted in surprise at something she read.

Before he had the chance to ask, he heard her exclaim, "No!"

Still clutching the cellphone, her hands dropped to her lap. Gone was the pert nose and soft lips as she turned her head away to look out the passenger window. The slim fingers clenched the phone.

"Hollie? What is it? What did you find?"

When she swung her head back in his direction—one quick glance at her plaintive eyes made him suck in his breath.

"I'm sorry," she whispered.

"Sorry?" That floored him. "What for?"

Her gaze dropped to the phone in her hands. "I—you said that the explosions in your neighborhood were a nationwide news event—"

His stomach dropped. Plummeted was more like it.

"I didn't mean to search," she defended. "But I wanted to know why the press would be hounding you."

"It's okay, Hollie," he assured, his throat tight. "I have no secrets."

"I'm so sorry. I had no idea." Her hands trembled.

"It happened a long time ago." Hollow words.

"Your wife—I didn't realize—"

If he wasn't driving, he would squeeze his eyes shut and keep them shut.

"I traveled. I traveled way too much," he heard himself say as if it was a stranger reciting a foreign tale. "I was out of state when it happened. Whitney should have been at work, but—"

She was home, packing.

"Todd—" Hollie pleaded from beside him. "You don't have to tell me. You don't have to say anything."

Keeping his eyes trained on the highway, he was grateful for the excuse not to make eye contact. He didn't want her to see the guilt. He didn't want *anyone* to see the guilt.

"It's only fair," he replied in a clipped tone. "You shared your tale with me."

He took her silence as a cue to continue. He *needed* to continue. A confession to a woman about to board a plane and never be seen again was the perfect outlet. But if he dared to glimpse at her, he would realize that she was more than an outlet.

"Whitney wasn't even in the house," he recounted hoarsely. "She was out front, getting the mail. The explosion—" it was hard to swallow, "—shredded the house and sent pieces flying. It was that debris that got her."

At the sound of Hollie's gasp, he added, "They tell me her death was instantaneous. No suffering."

A shaky hand hovered over his arm, too afraid to settle on it. Finally she returned it to her lap.

"I can't even find words to express how sorry I am," she choked.

Todd lifted his arm back to the steering wheel, out of reach.

"There is no reason for you to be sorry. You didn't know her. You don't know me. I mean, hell, we were in the process of separating at the time. That's supposed to make it all better, right? Our relationship was falling apart because we were rarely together. So that's supposed to make it all easier on me, right? Well, it doesn't. There isn't a moment of any day that I don't feel pain and regret." He bumped his head back against the headrest. "There isn't any day that I don't feel guilt."

The hand that had reached out to touch him was gone completely. He dared not even look at her.

Way to go, Hewitt.

This is why you can't interact with the public. This is why you have to stay in your farmhouse.

"You've been in that farmhouse alone for three years."

No matter how wistful the voice was, he refused to glance her way. Imagine the relief she must feel that she was on her way to the airport—away from him.

"It says here that a lawsuit was settled with the gas company and each of the parties affected received an *adequate* compensation." Hollie cleared her throat. "There is *no* compensation adequate for the loss of a loved one."

Todd's throat pumped and his fingers gripped the steering wheel with inhuman strength.

"So you took that money, bought that farmhouse, quit traveling, and have lived a life of seclusion."

PHILADELPHIA AIRPORT — 2 MILES

Halleluiah.

"Yep. That pretty much sums it up."

There was no point in hiding the bitterness.

The other half of the car remained silent, which suited him just fine. After a few minutes he surrendered to the temptation to look at her. It startled him when their eyes collided. He snapped his back to the off-ramp.

"I am sorry, Todd," she whispered huskily. "I am sorry for you. I am sorry for her. I—"

"Look. There's no reason for you to be."

He pulled into the short-term parking lot, parked, and shut off the ignition, staring straight ahead.

"I'll walk you in if you'd like," he offered, "or if you don't want me to, I understand."

"Todd." Her voice beckoned, but he refused to turn.

"Todd." She tried again. "Look at me."

Hands still locked on the wheel, he swiveled his head in her direction. She was turned sideways in her seat, looking directly at him with a sincerity he felt he didn't deserve.

"It was a tragedy. It should have never happened, but don't let guilt consume you. I grew up watching that happen to my father. He couldn't make it to the boat outing that my mother went on. He was busy. She passed away that day, but I lost my father that day as well. He was never the same. Don't lose your life to that."

A sharp cramp seized his chest like a giant fist squeezing his heart. So much loss in this world. This woman's mother, her father, her troubled search to locate a memory. Whitney—and before that, the loss of a relationship that was once so strong.

Powerless fingers slipped from the steering wheel and landed on his thighs.

"You didn't even get a chance to look up Nina yet," he said, staring down at his empty hands. "You spent the whole ride looking up my miserable life."

"Not miserable." Tentative fingers reached for and rested atop his hand. "There are always bright times. Focus on them."

Like now?

His head flinched as if he could toss aside the notion.

"You have my number." He studied her hand. Slightly tanned. No nail polish. Short nails. "Keep me posted on your search. And I'll let you know if I find anything more in the house."

Hollie withdrew her touch. "Sounds like a plan." She reached for the door handle and looked back at him. "Will you walk in with me?"

Todd skewed a look at her and this time his smile was genuine.

"I said I would."

Watching from behind the line as Hollie checked in, he could see her hands flail in animation, no doubt defending why she had to change her flight. It would be of no use. They would still charge her the change fee.

As she walked toward him with her ticket in hand, he felt his heart kick up a notch.

"It's like arguing with a brick wall," she complained once she joined him.

"Occasionally you'll find a porous brick."

Her giggle was genuine as she fell into step alongside him. It seemed like their pace was intentionally slow, lingering on the outskirts of the security line. Finally, Hollie glanced at her watch and sighed.

"I guess I better go through now."

"Yeah, you don't want to miss your flight after all this." *That wouldn't be so bad.* "Do you want me to follow up with the police about the accident?" he offered.

"No, I'll call them when I get home." She hesitated, looking everywhere before she finally returned to his eyes. "I don't know how to thank you." Her shoulders slumped. "You put up with me and my crazy search for something—"

"Unattainable?" he suggested thickly.

"Yes." She nodded, still searching his eyes.

For the longest time they stood in that throng of travelers, staring at each other, standing close enough that no one dared pass between them.

This woman had appeared on his doorstep and rattled his life like a can of marbles, letting them spill out and roll in every direction. And now he was saying goodbye to that beautiful chaos.

Without thinking, he reached up and hooked his finger under her chin, urging it up as he bent down to kiss her. It was a soft brush of lips, gently coaxing the tension from her. Settling into it, he felt her tentative response grow in confidence. It could have ended at just that, but neither seemed to want to break from it. Each pass lingered longer than the previous until he felt he could never stop.

Withdrawing from that sweet temptation, he found her chin tilted up in anticipation, and her eyes pressed closed. They fluttered open with big black pupils eclipsing the bronze rim.

"Look." His voice was hoarse. "Don't analyze that. It was just something I wanted to do, okay?"

Hollie nodded mutely, her eyes still wide until she blinked a few more times and took a tentative step backwards. It was when her gaze dropped to his lips that he nearly reached to haul her against him.

Nearly.

"You better put on some sunglasses, Mr. Hewitt."

"Why is that?"

She winked. "The press might recognize you."

A growl began low in his throat but he swallowed it before it could surface.

"You better get on that plane, Miss Musgrave."

Before I do something stupid.

The mischievous smile was gone as she retreated another step and merged into the growing line. A boisterous family fell in behind her, obliterating his view to just an outline of smooth chocolate hair slipping across a shoulder. At that moment she turned and flashed a smile at him before the crowd swallowed her.

Damn.

CHAPTER ELEVEN

It was hard to do much of a search on her cell phone, and Hollie's mind wasn't into it. All the tiny text about the Nina Marianis of the world faded as her thoughts drifted to that kiss. Even now, sitting on the plane, waiting to pull back from the gate, her face flushed at the recollection.

Don't analyze that.

It was just a congenial kiss goodbye—after all they had been through over the last twenty-four hours. She had slept in his house, used his shower—waded through his cellar.

But friendly goodbye kisses should be simple pecks—not simmering smooth strokes.

What did it matter? The plane was pulling onto the taxiway now. This adventure was over. She had lost the zeal for the search of her memories upon discovering his. The man had lost his wife. There were people out there with challenges far greater than hers.

Did those people receive, *STAY AWAY FROM THIS HOUSE, HOLLIE* notes?

So many questions roiled through her mind. She tipped her head back against the seat and fell into a fitful sleep.

The door loomed. She reached for it, but it never opened. Instead she felt as if she was being sucked away from it—hauled back into a black tunnel.

Hollie jolted the second the plane's tires hit the runway. Outside, the hulking outline of the football stadium paralleling the runway provided a stark contrast against the sunny sky.

She was back home.

The farmhouse.

The accident.

The note.

The kiss.

She tried to distance herself from it.

Todd.

An image of him propped against the kitchen counter, long legs crossed, arms crossed, a black t-shirt stretched tight across wide shoulders, a shadow of dark scruff across a chiseled jaw, and sandy hair with no style in mind. A private man. A grieving man. A lost man. A sexy man.

Ding.

The passengers surged to their feet in a bulky shuffle toward the door.

It was back to reality.

"So, you should look!" Flo demanded.

Hollie had made it as far as the lobby before being assaulted by the team.

"It's going to take some time—"

Frank thrust her half-drank cup of coffee at Hollie. "Here, sit down. Have coffee."

"It would be easier on my laptop, which is still in the car."

"We'll wait here."

Florence and Francine dropped down onto the loveseat in unison, their arms crossed. Hollie's gaze fled to Maryann who was seated across from them. She shrugged in defense.

"Ladies, can't Hollie get settled? She just got back."

Frank patted the cushion between her and Flo. "What's more comfortable than a seat between friends?"

Hollie raised her eyebrow and succumbed to a giggle.

"All right. I'll get my laptop out of the car and be right back."

Flo glanced at the digital clock mounted in the corner. "It's almost suppertime. We can order Chinese from next door!"

Yum. Leftover coffee with beef and broccoli.

Hollie's stomach rolled at the thought, but she smiled as she made her way outside. Grabbing some cash out of her purse to pay for dinner she saw Todd's business card sticking out of her wallet.

TODD HEWITT
Printed Circuit Board Services
TLH LLC

It listed a phone number and an email, but there was no fancy logo.

Should she text him just to say she made it home safely?

No. He was probably happy to have his quiet life restored.

Slipping the card back into her purse she grabbed her laptop and returned through the sliding glass doors. The lobby and these ladies would keep her from the temptation to contact him.

Hollie gave a simplified version of her trip north, omitting the accident, the note…and the kiss. It didn't matter. All the trio heard was, "*man*."

"What did he look like?"

"I bet he had black hair."

"And blue eyes."

"And wore flannel shirts and boots."

"Flannel shirts and boots?" Hollie repeated, laughing. "It's the summer."

"Well, it's Pennsylvania," Flo observed. "It's cooler up north."

Shaking her head with a smile, Hollie tuned them out for a moment to continue her internet search.

There was a surprising number of Nina Marianis in the world. Even a surprising number in Pennsylvania. Adding the word *deceased* to the search narrowed it down to zero hits. Changing tactics she found a site that just searched obituaries. It was a morbid task, but it yielded a few results. There were two Mariani obituaries listed in the vicinity of Todd's farmhouse that seemed to fit in the timeframe. Only one was a female with the name *Nina*.

Nina M. Mariani
Doylestown, PA
Born: October 9, 1982
Passed Away: December 15, 1987

Hollie felt the air conditioner drill down on her bare arms.

"They say when you're real young you can remember your former life. But when you grow up you forget about it."

Her mother's words echoed hollowly.

Maryann was seated next to her and picked up on her change in demeanor.

"What is it, Hollie? Did you find something?"

Francine and Flo were still busy rambling on about the man.

"This—there's a girl—" Hollie stuttered for just Maryann to hear. "The city, name, and timeframe seem to work." She swallowed slowly and met Maryann's curious gaze. "She died nine days before I was born."

The elderly woman clutched the collar of her duster.

"Coincidence, Hol," she stuttered, but the doubt in her eyes mirrored Hollie's.

"You two look like you've seen a ghost," Frank remarked. "Did you find something?"

Maryann explained as Hollie stared at the numbers.

"Oh my." Florence crossed herself.

When Hollie looked up she found the ladies staring at her as if she would sprout a ghostly veil and levitate two feet off the floor.

"Don't be silly," she chastised them.

Setting the laptop aside and making a show of eating her beef and broccoli, Hollie listened to them ramble on with fantastic theories. The more ludicrous their concepts, the more comforted she felt. But, honestly, she wanted to share this news with Todd.

Would he care?

Maryann patted her hand. Hollie reached and curled her fingers around the woman's. She squeezed.

I'm okay.

"Why don't we let Hollie get some rest?" Maryann suggested. "You have to work tomorrow, don't you?"

Friend, mother, or personal assistant. Hollie adored Maryann Baumann.

As exhausted as she was, sleep was still a fitful companion. Trudging to the shower she let cold water restore some vitality, and then dressed in a hurry, knowing she would have some catch-up editing to tackle.

The lobby was empty. None of the ladies were up yet. Last night she all but had to muzzle them to keep from telling anyone who walked through the door that, *"Hollie is reincarnated."*

Slinking her laptop and camera bag over her shoulder, Hollie reached up and finger-combed her still moist hair as she triggered the sliding glass door out into the parking lot. A wave of humid air thwarted the attempts of her fingers. She breathed in the briny scent and jogged over to her Altima parked under a sweep of Spanish moss.

"Damn spam," she grumbled as she pulled the pamphlet out from under her windshield wiper.

It was a menu for a local BBQ restaurant. Cold fingers of fear invaded the sultry heat as she felt an uncanny notion that she was being watched.

Her head snapped up. She searched the parking lot. There was a smattering of cars, but no pedestrians. The top of a yacht passed by through the Intracoastal waterway and a pack of seagulls scavenged a dumpster on the side of the building.

All was quiet. Peaceful. No one watched her. No one cared.

Still, the notion of that note found on Todd's front doorstep had spooked her. It also spiked her anger.

When someone tells a child not to touch something, that only spurs their curiosity. That was the state she was in. The dreams. The reality of seeing a delusory house that actually existed—and the cryptic handwritten warning. These were all motivators.

In her shared office outside the stadium grounds Hollie caught up on outstanding emails and assignments. At the first opportunity, she reached for her phone and called her father. It was early in Arizona, but she knew he would be up.

"Hermey!" Stuart Musgrave's happy voice filled her ear.

"Hi Dad."

"Everything okay? You usually call on Saturdays."

Her father was the ultimate creature of habit.

"Yes, yes. I just wanted to see how you're doing."

"Oh," he sounded congenial. "I'm fine, just surprised to hear from you on a Wednesday."

Might as well get to the point.

"Dad, do you remember those dreams I always had?" She tested out the subject.

"The house?"

"Yeah." If she admitted that she visited the house in person she was afraid her father might check her into a clinic. Instead she modified the tale. "Well, I finally saw a house number in my dream, and I—I think I found a possible match. A farmhouse in Pennsylvania."

Silence.

Oh dear.

"You've never been to Pennsylvania," her father remarked carefully. "Well, not as a child, anyway. I don't know if your work might have taken you there."

"Are you sure? Maybe when Mom took me to see Grandma?"

Silence.

She knew it hurt anytime her mother was mentioned. Stuart Musgrave distanced himself from Florida to escape from the pain. In doing so, he detached himself from his daughter because of her close resemblance to her mother.

"No. You only went once or twice, and your mom would call me several times a day. I always knew where you two were."

"Okay."

There was no sense in hashing out this topic with him. Her father wasn't big into unsolvable mysteries. That was more of her mother's talent. Instead, she turned the topic to tee times and mentioned a couple pro golfers she had worked with a few weeks ago. That set him into a cheerful shift, and they ended up hanging up with a promise to chat on Saturday.

Stifling a yawn, Hollie noticed her officemates packing up for the day. The sooner she left here, the sooner she could get a jump on her Mariani stalking.

Okay, yes, one could claim she was an internet stalker. But there was no way to explain her familiarity with that farmhouse. The thirst for knowledge crawled under her skin and twitched like a thousand cricket legs.

Traveling across the Courtney Campbell Causeway, Hollie watched families with fishing poles pulled over on the side. Her dad used to take her to do the same thing. Before the accident. After that he didn't like to be near the bay. They went fishing at local lakes instead.

Lost in her thoughts, she finally noticed the sedan tailgating her. It wasn't uncommon. There was always traffic along 60. She switched lanes and the vehicle followed.

Peering into the rearview mirror, she couldn't see the driver behind the heavily tinted windshield. Brake lights in front of her forced her to tap her own. The black sedan pulled up within a few inches of her bumper. She raised her hands.

Back the hell off.

Instead, the sedan saw a break in the traffic and slipped into the right lane.

Good. Get lost.

Still locked in place by the traffic ahead, Hollie sat nearly idle as the sedan pulled up alongside her. There was space in its lane for it to continue on past, but it paralleled her and hovered at her side. She could vaguely see a profile behind the tinted window. That profile appeared to be angled in her direction as the car remained neck and neck with her.

"Go, damn you!" she called out, irritated.

It slowed down and dropped in behind her again.

Hollie gripped the steering wheel and slid her Altima into the right lane. Instantly the sedan slowed down and slipped in after her.

The first inkling of fear began an insidious crawl under her scalp. It was nonsense, of course. This was a case of mild road rage, or just someone's absurd idea of entertainment.

On this causeway there was nowhere to go. Two lanes sliced across the wide bay. She could turn off to one of the many fishing access points, but if it was some sort of psycho tailing her, those exits would prove too vulnerable.

Holding steady with the sedan tight on her bumper, she took a deep breath when the opposite shoreline came into view. Once the water was behind her, Hollie took the first right possible, and cursed when the sedan followed. Another hasty left was mimicked by her tail.

Perspiration bubbled on her forehead.

At one point she charged the end of a yellow traffic light and thought surely she would lose him, but the sedan burst across the intersection to a chorus of horns. Nearing her neighborhood, rather than lead this person directly to her home, she pulled into the Publix parking lot, straight into a spot at the front of the store. She got out of the car, and made a show of extracting her cell phone and pounding keys on it.

That's right. 9-1-1, you bastard.

She wasn't really calling it. She was waiting to see what the driver did.

The black sedan executed a slow drive-by, tapping the brakes to idle a few feet away. Through the tinted glass she could see that the figure was wearing sunglasses, but aside from that small fact she couldn't even confirm what sex it was.

She stood in the crook of her open car door, staring down the shady figure until a woman with two children and a shopping cart crossed between them. At that moment the sedan pulled away and exited the parking lot.

Hollie slumped back down into her car with her legs jutting out onto the blacktop. After a few sustaining breaths she walked into the store and paced around for an hour. On each lap around the pharmacy section she'd cast a glance out the windows. Finally satisfied, she drove home, her eyes glued to the rearview mirror. There was no black sedan. And even though the encroaching night cast heavy pockets of darkness in her parking lot, there were no unexpected vehicles lurking there.

On edge, she bolted toward the entryway. It was too late for the ladies to be congregated in the lobby. She rushed up to her floor and closed the door behind her, careful to throw the dead bolt.

Two days later Hollie was convinced it had all been coincidence. There was traffic on the causeway. Everyone was maneuvering to gain a lead. The drive-by in the Publix parking lot couldn't be so easily explained, but there had been no similar incidents since then.

There was little yielded from her internet searches for Nina Mariani other than the dates of her birth and death.

The surname wasn't Smith, but damn, there were a lot of hits on the name. There was a restaurant in Norristown, Pennsylvania called *Marianis*. There were Mariani cabinetmakers, Mariani plumbers, Mariani lawyers. Marianis who had been convicted and Marianis who were in the clergy…but none had a correlation to Nina.

Hollie stepped outside her office building on Dale Mabry and cupped a hand over her eyes to shield them from the sun.

It wasn't sun glare that caused the apparition outside. Across the street, the black sedan was pulled over to the curb with the same sunglass-wearing profile behind the tinted windows, watching her.

A quick glance up and down the side street produced no hope for aid. No police. No pedestrians. Hollie hoisted her phone out of her purse and made a show of pointing at it. Tinted windows or not, there was no mistaking the waggling of a finger behind that veneer.

If she pressed 9-1-1, what would happen? She'd report that someone was following her and by the time the police arrived, the car would be gone. She'd file a report, and in an hour she'd still be faced with the long ride home alone. Alternatively, she could walk over to the car and pound on the window, demanding answers. So tempting was that thought, she took a step off the sidewalk.

The engine revved across the street.

A warning?

This was absurd. Was it a disgruntled fan? Someone who felt their sports hero was not featured adequately by her?

The car was standard. A Camry, an Accord, a Malibu. Whatever. There was none of the flash associated with athletes. And if one of them wanted to stalk her, they wouldn't usually hide behind tinted glass. They would blatantly flirt in her face.

Hollie turned around and climbed the front steps back into her office building, fastening the lock to the front door as soon as she was inside.

Through that glass barrier she watched the window of the sedan slide down and a man in a white short-sleeved shirt considered her from behind reflective sunglasses. In slow motion, his hand extended to form the shape of a gun as his fingers mimicked shooting. His fist recoiled and the window slid back up.

The sedan pulled away.

Hollie stood at her office window, staring down at the street. It was empty with the exception of a few utility vehicles passing through to a nearby construction site. It was 6:35 PM. On Fridays the team was usually long gone by 5:00 PM, prepping for whatever events they had to cover on the weekend.

Too afraid to drive home alone, she considered her possibilities.

Of the ladies she lived with, only Francine had a driver's license, but she would never drive across the causeway, or—*gasp*—into the city.

For a moment, Hollie considered calling the putz she had dated awhile back, but that would be mortifying. Even more absurd was her desire to call Todd. She doubted he would even answer the phone. One, he clearly wanted his privacy. Two, he probably thought she was a lunatic.

But, he had been sympathetic—

He had been protective—

He had kissed her—

No. She couldn't call Todd. What could he do a thousand miles away?

Listen.

Offer advice.

No. It was a silly notion.

Resuming her stance at the window, Hollie clasped her phone so tight that her palm cramped.

6:37.

She crossed over to her desk and drew Todd's business card out of her purse.

CHAPTER TWELVE

Todd stared at the incoming number long enough that the call nearly went to voicemail. His thumb finally swiped.

"Hello?"

There was silence. She must have hung up already.

"Hi, Todd."

Hollie's voice was so soft he nearly cupped a hand over his right ear.

"Is everything okay? Did you find something?"

The sigh on the other end was unmistakable. Not an impatient sound—more like relief.

"No. Not really."

Frowning, he pulled back the kitchen chair and dropped down onto it.

He had been fighting the urge to call her for 48 hours now. It would have been simple to explain it away as curiosity. *Oh, just calling to see if you found out anything more about Nina.* When in fact, all he could think about was their farewell at the airport.

For 48 hours he tormented over the fact that he'd kissed a woman other than his wife. Granted, from what he had gathered, Whitney had been kissing other men while he was on the road—but that wasn't his style. As rocky as the marriage was, it wasn't something he entertained.

Till death do us part.

He flinched at the words.

"I don't know why I called," Hollie's voice arrested his attention. "You're going to think I'm crazy."

"Again?" he joked.

A small chuckle nearly tickled his ear.

"Yes, again."

"Okay, shoot."

"Ouch," she exclaimed. "Poor choice of words."

She then explained about the black sedan that she first wrote off as a fluke, but how the driver had returned and made a gun gesture with his fingers.

Todd's slouch in the kitchen chair stiffened as her tale unfolded. His hand curled into a fist on the table.

"And where are you right now?" he asked.

"In my office. He's gone, but—" she hesitated, "—I'm just worried that the moment I leave he might reappear behind me. This is so sad, but I'm literally afraid to drive home."

Before Todd could respond she added, "I mean, I know I can't hide up here forever. And well, damn, I have to commute to work every day. I can't let this guy scare me. I just don't know—" again, another pause, "—I don't know why this is happening."

"Let me ask you this," he tried to rationalize. "Prior to visiting my house, had you ever noticed anyone following you—had you received any notes on your doorstep?"

"No. Not that I'm aware of."

That disturbed him. What was it about his house that put this woman in potential danger?

"Have you called the police?"

"And say what? You know how they'll react."

"You can call the officer up here. He has a report that you were t-boned by a hit-and-run driver. Combine that with these other incidents and he can't discount it."

"Maybe not, but what *can* he do? Seriously? There's nothing concrete to go after. It's just harassment. Nothing more than you've experienced by the press."

"It's different," he countered. "No one threatened me."

"I don't know." She sounded dispirited.

"How about an Uber?"

"Not sure I'd even trust a stranger right now."

"You have no one you can ride home with?"

"If I said no would that make me pathetic?"

Todd grinned and his fist uncurled. "Can the man who lives like a recluse and is afraid of his own basement even answer that?"

This time she laughed. It was such an honest, pleasant sound.

"I mean—," she continued, "—no one that I want to ask."

"Well, if I was there you wouldn't have to ask."

There was no response, which made him want to smack his forehead on the kitchen table.

"I wish you were," she whispered.

What?

"Look—" He took a breath. "Here's what we can do. How long is the drive home?"

"40 minutes-ish."

"Okay. Can you go hands-free on your phone?"

"Yes." He heard the first bite of enthusiasm.

"You stay on the phone with me. Get in your car. And I'll be with you." To justify his action he added, "I have news to share, anyway."

"News?" She perked up.

"Yep. I had another chat with my dear neighbor."

The sound of Hollie in motion came through. "Now you have my interest."

"Damn, and I didn't before?"

The banter was light, meant to distract her unease, but it also felt remarkably natural. Truth be told, he was about to call her with his recent findings…he had just been too busy trying to talk himself out of it.

Once Hollie was in her car her voice echoed slightly through the speaker in her dashboard.

"It looks clear," she observed, talking loud as if he couldn't hear her.

When her head turned, her voice wavered. "I'm starting to feel like an idiot again."

"Yeah, yeah," he chided amiably. "Just keep your eyes on the road."

"It's more of what's behind me that makes me nervous."

"You're on a busy street. Keep that in mind."

"So—what is this news?"

Todd rose and paced across the kitchen floor, listening to the floorboards creak. "Well, I couldn't get too much. Old Mr. Stein showed up."

"How did you even get the Mrs. to talk?"

"Charm, of course."

Hollie's snort sounded through the phone. It was a sound he was growing familiar with, and would do anything to incite.

"All right," he confessed. "The truth is that I found out very little, but I just wanted to talk to you."

A blinker sounded in the background. It took a moment for Hollie to respond.

"Careful, Mr. Hewitt," she warned. "I might suspect you're flirting with me."

Todd drew open the refrigerator door. "I wouldn't have a friggin clue how to flirt."

A siren sounded on the other end.

"Everything okay?" he asked quickly.

"Fire engine. All is well."

Leaning into the cool bowels of the refrigerator, he grinned. "Well, what our chatty Mrs. Stein attempted to emphasize was that the previous owners of my bachelor pad were indeed the *Johnsons*. She doesn't know where I picked up the name Mariani, even though I pointed out that it was from her own mouth. She insisted I must be mistaken."

"Odd." Hollie's voice sounded tinny.

"She did share that the *Johnsons* had two adult sons, and one granddaughter."

"Nina?"

Closing the door with his hip, Todd pulled out a Tupperware container of chicken nuggets. "She wouldn't say the name, but she did state that the girl died young, just before the Steins moved in. And evidently, shortly after that, so did the girl's father."

"I found a listing for Nina Mariani's death online. Not an obituary—just a record of her death." The blinker sounded again and Hollie returned with a subdued tone. "Tell me that it's just coincidence that Nina Mariani passed away a week before I was born, and that I dream about the farmhouse she lived in."

Todd set down the nugget in his hand. He stared out the window at the split-rail fence with clumps of high grass circling the posts.

"It's coincidence," he murmured, unconvinced.

There was another gap of mutual silence. He felt powerless. It was just another occasion of him being too far away to protect someone.

Someone he cared about.

"Look—" he hesitated, "—I haven't taken a vacation in a long time. I was thinking—"

"Todd, I think I see him!" Hollie cried.

Todd gripped the rim of the kitchen counter. "Hollie, be careful. If you're sure, call the police. Do you want me to call them? What highway are you on?"

"Hold on."

There was a distinct rev of the engine.

"Hol, what's happening?" He left the kitchen, bounding upstairs, ready to—

To what?

Pack?

"I don't know. Maybe it wasn't him," she declared, halting him halfway up the stairs. "Dammit, I hate being this paranoid. I'm not the type to jump at shadows."

Holding onto the bannister, Todd lowered himself down onto a step.

"I should have never called you," she continued. "I don't know why I did. I went up to find your farmhouse, and ever since then, I feel like I'm being watched. It must be some idiot from work."

The idea of an idiot from work sat about as well with him as an unidentified psycho. He had to pose the question.

"Could an old boyfriend be stalking you?"

He could hear her fingers drumming against the steering wheel.

"It would have to be a *really old* boyfriend. I haven't been seeing anyone in quite some time. I've been going through the *men suck* phase for about a year."

"Ouch." He flinched.

Hollie laughed. "Well, maybe they don't *all* suck," she added. "But in answer to your question, I highly doubt anyone from my past gave me a second thought after they left me."

"I wouldn't exactly call you forgettable."

"Well, with you I made quite an impact…literally."

Although she rendered her accident outside his driveway a joke, neither of them thought of it as one.

"You were saying something about a vacation before I rudely interrupted you." Her voice was soft again, to the point he pressed the phone tight against his ear.

"I was."

Great. I'm coming across as a stalker.

"You would like Clearwater Beach."

Not an outright rejection.

"—and it would be good to see you again."

Todd tried to squelch the pleasure that statement elicited even as he began to calculate plans for a getaway.

Why the hell not? He had not had a vacation in years.

"Well, yeah, I thought maybe I could take in the beach." *I do like to fish.* "And maybe we could put our heads together and figure out what your connection is to my house."

That sounded legit, right? Not overly enthusiastic?

"I'd appreciate the help," she said sincerely. "I just hope you don't think I'm insane."

"Maybe I'll be able to figure that out in person."

It was meant as humorous, but perhaps a little too much truth rang out.

As soon as Hollie was parked and safely in her condominium lot, some of the tension finally eased.

"I'd really like to see you," she admitted, "but don't—don't come down here because you feel sorry for me. I mean—I'm just jumping at shadows here. I wouldn't want you to come down here under some misguided notion that you need to protect me. That would just be silly." Her voice dropped off.

Todd rubbed his forehead and waited a moment before responding.

"I do things because I want to, Hollie. I'd like to see you again. I can try to justify it by saying I want a vacation, etcetera. But that's just the truth of it."

It was easier confessing something like that over the phone. If neither liked where the conversation was heading they could just hang up.

"If that's too much—" he murmured, "—I get it. Trust me, it's not like me to do anything like this."

To his surprise there was a soft laugh on the other side. "I think I've gathered that about you already."

His lips hiked up, but he remained silent.

"How soon can you come down?" she asked.

Now his smile developed into something real.

"Let me look at flights and I'll let you know what I find. In the meantime, be careful. Call me—"

"I'll call if I see anything," she assured, her voice gaining confidence. "I have to work offsite tomorrow."

"Will you have people around you? People you know?"

"Yeah. I'll be okay."

She didn't sound a hundred percent sure.

It might have been wise to hang up and dismiss this whole crazy idea. Yeah, that might have been wise.

Wisdom wasn't a prized possession right now. Not since that kiss at the airport.

Hell—not since a midnight meal of cold pizza and a charming snort of a laugh.

If Todd thought it was going to be awkward, Hollie sure didn't make it so. To his surprise she was there waiting for him at the bottom of the escalator.

Trapped in a throng of passengers, he could only stand still and watch her as the stairway glided down.

She was dressed in jean capris with frayed bottoms, and a white sleeveless blouse that showed off sun-kissed arms. A warm smile lit up her face when she spotted him.

In all those years of weekly travel through airports—when was the last time someone had been at the bottom of the escalator to welcome him?

Still holding his duffle bag, he gave her a one-armed hug, lingering long enough to smell the lemon in her hair.

"Welcome to the Sunshine state," she beamed.

"You know, I've been to Florida before," he reminded her with a quick grin. "Probably not a state in this fine country of ours that I haven't worked in."

"You haven't traveled in a few years. Has the routine changed much?"

Todd glanced over her head at the melee near the baggage carousel. "No. I'll admit I don't miss it."

"Regrets already?" Her bottom lip plumped up.

"No." His smile felt genuine. It felt good. "I may not like traveling, but I don't mind being here."

"I guess, *I don't mind,* is as good as I can hope for given the circumstances."

Opposing thoughts took up a genuine fist fight inside his head. Trying to tame them he focused on his foremost concern by scanning the crowd to see if anyone's gaze lingered on Hollie too long. His wandering glance came to a halt on the woman looking up at him. Tremulous lines tugged at the corners of her eyes and shadows pooled beneath them. Signs of distress and lack of sleep were blatant on an otherwise striking face. She searched his eyes, her smile fading with each passing second.

"There's something we need to address," he stated throatily.

"Oh?"

He dropped the bag and wound his hand beneath her hair, his fingertips grazing the curve of her neck.

In that split second of indecision, he caught the flash of dark caramel eyes, warm and sweet—filled with temptation. Even as he dipped closer, he took in every detail—the soft fan of dark lashes, the sultry scent of her skin. The quick breath that smelled of cinnamon. Then his mouth connected with hers and his eyes dropped closed.

Each brush of his lips against hers elicited new sensations. Not just the raw physical pleasure of the taste of her, but far more erotic temptations.

Fusion.

Balance.

A sense of belonging.

When her palm cupped his shoulder, the tension left her spine and she relaxed into him, the kiss taking a turn in intensity.

Were it not for the luggage cart that rolled over his toe, he would have been in no rush to come up for air. A wayward elbow struck him in the ribs and the hastily muttered, *Get a room*, actually made him pull back and laugh.

Hollie wrapped the hand that had been on his shoulder across her mouth, but mirth brimmed in her eyes.

"Well—wow," he reeled, "that was *not* how I planned to act when I saw you."

"Were you thinking more along the lines of a civil handshake?" She extended her hand.

Instead of shaking it, he took it in his own and used the grip to steer her toward the exit.

"You may find this hard to believe, but I consider myself a tad reserved."

"Reserved?" She slanted a glance at him and slowly extracted her fingers from his to reach in her purse for her keys. "Stuffy, you mean?"

Before he could answer they both had to focus on darting through the line of cars and busses at the arrivals entrance.

Once across, and walking through the parking deck, Hollie asked, "And what was it that we needed to address?"

"I was going to say—" He cleared his throat. "I was going to address that kiss when you left, and say something commendable like, I stepped over the line. And—and I was going to apologize if it seemed like it went too far."

Hollie stopped. The sound of cars climbing the ramps seemed distant. They were cloistered in a corner of the parking deck where a humid breeze whistled between the gaps in the cement walls.

"And where did that speech go?"

A knot formed in his throat, but his lips twitched. "Out the window the moment I saw you at the bottom of the escalator."

Her eyes flared, but she waited for him to continue.

"And I just wanted to kiss you again." Another swallow. "Which pretty much invalidated the whole speech."

Her prolonged silence tortured him. Equally as agonizing was the cryptic dark stare.

Finally a smile toyed with the lips that he had just savored.

"Do you think you might kiss me again sometime?"

It was a demure question that managed to clear the obstruction in his throat.

"I just might."

Their silent face-off was charged, as if the lightning from a thunderstorm on the distant horizon ricocheted its energy between them.

Hollie fiddled with her purse strap and her glance slipped to his mouth, lingering there.

Mercy.

"How is your foot?"

"My *foot*?"

"That luggage cart ran over it."

Todd drew in a deep breath filled with a blend of exhaust and moisture. When he released it, a soft whistle crossed his lips.

"My foot is just fine, Miss Musgrave." He smirked, tossing his bag into the trunk she just opened.

As he slid into the passenger seat beside her, he watched a slim limb reaching for the ignition.

"Just so we're clear," he said. "I'm not just here to make an apparent fool of myself. I'm down here to help you find out more about the Marianis. I mean, after all, it is my house you are remembering."

A sublime grin made his stomach quake like an inverted turtle's legs.

"And to take a little vacation," she added.

"Right." He stared straight ahead. "A little vacation."

They pulled into a parking lot flanked by squat palm trees. Hollie parked under a tall oak veiled in Spanish moss. Fists clenched around the steering wheel, as she just sat there, making no move to get out.

Todd followed her blank gaze.

"Do you see someone?"

Jolted out of her reverie, she slid her glance in the opposite direction of him, toward the front of an eight-story building.

"No," she sighed. "How patient are you?"

"Patient?" Odd question. "Once upon a time I would admit I wasn't patient at all. Lately—" he paused, "—I guess with age I've calmed down."

"Calm?" Her eyes swung back toward him. "Would you classify yourself as calm when you welcomed me on your doorstep?"

Touché.

"I said *lately*. Like in the past few days."

Hollie laughed. When she did so it was loud and genuine, not a feminine titter. An odd sound to emit from such a pretty face…and entirely addictive. He could sit here all day and crack jokes just to hear that distinctive snort.

Patient? Yeah.

"All right, then." She put her hand on the door handle. "Just remember—patience."

An intriguing warning.

Sliding out of the passenger seat, he felt the hot air assault him. Perspiration dotted the back of his neck, but a soft breeze channeled through the waterway offering some relief. He hiked his duffle bag over his shoulder and discreetly surveyed the parking lot. It was nearly five o'clock, but all cars were idly parked and no one stood outside. Ahead, he caught the angle of Hollie's head, her dark hair rustling between her bare shoulders. She too was watching. When her head dropped forward again he gathered she did not recognize anything out of place.

At the sliding glass door entryway she stopped, waiting for him to fall in beside her.

"Welcome to the Harbor Breeze," she announced, sweeping her arm out and stepping on the doormat that triggered the glass panels to open.

A blast of cold air slipped through the gap in the doorway and he gladly stepped inside. The lobby was sedate. A sand-tiled floor with peach-colored walls ran the length of the building to reveal a bank of floor-length windows on the other side. To his right was a wraparound counter with an empty desk chair behind it. To his left was a seating area with teal love seats set u-shaped around a coffee table, and beyond that appeared to be a communal breakfast nook.

As he took another step, three heads turned around like synchronized prairie dogs. All three were well into their seventies, or possibly eighties. The one closest to him seemed larger than the others, or perhaps that was perspective. Beside her on the loveseat was a short woman with harsh red hair scarred by a vivid white stripe.

Rounding the corner of the loveseats was an elderly woman with silver hair and a pleasant smile. That smile broadened at the sight of Hollie.

"Patience," Hollie whispered to him.

"Hollie!" The stout woman took two attempts and finally hoisted herself off the couch, leaning on her walker. "Introduce us to your friend."

Hollie cringed and turned to Todd, her dark eyes pleading.

"Ladies, this is Todd. A *friend* of mine."

"Oh!" The one with the snowy stripe blinked like an owl.

"Todd—" Hollie smiled at him, "—meet my friends."

There was a challenge in her eyes. Perhaps defensive. Maybe protective. A lioness guarding her pack.

"Ladies, it's lovely to meet you." He grinned.

The upright woman released her walker and thrust her hand at him.

"Francine Lentine," she announced.

Todd clasped the hand with equal zeal. "You must be Frank," he surmised with an easy smile. "Hollie has told me so much about you."

"Oh really?" A black-penciled eyebrow rose and she pursed her lips in Hollie's direction. "She hasn't told us nearly enough about you."

Hollie frowned. "Todd is just a friend."

"Mmm-hmm." Frank ran narrowed eyes up and down his body. "I want a *friend* too."

Witnessing the infusion of pink in Hollie's cheeks was well worth this awkward introduction.

"Todd, this is Flo." Hollie nodded at the seated woman eclipsed by Francine.

"Pleasure to meet you, Flo."

Flo's mouth dropped open as she stared up at him. An inarticulate grunt might have been a greeting of sorts.

Casting a curious glance at Hollie, she shrugged her shoulders and smiled at the last woman who just now rose to her feet.

"Please," Todd rushed, "there's no need for anyone to get up on my account. I'm the one who interrupted your summit."

"Summit," Frank repeated. "He's a hoot."

The woman with short, fashionably-cut silver hair smiled congenially at him.

"It's so very nice to meet you, Todd," she said, unable to reach his hand with the coffee table in her way.

Compensating, Todd leaned forward, extending his arm lengthwise across the glass table and clasping her thin hand in his.

"Todd, this is Maryann Baumann."

"Maryann." He nodded. "Your next door neighbor?"

Maryann's smile broadened.

"So why have you been hiding this handsome fellow from us?" Frank interrupted.

"I have not been *hiding* him. We're busy working on something together."

Todd caught an expressive look in Maryann's shrewd eyes. He gathered she knew more about him than the other ladies.

My best friend, Hollie had mentioned.

As Francine continued to grill Hollie, and Flo continued to gape—it was to Maryann that Todd offered a relieved smile. There was wisdom in the woman's blue eyes...and patience.

"He looks good, but he doesn't say much," Frank observed, plopping back down onto the loveseat with enough force to nearly eject Flo.

"I apologize." He bowed his head. "I just got off a plane and the stress of travel has stolen some of my socializing skills."

Francine's eyebrow rose as she crossed her arms over an ample chest.

"Travel? Where from?"

"P—"

"Simmer ladies," Hollie interjected. "I'll bring Todd back down later. We have some work to do."

"Work." Frank snorted. "That's what they're calling it these days." She jabbed an elbow into the red-headed guppy next to her.

The action broke Flo from her stupor, though she still stared up at Todd as she blindly fumbled inside the purse sitting on her lap. Eyes glued to him, she thrust out an envelope in Hollie's general vicinity, missing her by nearly a foot.

"This came for you, Hol," she said, gaping at Todd.

Hollie tucked it into her handbag and gave a quick jerk of her head, motioning him away from the awkward inquisition.

"Ladies, it was wonderful to meet you all, but it looks like Hollie is calling me away."

Francine's lips plumped into a pout, and Flo's red lips finally closed the gap. It was Maryann that called out to him as he turned away.

"Todd," she called.

Hesitating, he looked back at her.

"I am so happy you are here." The soft German accent was comforting. "Have Hollie bring you over for cookies later."

Another first for him. It had been a long-ass time since he was invited anywhere for cookies.

With a quick grin and nod, *yes*, he hastened after Hollie who was holding open an elevator door for him.

Inside Hollie's condo, Todd was riveted to the wall of windows overlooking the waterway where a slanted bridge crossed over to a white sand strip stacked with high-rises. He took a brief glance around the living room and the open access to the kitchen. The décor was a blend of white and tan, subliminally plain, meant to draw ones attention to the bank of windows and the diverse colors beyond them.

"Wow," he remarked. "This place is the *anti*-my house."

He felt her move in beside him and was no longer interested in the view outside.

"Yes. I grew up a block away from the beach. Palm trees. Spanish moss. Lovebugs. Cigars." She waved her hand. "You can certainly imagine how your farmhouse has seemed so out of place in my dreams."

"You smoke cigars?" he asked, surprised.

"No." She punched him gently in the arm. "That's just what we're known for here."

He knew that, but he enjoyed seeing her smile.

"And now? Since you've been to my house, are you still having the dreams?"

There was a flash of dismay in her eyes.

"Maybe less frequently," she muttered.

Turning to face her, he resisted the urge to glide his fingers down her tanned arms.

"We're going to figure this out," he vowed.

Dubious eyes stared up at him. She gave herself a mental shake and plastered on a smile. "You survived the ladies. That's admirable."

"They look out for you, don't they?"

"It's their favorite pastime."

It was a comforting notion. "I like them. Both of my grandmothers are gone. Your ladies kind of made me feel young again."

Hollie gave a quick nod of understanding and then shuffled past him toward a granite-topped island, opening the stainless steel refrigerator behind it.

"You must be starving. I don't have much to choose from." She peeked at him over the refrigerator door. "We can go out?"

Rounding the island, he leaned over and peered around her tempting curves.

"Looks like some perfectly good Chinese food containers."

"You have no idea how old they are."

"Less than a week?" he asked optimistically.

A smile surfaced. "Last night's dinner. I wasn't too hungry. I hope you like Sesame Chicken." She poked her head back in. "And red wine or iced tea?"

"Both," he considered. Noting her curious glance he added, "I'm thirsty, and I think we need to relax."

"Amen to that."

She pulled the items out and shut the door with her hip.

As he was helping her to dish out the food, she plugged in her laptop. After grabbing his own from his duffle bag, Todd hiked up onto a barstool to gauge the woman seated across from him.

"Have there been any other dreams?" he asked. "I mean besides the one about the farmhouse."

Hollie's lips left the rim of her wine glass to shake her head.

"No other memories of travel? No photos?"

"Nope."

"Do you have it? The picture of her?"

There was no need to clarify. Hollie pulled the tarnished picture of Nina out of her purse, and in doing so noticed the plain white business envelope Flo had given her. She frowned at it and held onto it as she slid the photo over the granite toward him.

Opening the envelope and extracting a yellow sheet of paper, Hollie's face blanched. Her fingers trembled.

"What is it?" he asked, abandoning the photo.

Hesitating, she finally handed him the folded note.

STOP YOUR SEARCH.

SOMEONE WILL GET HURT.

Todd stared at the words as the first inklings of doubt wormed into his mind.

What was he doing here? Trouble shadowed this woman. More than trouble. Danger. A few days ago *danger* played no role in his life…and it was good.

"You should go."

The words were husky. Uttered from a woman who was struggling to maintain her composure. Sun-kissed skin paled as it was pulled taut across high cheekbones, making the shadows below her eyes more prevalent.

He considered her warning. Seriously considered it.

"I should," he hedged. "But I won't."

"For God's sake, why? You don't need this. It was a big mistake for you to come down here. I was a fool to encourage you."

Setting aside any reservations he might have, he couldn't stand to see her fighting to hold herself together. Someone was tormenting this woman and it pissed him off.

"Look," he set the note down, watching her eyes follow the motion. "I could point out that it's not just about you. Whatever is going on, whatever these warnings are—they clearly deal with the house I'm living in. Everything that has happened to you happened directly after visiting my home. That makes it personal for me." He paused. "Yeah, there's that—or—" *deep breath*, "—I could admit that for the first time in three years I've met someone I'd like to know more about—that I'd like to spend time with."

A shrug that didn't come easily hefted his shoulders. "And you're right. I have to decide if my desire to spend time with you is strong enough to deal with these threats that you've been subjected to. Do I really want that sort of conflict in my very quiet, very private life?"

Hollie's face pinched in pain and she looked away. "I guess I know the answer to that."

"Do you?"

Uncertainty darkened the gaze that returned to meet his.

"No," she whispered. "I don't know the answer. I don't know *any* answers. I only have questions." She grabbed the note. "Who is sending me these letters? And who is following me? And why do I remember *your* farmhouse?"

Potent questions.

Who could answer?

Her family?

Evidently not.

The police?

They might assist in protection for a short time, but they wouldn't answer the questions.

The Steins?

That source was pretty much tapped out.

"Look—" He took a solid breath and stared straight into those tumultuous eyes. "We'll tackle it one thing at a time. All those questions combined are overwhelming. But let me just answer one. Yes—yes, I want to be with you. I don't scare off easily, so unless you specifically tell me to go, you're stuck in your promise to show me the beach."

It was as if he had chiseled away the exoskeleton that supported her. She melted down into her stool.

"I'd like you stay." Her voice was barely audible. "I guess I'm selfish."

Todd's lips clamped into a crooked smile. "That makes two of us." Releasing his grip on the granite, he rubbed his palms together and reached for the laptop.

"Okay, let's start with, *who were the Marianis*? I think I might have found something on that while I was waiting for the plane."

Tension eased from Hollie's face. She took a sip of her wine and then dropped her elbow on the counter, cupping her chin in her palm.

"You've been holding out on me," she claimed. "What did you find?"

Todd took a tentative bite of chicken. It was pretty darn good.

"Well, it's hard to tell if its related or not, but when I started searching for Marianis, without any geographical restriction, I found a bunch of references to a man with mob affiliations who was sent to prison back in the eighties."

Hollie chuckled and jabbed a piece of chicken with her fork. "There you have it. I'm actually a mafia princess." Frowning, she chewed and spoke with a mouthful. "Tell me more."

Todd grabbed the note.

STOP SEARCHING.

SOMEONE WILL GET HURT.

Hollie leaned over to read it again with him.

"Seriously, maybe we should just let it go." This time she sounded resolved to the fact. "I mean, the hypnotherapist gave me some tricks to help with the dreams. Maybe they'll start to work."

Soft brown eyelashes fanned across solemn eyes as she stared hard at the letter.

The note truly bothered him. It was a blatant threat, and even if she was to drop her search, it meant someone was watching her…waiting to see what her next move would be. He remembered what it was like to be watched all the time, but it was so much different in his case.

More troubling was that there had been two notes. One at his farmhouse, and one down here. That either meant a collusive effort, or someone was following her no matter where she went.

"If someone is upset that you went to my house, maybe being back here will assure them that you're putting it behind you."

Hollie looked as dubious as he felt. "And this note...and the guy outside my office building?"

"I don't like that one damn bit. I'll drive you to work if you have to go. I'd like to have a word with anyone who is harassing you."

Her lips parted in astonishment. "That's really nice of you, but you can't escort me everywhere. If someone is harassing me, I'll damn well corner them myself."

Todd set down his fork and sat atop the bar stool with his arms crossed. "I don't doubt that. You don't strike me as someone easily intimidated. But you don't know who this is. I mean, have you talked about your dreams at work? Or your trip? Could someone at work, or in your social circle have some beef with you?"

"You just met my social circle. They are also the only people I've discussed my dreams with—or my trip."

Caught staring at her, he swiped a hand over his face in contemplation.

Hollie's eyebrows rose. "What?"

"Your social circle." He grinned. "I like them."

Relaxing slightly, she managed to shrug. "Don't judge me. I do go out with people from work—people my age. These ladies—" she waved her hand toward the front door, "—they are my family."

Todd held his hand up. "Don't be defensive. I'm not judging you. I meant it. I really like them. But, let's talk about those people from work that you go out with. Anyone hold a grudge? Anyone that just might know about your inquiries?"

She mulled that over while taking a sip of wine.

"I *did* do some internet searches at work," she conceded. "And I guess there were people working around me at the time. I get along with most of my coworkers."

"Most?"

"Well, there's one—" Her voice drifted off as she looked away.

No need to press her. She knew this was for her own benefit.

"Maryann calls him the "M"—word."

"M—word?"

"Mark." She took another sip of wine. "An ex. I mean, we were only together—if you call it that—for a few months. And I doubt there was animosity on his end. If there was to be any animosity, it would be from me."

Todd sat up, alert. "What happened?"

Hollie met his eyes briefly and then shook her head. "Of all the clichés—a cheerleader. A cheerleader happened."

Before he could offer his opinion of the loser, he witnessed Hollie's eyes widen as she sucked in a breath. Her gaze jerked up to his.

"The M-word. Mark. His schedule was on our calendar. He was in New York at the same time I was up there."

Todd drummed his fingers on the table.

"Okay," he said, pushing his irrational anger at the M-word aside. "That's something to look into, at least. Is he back?"

Hollie nodded mutely.

And so were the notes.

"You never told him about the dreams?" He hated to ask the next question, but he was trying to help her. "I mean, did he witness them?"

Blanching, Hollie reached for the wine glass and took a hearty sip.

"No," she choked. "The dreams—" she hesitated, "—they went away when I was a child, and for some reason they just started up again. Pretty recently—I mean, *after* I was seeing Mark."

Both uncomfortable with the subject, they ate contemplatively until Hollie cleared her throat and said, "You mentioned about a trial?"

"Oh. Right." He reached for his phone and typed a hasty statement. "Here it is. Joseph *Sprinkles* Mariani—"

Hollie giggled over a piece of broccoli. "Sprinkles? Seriously?"

"Just reading the article," he chuckled. "Anyway, *Sprinkles* Mariani was convicted of gun trafficking, loan-sharking, gambling, skimming of union construction, and assault in March of 1991."

"Sounds like a charming guy." Hollie raised her eyebrows.

"But wait—the interesting part is that they mention his brother, Richard, who was wanted for questioning by the FBI, but could not be located—presumably having left the country."

Awareness flashed in her eyes. "Brothers?"

"Exactly. I didn't see a picture of Richard, but there is one of Joseph, aka Sprinkles, during his trial."

He turned the phone around for her to see.

She leaned in and gasped. "He was in the picture down in your basement!"

"Exactly."

Slim dark brows lowered as she focused on the screen.

"This trial was in New York," she read. "Yet they lived in a farmhouse in Pennsylvania?"

"The article states he was from New York, but traveled for business. It mentions nothing about property in Pennsylvania."

Hollie sat back, staring out the sliding glass doors at the darkening skyline. "I was so busy searching for Nina in Pennsylvania, I didn't think to just search for the last name. There were so many Marianis in the country."

She reached up to cup her forehead in her open palms, sliding her fingers through her hair in thought. "But what does Joseph Mariani have to do with me? How do I know that house?"

"Your father is probably the only one left to tell," Todd offered, hating to see her crestfallen expression.

A sheen veiled her bright eyes as she looked up at him. "I've asked. Over and over and over. He knows nothing about it. I even called yesterday and mentioned Nina's name. He started reciting my childhood friends. It seemed pointless to interrupt him and explain that Nina died just before I was born. He clearly didn't recognize the name."

"Any connection between the M-word and the Marianis?" he wondered aloud.

Hollie snickered. "You called him the M-word. That's hilarious."

"It's better than what I'd prefer to call him."

The misty shroud over her eyes evaporated and a pleased smile toyed with her lips. She didn't speak for a moment and then she shot up, startling him.

"None that I'm aware of," she stated. "But I've got some serious investigating to do tonight."

Before she could burrow into her laptop, his voice arrested her.

"We," he corrected. "*We* have some research to do."

A pointed look over the rim of the monitor teetered between challenge and grateful acceptance.

"So what's this tool's name?" he segued over a bite of chicken.

"Mark Longtree," she replied, carrying over her laptop.

Todd coughed up the piece of chicken and swallowed it again.

"You're kidding, right?" His eyes watered with mirth.

"No," she deadpanned.

"That's like some porn star name."

"I wouldn't know." She pursed her lips and looked down her nose at him before cracking a grin.

They both erupted into laughter. Hollie tried to control hers, but couldn't stop giggling.

"All right," she admitted, stifling a snort. "I was not in the right mindset at the time. Maryann was the only one to have met him from the posse downstairs, and she gave me the same look you're giving me right now. He flirted with me at work, and one day I was just too lonely to go home so I went out to dinner with him."

She paused for a sip of wine.

"I think I knew already by that night what his character was really like, but I tried to make it work." She hung her head, and then typed on the laptop as a diversion.

"I can imagine your opinion of me is really low," she added, not looking up at him. "A desperate woman who hangs out with old ladies and can't even keep a loser boyfriend...oh, and is also off the deep-end crazy."

Todd hitched his leg up on the bottom barstool rung.

"We all have things in our past that we wish were different."

Left staring wistfully at the screen, Hollie finally glanced up.

"Tell me more about this trial."

She wasn't one to dwell on people's perceptions, he gathered. It was refreshing. Not too many eggshells with this peculiar woman.

Moving to the couch so that they could share her laptop screen, the act of doing so joined their thighs as a mutual table. That heat and soft pressure was making it hard for him to concentrate, combined with the glossy tendrils of hair that brushed his arm each time she leaned forward.

"He died in prison." She read. "Under suspicious circumstances."

"Let's try this—" Todd collided with her fingers as he took control of the keyboard. He typed two words in the search box.

LONGTREE MARIANI

Hollie collapsed back against the cushions and exhaled.

"Yeah, he's a schmuck, but I seriously don't think he'd be leaving me threatening letters."

The words were valiant, but the inflection was not. In fact, her chin angled away in consideration.

"What are you thinking?"

"Well," she started, "of course it's ridiculous, but the guy in the car across the street from me—the one who made the motion of a gun with his hand. He was all in black, and with dark sunglasses on. He was also standing under the shade of a tree so I couldn't make out many details."

"But—"

"But he was Mark's height."

A growl climbed up his throat.

"So are most men." She glanced down between them at his thigh pressed against hers. "Well, not you. You're a bit taller."

This close, he could hear her slow swallow. It did little to temper his growl.

They continued to search, discovering more about Joseph and Richard Mariani, but nothing to tie the condemned mobster with Todd's farmhouse. And no correlation or mention of Nina Mariani.

So engrossed with crafting proper search phrases, Todd jolted when he felt a weight slump against his shoulder. Dark hair infused with highlights from the nearby lamp cascaded down his arm and the soft breath of slumber moistened the skin exposed by his short-sleeved shirt.

Holding his breath, he dared not move and risk disturbing her. It was evident that sleep was something she needed desperately. That she felt comfortable enough to do so against him caused a rumbling in his chest.

Carefully setting the laptop aside, he used his toes to haul off his shoes and then stretched his legs out onto the coffee table, slouching into a position that would better comfort her. For several moments he sat perfectly still just relishing in the impression of her body and the trusting submission that allowed her to fall asleep in such a fashion.

It felt good.

So good.

He wanted to wrap his arm around her but didn't dare chance waking her.

Beside his socked feet he noticed the folded note sitting on the coffee table.

No one was going to threaten her. Not when he was here at her side.

In time, his head lolled atop hers and he fell into a contented sleep filled with citrus, satin...and a primal sense of peace.

CHAPTER THIRTEEN

Hollie's hand curled into a fist. Instead of rapping against the front door, her knuckles landed on a firm, yet pliant surface.

Beneath her cheek, the steady drum of a heartbeat provided the hypnotic effect of a metronome. Keeping her eyes closed, she drew in a deep breath tinged with detergent and a masculine musk as she grasped the position she was in.

Todd's long body stretched the length of her couch and she was tucked in against the backrest, sprawled nearly on top of him. There was no possible way to move discreetly so she let her muscles relax and her head dropped back down into the crook of his arm and chest.

"Dreaming?" A husky sound rumbled close to her ear.

Her palm laid flat on his chest. She had to command her fingers to stay still. They wanted to massage and investigate the terrain.

"Yes, but—" she hesitated, "—I don't feel so anxious tonight. Maybe it's the work of the hypnotherapist, or maybe—"

"Maybe it's that you're not alone."

That much was true. When she woke, she felt his arms around her. It was the safest and most content she had been since the dreams had returned.

Now she tried awkwardly to hike herself up.

"I guess we were both exhausted," she suggested feebly. "I'm sorry I fell asleep on you." She glanced at her watch. "Whoa. 1:30. I'm *really* sorry."

In an ungainly attempt to extract herself from the embrace, Hollie ended up with her thigh wedged between his legs and her chest suspended above his head.

"I'm not."

Hollie looked down at the strong jaw dusted with copper bristles as her eyes mutinously drifted to his full lips.

A calloused hand reached up and brushed against her cheek, pushing her tumbling hair behind her ear.

"I guess I better get going and find a hotel," he suggested in a rough voice.

Dipping her head ever so slightly into his touch, she managed a soft response.

"You could," she considered. "Or you could pretend we never woke just now."

The palm against her cheek froze and it seemed as if his very breath had come to a halt. That hand moved again, roaming down to her shoulder where he gently urged her back into her reclined position against him. Hollie responded stiffly until the rhythm of his heart was once again beneath her ear.

"You're pretty muscular for a guy who works with circuit boards," she muttered lethargically.

A masculine chuckle purred under her cheek.

"Sleep, Hollie," he whispered. "Sleep before I change my mind and keep you up."

Wishing for the sensual wakefulness he threatened, she rubbed her nose against his neck, stretching languidly against him. His lips found hers and he kissed her hard, strong fingers twisting into her hair. Her hips arched in response and her lips parted, savoring the hot assault of her mouth.

"Hollie," he rasped against it.

"Mmmm."

"Hollie," he whispered again, this time pulling temptation away.

"I want you," he said hoarsely. "I think you can pretty much gather that."

With her hips inclined the way they were, she indeed could confirm that fact.

"But—I don't know—maybe I'm—" he answered her soft brush of the lips before pulling back again, "—maybe I'm old-fashioned or something, but I didn't fly down here just for sex. That's the last thing I want you to think."

He regained some of his wits and shifted slightly, making her body want to stalk that withdrawal.

"I think we both know this is coming for us," he continued, but—you're exhausted—hell, I'm exhausted. Sleep with me. Like this. Right here. Sleep in my arms on this couch, because honestly, I've never felt more comfortable in my life."

Testifying to that fact, his arms curled tight around her and she soaked up the embrace, snuggling closer, and breathing in the heat of his skin.

She wanted to protest. She wanted to see this man naked. But the soft, incoherent murmurs and the warm cocoon were a temptation too strong to resist.

With a contented smile on her face, she fell asleep. It was an undisturbed respite that lasted until the sun filled the balcony doors. Beneath her, the toned abdomen stirred in an indolent stretch.

Hollie propped herself up on her elbow, staring at her hand resting on his chest as if it belonged to someone else.

"Good morning," she said awkwardly.

Tawny eyelashes fanned around his lowered eyelids. "Good morning."

Those eyes cracked open into a golden sunrise.

"You look well rested," he murmured.

"You look uncomfortable," she countered with a grin.

"Oh, trust me—this is the most comfortable I've been in a long time. I may require a chiropractor, but it was worth it."

In an effort to ease his torment, Hollie tried to dislodge herself. Lifting one leg over him she jabbed with that foot to locate the floor.

"Uh, Hollie," Todd's words were clipped. "You might—"

There was no need for him to complete his sentence. Her maneuver had placed her in a direct straddle across his lap, and there was no disguising the effect it had caused.

"Oh. Oh."

What now?

Sliding either way was only going to intensify the predicament. She tried to use her knee to shove off the couch, but Todd's hands clasped around her hips holding her still in a position that was starting to make her breathing heavy and her lips grow slack.

That strong grip on her hips lifted into her hair and cupped her head, urging her face closer as his head rose off the arm rest.

The kiss he gave her was so soft and so contradictory to the heat that was ramping up literally between them. He took his time and caressed her lips with a gentleness that was exquisitely frustrating. In response her hips mutinously began to rock, which caused a deep rumble in his throat. His hands dropped from her face back down to her waist where he quickly hiked her off him. In one sure transfer, both her feet landed safely on the carpeting.

She stood there, breathless. Feeling her heart drum a little unsteady, she watched the brawny man slip up into a seated position, resting his elbows on his spread knees, massaging the back of his neck with one hand.

"We'll get back to that, Miss Musgrave," he uttered, finally looking up at her with eyes darkened by desire. "I promise."

Now.

"First concern is your safety," he vowed. "I'm supposed to be tucked away in some hotel, meeting up with you for lunch or dinner like any respectful acquaintance."

Gaining some composure, Hollie straightened her blouse around her hips.

"I slept on top of you. I'd say you're more than an acquaintance by now."

Todd's eyebrow hiked up and he grinned. Amber hair spiked up on one side, clashing with the dark unshaven jaw.

"I have to get ready for work," she announced shakily. "I'll put some coffee on, and there's a shower in the guest bathroom."

Unsure what to do with her hands, she tucked them in her back pockets and gave a quick nod before turning away.

"Hollie," his voice arrested her.

She stopped, peering back at him. In two steps he had her, his hands on her shoulders turning her to face him as his mouth captured hers with a scorching kiss— hot, hard, and screaming *now!* And then he was gone— retreating a step with his chest rising and falling.

"As I said—we'll come back to that later. For now, I'll go shower and tag along on the ride to work to make sure you're safe."

Unable to speak, Hollie touched her fingertips to her lips and managed an affirmative bleat before fleeing to her bedroom. If she didn't, she just might reach for his hand and yank him along with her.

With the door shut, Hollie leaned back against it and listened to the pounding of her heart. Never had a man had this much of an effect on her. In the past, and most recently with the M-word, it had simply been a matter of not wanting to be alone—not wanting to be the dateless woman in the office. When he had kissed her it had been a quiet state of, *okay, this is what I'm supposed to be doing.*

Todd on the other hand was all about wanting. He made her feel feverish any time he touched her. When he kissed her—well—a buzzing filled her ears as if she was lying in a grass field with the leaves on the trees rustling and the summer bugs serenading her.

Last night, curled up in his embrace—that was one of the most cozy and stimulating moments of her adult life. Any of the recent threats, perceived or real, faded in that secure haven.

Don't blow this.

Surely it had to be her. What were the odds of meeting so many men who did not bring on the sound of rustling leaves and serenading bugs?

No. It was him. He alone had that impact. Even now, just the mere thought of Todd in her guest bathroom—in that awfully tight shower that barely fit a man of his size—*bzzzzz.*

Using her palms she propelled off the door and kicked into gear. It had been unnecessary to set an alarm in the past few weeks. This morning, though, she had slept too late. If the drapes had not been parted, allowing the sun to zap her in the eyes, she might still be nestled against the muscular contours of Todd Hewitt.

Bzzzz.

"Good morning!" Francine announced their emergence from the elevator with the subtlety of a drill sergeant.

Beside her, Flo's magazine fell to her lap and she gaped at Todd.

"Has that woman ever seen a man before?" He leaned into Hollie's shoulder to whisper.

She snorted and her cheeks burned at the woman's frank assessment of his wardrobe.

"I see you brought a change of clothes with you. Smart thinking."

"Francine," Maryann hissed. "Good morning, Hollie," she inclined her head and smiled. "Todd." She nodded.

"Good morning, ladies." His enthusiasm matched their curiosity. "What are you all up to this morning?"

"Coffee and donuts," Frank waved her hand at the opened box of glazed treats on the table. "Please, come have some."

Hollie caught his side glimpse and shook her head.

"I'd love to," he went so far as to place a hand over his heart, "but your Miss Musgrave here is dragging me off."

"I don't blame her," Frank hiked up a bushy eyebrow and stared levelly at Hollie.

Sighing, Hollie grabbed Todd's arm and tugged him.

"See?" he announced. "But if you all are here when we return, I'll take you up on the invitation."

Three sets of eyes brightened and Frank quickly ducked her head and drilled Flo. "We have to run to the store for later."

Flo nodded mutely.

Maryann perked up as well. "Oh, those lemon cakes. We need those.

"Lemon cakes," Frank scoffed. "Does he look like a man who likes lemon cakes? Brownies. We will get brownies."

"Macaroons!" Flo exclaimed, breaking her silence and clapping her hands together.

With the ladies animated and distracted, Hollie seized the opportunity and tugged Todd again. He surrendered to her pull with a smile.

Crossing the parking lot she teased, "So, you just arrive in Florida and already you have a date with four ladies."

"Four?"

"Well, I'm included in the fray, aren't I?"

"Ah," he grinned at her across the roof of her car. "So it's a *date* I have with you, then?"

Reveling in the banter, she smirked back. "You're going to need your vitamins for this one."

The flash of white teeth and a dimple to boot made her stomach quiver.

Reality came crashing back as she saw his gaze slide beyond her, carefully scrutinizing the parking lot for any sign of trespassers. Sighing at this new way of life for her, she searched the front and back windshield for any unwanted notes.

Some of the tension left Todd's face and a cautious smile returned.

"For the record," he said. "I don't mind lemon cakes."

"You have my cell number," Todd reminded. "Any notes. Any strangers. Anything out of the ordinary, just call me. I will be close by." He glanced down the thoroughfare of palm trees. "I saw on the map that the library is near here."

"It is," Hollie asserted, tipping her head in the general vicinity of the stately brick building. "But I don't want you to be bored. I'll take tomorrow off and show you the area. I just had some assignments that have to be wrapped up today."

A raised hand stopped her.

"I'm going to see what I can dig up on the Marianis. As much as I tried to search last night—" he flattened his hand against the jagged trunk of a palm, "—it was a little difficult to focus."

Bzzzz.

"I know what you mean."

Todd's eyes locked with hers as traffic rolled by. The disarming grin on his face drew her lips up into a reciprocal smile. Her cheeks burned.

"I can't tell you how much I would rather come with you to the library than go to work right now."

Todd reached out and grazed her bare arm with his fingertips.

"Watch it, Miss Musgrave. I might think you're starting to like me."

Hollie looked at those fingers on her arm. A scar crossed one of his knuckles. Shockwaves pulsed through her arm from his touch.

"Don't get cocky, Mr. Hewitt."

Conversation on the doorstep of her office building drew her attention. A few people congregated at the top of the stairs. When she looked back at Todd she found him studying them guardedly.

"There's a place around the corner that serves great Cuban sandwiches. We could have lunch?"

His affirmative nod replenished her smile.

"But I will come meet you here," he hedged.

The warning tempered her reaction. "This is silly, Todd. I can't really believe someone means to harm me. It makes no sense."

"Hollie. Someone left a note for you on my doorstep. And someone left a note for you here in Tampa. That's too disturbing to consider trivial. If there is another incident we're going to the police."

It was sobering advice. Going to the police meant there was a legitimate threat, and she didn't want to accept that. She wanted to explain this all away as an innocent prank. It really could be Mark screwing with her. At what gain, though? Was he through with his cheerleading coach and this was his absurd way to get her attention?

Reading her anxiety, Todd reached for both her arms, his hands sliding down until they connected with her fingers with a squeeze of assurance. He ducked his head to meet her downcast eyes.

"Noon," he confirmed. "I'll be back at noon unless you call me earlier."

Noon.

Four hours away.

"Noon it is," she remarked with a quirk of her lip.

Todd studied her, his eyes sliding over her face as if committing it to memory. He leaned in and gave a quick kiss on her cheek. When he pulled back he laughed.

"You should see your expression right now," he chuckled. "Trust me, the kiss on the cheek was so that I could walk away. A kiss on the lips and you wouldn't be going to work right now."

"Grrrr."

"Did you just growl at me?"

"That I did," she murmured. "See you at noon."

Forcing herself to turn away, she could feel his eyes on her back until she disappeared inside the building.

Lunch had been all too short, filled with questions about Todd's investigation. He learned nothing of Nina Mariani, and his search for the Johnsons, cross-referenced by his address yielded little either. Lured back to the Mariani trial, it was the only connection he could establish with his farmhouse. The image of Joseph Mariani in the courtroom seemed the likeness of one of the two men in the photograph located in his cellar.

He assured Hollie that he was content spending the afternoon at the library, but warned that he'd be on the office doorstep at five on the nose.

Normally, she didn't keep punctual hours. In fact, she often worked late because she liked the quiet time when everyone cleared out. Today would be an exception, though. Slamming her laptop shut at 4:59, she muttered a hasty farewell to those sitting around her.

Mark Longtree rose from his corner desk and blocked her path to the door.

"Where are you off to in such a hurry?"

A flurry of profane retorts came to mind, but she just hiked up her purse strap and shouldered by him.

"Hey," he called after her. "That's no way to be. I was going to ask you to go out for a drink."

Hollie stopped in her tracks and glared over her shoulder.

Loser.

That was the word that came to mind as she looked at the guy who thought he was *all that*. Thinning dark hair and a paunch midsection were not the drawbacks to this man's appearance. It was the insincere smile. How she had not noticed it the first time around was a flaw in her character. But life taught lessons, and this was one she would never forget.

It wasn't even worth responding. She turned her back on him and headed downstairs. Mark was a distant memory by the time she saw the sexy man resting against the railing outside. So happy to see him, she opened the door and reached out with her free arm to loop it through his and squeeze.

"Hey—" He smiled. "Happy to see me?"

"Quite." She beamed.

The sound of the door opening behind her and Todd's guarded frown over her head had her swiveling around.

"Let me guess," he murmured into her hair, "the porn star."

She jabbed an elbow into his rib, but laughed while doing it. Her laugh waned when Mark ambled toward them.

"Well, no wonder you were in such a rush to leave," he simpered, his icy eyes latching onto Todd's hand on her hip.

"This guy dumped *you*?" Todd grunted as she felt him skillfully slide in front of her.

"Mark, is it?" Todd asked the man.

Oh no. Hollie cringed.

"Yeah." Mark strolled forward, puffing his chest out, which also bloated the roll over his belt.

"Maybe you can help us," Todd suggested.

Hollie's head snapped up at him. *What?*

"Someone has been leaving notes on Hollie's car," he explained. "And following her home from work."

Mark crossed his arms and frowned. "Guys will be guys, I guess."

"Come again."

Hollie could feel the tension in Todd, his arm a taut rubber band ready to sling at Mark.

"I mean, she works around a lot of men, and despite their best efforts to be nice she doesn't always give them the time of day." Mark's slight shoulders nearly reached up to his ears and then fell. "I wouldn't be surprised if someone is trying to get her attention."

A stabilizing breath coursed through Todd before he asked evenly, "And what about you? I understand you dumped her several months ago. Are you trying to get her attention again?"

"Hey!" The man stood at attention but that only brought him to about five or six inches below Todd. "I didn't dump her. She just didn't seem that into me. Trust me, bro. She'll do the same to you."

Hollie clasped Todd's arm, sensing the threat to his control.

"Well, *bro*, that is entirely up to Hollie. But if I find out you are harassing her—"

As Todd leaned in, Mark edged backwards, his chin angled in a retreating challenge.

"I don't know what you're talking about. She's cute and all, but she's pretty much a loner. I was just trying to give her a bit of a social life."

Hollie stepped around Todd, her face infused with the late afternoon sun.

"I am not a charity case, Mark. You want a social life, go back to the cheerleading squad—or have they all wizened up?"

Mark turned red, the crimson inching up his high forehead and into the recesses of the thin hair.

"Whatever," he spurned, batting his hand in the air.

Adjusting his collar, and glancing around, satisfied that there was no audience, Mark pivoted and marched back into the building.

It was impossible to even meet Todd's eyes after that humiliating exchange. Keeping her gaze averted, she started down the stairs, prepared to make a beeline to her car parked down the street.

"Hey." The masculine rumble sounded behind her.

She drew to a halt but did not turn around and let him glimpse the flames in her cheeks.

"What?"

"Hollie, look at me."

It was impossible to resist the soft command. There was no censure in it and she turned to find a tolerant smile and a pleasant flash of mischief in the golden eyes.

"He's a tool. Let it go."

Let it go.

"I am mortified, Todd. And worse than that, I'm starting to suspect he might be behind these notes. I mean, what are the odds that he's up north at the same time I receive a note on your door?"

Todd's features clouded as if the sun had set and the heavy shadows of night scored his angular cheekbones.

"If he did, I will find out, and he's not going to be able to visit cheerleaders for the foreseeable future." Tempering his reaction he added, "And as far as you being mortified. Why, because you once dated that guy? We've all dated people no one would ever imagine. Or is it that he called you a loner? Because I happen to have a certain fondness for loners."

With that, he stepped forward and reached for her hand, lacing his fingers with hers. "And I happen to like you."

He leaned down and kissed her. A gentle kiss. A transfer of confidence, and a pledge that he meant it.

Further mortification came when she felt moisture inch up behind her eyes. She kept them closed until control returned, and then looked up at him.

The sun was behind him, illuminating his hair with sparks of gold, and casting his face in contrast. All the hues and shadows made him look like a sandstorm in motion.

"I happen to like you too," she answered softly.

Not releasing her hand, he walked her to her car and cast a skeptical glance around them, but there were no suspicious vehicles around. No notes on the windshield. No one pointing finger guns at her.

"So," he said, once they were immersed in the Tampa traffic. "I was able to confirm, albeit indirectly, that Joseph Mariani's parents did indeed live in my house. And given the fact that the picture we found seems to be taken out front with him and his brother, and Nina…well, I can't tell you how much it gives me the creeps to find out that a mobster was once inside my home."

"I can imagine how that must make you uneasy," she mulled, glancing up at the rearview mirror. "But I've never been to your house before, so what can possibly tie me to someone from the mob? My parents never traveled—never really mixed socially." She swung her head and wrinkled her nose at him. "Yes, that's where I get it."

Turning her focus back to the traffic she said, "I don't understand. I don't understand the dreams."

With the sunroof cracked open, salty air filled the car. In her peripheral vision she could see Todd's sinewy hand resting on his knee, the scar shining white across the knuckle on the middle finger.

"If there is absolutely no correlation between you and that house, maybe we have to give consideration to the first theory."

Her head swung toward him in disbelief, but quickly returned at the notice of brake lights ahead.

"Which is?"

"Reincarnation," he answered flatly.

Hollie snickered. "You would have gotten along well with my mother."

"I don't know, Hollie. We've dug up as much as we possibly could. I want answers too. They say this guy is suspected of several murders, but was not convicted for anything like that. I mean, the next step I suppose is to try and visit local government branches in Bucks County. Property records and stuff you can't research online."

"If they even volunteer that information." She doubted it. "There's another option—"

She felt Todd's eyes as he waited for her to elaborate.

"I could go back to the hypnotherapist. Maybe there's more—" She tapped the side of her head. "More in here."

"Oh, I've got no doubt there's more going on inside there." He chuckled. "But seriously, that might not be a bad idea."

Hollie gripped the steering wheel, relieved that his response seemed sincere and not judgmental. Drawing in a deep breath, she added, "I don't know how long you can stay, but if I can get an appointment tomorrow or the next day, would you come with me?"

Not, will you go to dinner with me?
Will you go to a movie with me?
Will you stroll along the beach with me?
No. Will you go to the hypnotherapist with me?
Yeah, you're a real catch, Musgrave.

"Yes."

The response almost went unheard in the melee of her mind.

"Yes?"

"One—of course I'd like to be there for moral support, but, two—" he rubbed his knee, "I think it just sounds plain fascinating. I'm curious."

A sense of peace settled over Hollie that she hadn't experienced in a long time—a sudden feeling of camaraderie. As much as she loved Maryann and the ladies, she still exhausted every effort to assure them of her well-being. For once she didn't have to pretend. She didn't lie or coddle to put someone at ease.

Without considering the move, she dropped her hand from the steering wheel to rest atop his. There might have been a slight tug of surprise, but in a second, strong fingers curled around hers and squeezed.

Not alone, they said.

She chanced a glance away from the windshield and caught the lion's gaze fixed on her. There was no trivial smile on those full lips. No false nods of assurance. The expression was solemn and sincere. It gave her more comfort than a snarky grin or a smooth wink.

When they pulled into the Harbor Breeze parking lot, she shut off the ignition and sat still, staring out in front of her. Todd made no move to exit the vehicle. Perhaps he was scanning the cars all parked in the prime spots near the front door—many of them with handicapped license plates. Or, maybe he was watching the landscaper trimming bushes on the far side of the building.

Or, perhaps like her, he was just trying to understand this vortex of feelings they were whirling about in.

Hollie leaned over the center console and placed her palm against his cheek, inching her head up to press her lips just above his jawline. A soft brush against warm, stubbled skin.

When she drew back, dark amber eyes searched hers. Neither of them spoke. They barely breathed. Her gaze dropped to his lips, slightly chapped, slightly moist, wholly tempting. They smoothed into a grin beneath her scrutiny.

"People haven't kissed me on the cheek since I was seven," he murmured huskily. "And it sure as hell didn't have the effect that kiss just did."

Heat infused her cheeks, but she remained huddled close, their foreheads nearly connecting. The air conditioning kicked on, blowing against her fevered flesh.

"I just wanted—I just wanted you to know how glad I am that you're here."

He drew back ever so slightly. Enough for her to catch his quick nod.

"You showed me so in the most tender of ways, Hollie."

"What type of effect did it have?" she tested.

A muscle pumped along his jaw. A quick jerk of tension and then it was gone.

"More," he whispered. "It felt like more."

Bang. Bang. Bang.

Hollie jumped high enough to nearly knock her head against the closed sunroof. She swiveled in startled disbelief to see the curved plastic handle of an umbrella tapping against the driver's side window.

"Come on you two lovebirds," Francine's hollowed shout invaded their moment. "The food is getting cold."

Todd's forehead dropped against her shoulder and she could hear his snicker in the cotton fabric there. "That's right," he muttered. "We have a party to attend."

Hollie's head sunk into his shoulder so that they were supported against each other across the console.

"Mortified again." Her words were muffled in the crook of his neck.

Todd angled his head and she felt his lips caress her cheek. They slid into her hair where he could whisper against her ear.

"I still want more."

"Come on," Frank bellowed. "You're steaming up the car."

"Maybe Mark was right," she sighed, straightening. "About me. This—" she swept her hand at the window, "—this is my group of friends. My social life."

Thick eyebrows knitted together. "We don't say the M-word around here, remember?" Todd reached for the door handle. "And do you think I look like someone who gives a damn what he thinks?"

The smile that rose to her lips was so liberating that she flashed it at Frank as she stepped out of the car.

"We have quiche!" Frank announced, cradling her umbrella in the basket of her walker as she ambled toward the front door.

"They have quiche," Hollie relayed over the roof.

Todd stuck a thumb up in the air and she giggled as he rounded the vehicle and caught up with her on the sidewalk. His hand curved warmly around her hip.

The shadows under the Spanish moss didn't seem so sinister this evening.

Todd deftly dodged the ladies most invasive questions, usually with a joke that would leave them cackling. Hollie sat next to him on the loveseat and leaned in, whispering, "And you thought the press was bad."

"They could take a lesson or two from these women."

Florence had finally considered him a member of the posse and gotten over her mute syndrome. Now she pressed just as hard as Frank, zinging the ultimate question.

"Have you had many girlfriends?"

Hollie felt Todd's arm stiffen. He clasped his plate in both hands, staring down at the floral carpet.

"Flo!" Maryann admonished, with a disapproving look down her long nose.

Florence clammed up again, shoving a piece of soggy dough in her mouth.

Hollie dusted her fingers over the tensed muscles in his forearm. He gave her a sidelong glance and a soft smile.

"It's alright," he assured her, and then looked up, adding, "I was married."

The swift intake of breath from the women on the opposite loveseat stole the oxygen from the lobby.

"My wife passed away," he continued.

The air flew back out, nearly brushing Hollie's bangs aside.

"Oh my." Frank clasped her hands around her stomach.

At least they had the decency not to ask what happened, but a blind man could see the curiosity brimming in their eyes.

Todd set the plate aside and laced his fingers together.

"It was an accident," he explained in a subdued voice. "An explosion."

In a soft purge, he relayed the fateful tale, feeling drained but somehow at peace.

Frank's walker shook. Her robust figure nudged to the edge of the seat cushion and then she launched upright, tottering for a moment before she prodded the aluminum go-cart forward.

Before Todd could prepare himself, she leaned past the handlebars and wrapped her plump arms about his neck. As if that wasn't enough of a shock, Flo quickly rose and shuffled toward him in her pink cotton dress, bending over to awkwardly pat him on the back.

Behind this melee, Hollie met Maryann's gaze. The woman raised slight shoulders and shook her head, smiling.

"Ladies," Todd took turns hugging each. "It's been several years, but I thank you. You have good hearts."

Maryann leaned forward and placed her hand atop his, squeezing.

"And so do you."

Tears formed behind Hollie's eyes, but when Todd's head finally poked through the foray to catch her glance, she beamed brightly. Perhaps her glistening eyes gave her away. There was a meaningful look on his face.

She rose and shooed the ladies back into their seats and the conversation quickly turned to the wedding of the maintenance man's daughter. The chatter then segued to the finest sponges in Tarpon Springs. This topic launched Francine to chronicle the best restaurants in Tarpon Springs—actually, restaurants anywhere. Flo contemplated what outfit to wear to church, and Frank chastised her for worrying about something that was almost a week away. Finally, the conversation was topped off with who was going to win *Dancing With The Stars*.

Watching Todd laugh at their stories, and offer his take on contestants that *should* have been in the competition, Hollie leaned back in the loveseat and reveled in this close haven. Her posse. She studied Todd's profile as he listened to Maryann talk about her collection of cuckoo clocks.

Chiseled.

A strong, angular jawline. A long, straight nose. Short tawny hair, with slightly darker stubble shadowing his face. She followed a corded muscle down the side of his neck that slipped into the white cotton shirt. The back of his neck was bronzed, his throat a little less so.

Engrossed in the conversation, Hollie was startled when his hand dropped off his thigh to wrap around hers. He squeezed it even as he laughed at one of Frank's jokes.

Affection took root deep in her chest as she squeezed back. The sliding glass entry opened, halting the conversation. Francine and Flo craned their heads, like two gazelles.

"Tony!" Frank screamed as if she hadn't seen the maintenance man in years, when he was usually milling about most of the day.

Tony Maillis was a small man from the nearby Greek community. Slight of stature, and sparse of dark hair, he had been a staple at Harbor Breeze since Hollie had moved in. It was what was held in the man's tanned hands that engrossed the posse. The remnants of what appeared to be a wedding cake with white icing and filigree patterns on it.

"Christina's cake!" Frank shrieked, hoisting up onto her walker and pushing it like it was a wheel barrow.

Flo followed suit, and even Maryann rose out of curiosity as the talk shifted to details of the wedding ceremony.

"And just like that—" Todd turned to Hollie with a smile, "—I am no longer the center of attention."

"I wouldn't say that." She winked, but it probably looked like an awkward muscle spasm.

The gesture worked and Todd laughed warmly.

"They'll be back," she assured, watching the congregation at the counter where the cake was being sliced.

Clearing her throat, she murmured, "Thank you for being so good with them."

Todd watched the small crowd across the lobby.

"They're wonderful." He seemed sincere. "And they adore you, which makes them high on my approval list."

"Where do I rank on that list?"

He was still in possession of her hand as his pointer finger caressed her palm. "Pretty damn high. Right up there with R2-D2."

Hollie clamped her hand around that finger. So simple. Just the touch of hands, like awkward teenagers. But the effect was no less than a cat's purr, the vibration humming inside her chest.

"They'll want us to have cake," she warned.

"Then we shall have cake. But first I have to hit the can. Way too much coffee." He glanced over her head toward the men's room.

"After the cake," she said. "We're done. We'll go upstairs."

Sunset eyes simmered. To her surprise, he lifted her hand and dusted his lips across the knuckles, causing her to shiver.

"I'll eat fast, then."

She knew her cheeks flushed, and she smiled brazenly, following him with her eyes as he walked away.

Pent-up air flew from her lips once she exhaled. She flicked a glance at the group standing by the counter, wondering if they had noticed her deflate. There were a few cackles, but they weren't at her expense. At the sliding glass door a man stood outside juggling a few grocery bags before setting two down by one of the cement-potted plants.

Hollie didn't recognize him, but there were often new people renting in Harbor Breeze. When the ladies didn't pay him any mind, she figured they either knew him or were too ingrained in their conversation.

Instead of ambling past to the elevator, the man made his way toward the conflux of loveseats, setting a Publix bag down on the coffee table.

He looked back at the group and then swung his gaze to her, murmuring, "Come with me."

Hollie's head jerked up.

A red baseball cap was drawn down low to conceal much of the face. A dark goatee circled plump lips, and equally dark hair poked out beneath the cap.

"Excuse me?" she asked, stealing a glimpse of the men's room door.

"If you don't want your boyfriend in there, or any of these ladies getting hurt, you'll leave here quietly with me."

"Hell no." She rose to her feet.

Turning so that his back faced the group behind him, the man reached into the shopping bag and exposed a handgun. Adroitly disengaging the safety and tucking his ring finger through the trigger, he looked up so that she could read the meaning in his black eyes.

"I could turn around and shoot everyone behind me and be out the door in mere seconds, and I am instructed to do so should you not comply. Your security cameras will just see a guy in a baseball cap, and the exterior cameras will not see my vehicle." He nudged the barrel of the gun up further. "So, can I count on your cooperation?"

Vomit inched up her throat. Anger could not stem the quaking of her limbs. Another glimpse at the men's room door only incited the man to step in closer.

"You better hope he doesn't come out."

Todd.

The ladies.

All that she valued.

"Move," the voice hissed.

If she could just get this man outside—away from any potential fallout—then she could try to run from him.

With one final assessment of the Harbor Breeze lobby, Hollie trudged on stiff legs toward the sliding doors. She didn't turn to see if the stranger followed. She felt his presence—a malignant cloud drifting in her wake.

Frank cackled at one of Tony's jokes, while Flo closed her eyes to savor the wedding cake. Maryann accepted a plate of the cake and shifted her glance at the last second, meeting Hollie's gaze. Hollie gave the slightest negative shake of her head and stepped through the doorway, hearing the closing hiss behind her.

One goal. Only one thing mattered. Get the gun out of range from anyone inside. With that in mind, her step off the curb was almost eager in its haste.

"This way."

A talon-like grip hauled her down the sidewalk, away from the parking lot. Hollie tugged against it, trying to free herself. The paper bag was thrust against her kidney, the blunt metal protrusion inside it emphasizing a point.

For as scared as she was, the shock of the situation gave her the bravado of disbelief.

"Who are you? What do you want from me?"

Losing sight of the front door of the Harbor Breeze she dug in, resisting his insistent tug.

Wild eyes scanned the street for anyone to call out to. Police. Pedestrians. There was nothing. The sun was setting and the shadow of night swallowed everything in its path.

With no relent from the merciless haul on her limb, her lungs filled in preparation. Before she could release the pent-up scream, a sharp strike to the side of her head rendered her world black.

CHAPTER FOURTEEN

Hollie woke, but the darkness had not receded. It took a few disconcerting minutes to realize that she was in an unlit room. A tiny red light gave off the faintest glow high above her. It reminded her of the unforgiving red eye of the *Terminator* machine. Squinting, she realized it was the small battery beacon of a fire alarm.

An electrical hum vibrated beside her. The drone only enhanced the pain in the back of her skull. Trying to reach for the ache, a shriek cracked in her dry throat. Her hands were fastened together. Tugging them, she felt the sharp slash of plastic into her flesh.

A zip tie.

What the hell?

She groaned against the pain and waited until her eyes could adjust to the soft red glow. It only lit the top half of the room. The floor she sat on was lost in shadow, harboring every unimaginable demon.

Tugging again, her shoulders protested at the effort, but the bindings would not yield. Curling her legs up beneath her, she was relieved to find that they were not secured. Pressing her back against what might have been a refrigerator with its relentless humming, she used her thigh muscles to inch her way off the floor. The effort cost her and she leaned heavily against the vibrating surface until the pounding pain abated.

Todd.

Did he know where she was? The last she remembered was looking over her shoulder toward the front doorway of the Harbor Breeze, but then—oblivion.

That freak in the baseball cap must have struck her, and taken her—

Where?

"Help!" she tried to scream, but it came out like a crow's caw.

"*Help*!" This time the shout had more zeal.

Creeping along the perimeter of the tight room, she maneuvered her hands behind her back to explore as best she could. Encountering a series of open shelves and the knobs of some closed cabinets, she gathered it to be a storage room of some sort. No windows. A basement perhaps? Todd's unease of such environments proved legitimate.

Shimmying her hands up and down a flat surface, she located a doorknob and whimpered, discovering that it was locked. Throwing her shoulder against the panel—more to draw attention than any ridiculous hope of knocking it down, she finally slid down into a crouch and steadied her breathing so that she could listen outside. Was there any telltale sound? Maybe? A bump or two above her. It was hard to hear over the hum of the icebox.

Pumping her thigh muscles back into a vertical stance she gravitated toward that hellish whine, awkwardly feeling her way around the moist refrigerator. Thrusting her bound hands behind it, she located the plug. With a few awkward yanks she finally jerked it from the outlet.

Silence.

Hollie leaned back against the moist cooler. It offered some relief against the perspiration rolling down her spine. Focusing on the stillness, she heard distant sounds—muted—undefinable.

One glaringly clear sound manifested, though. The unmistakable tread of someone approaching.

Torn between shouting for help or fearing that this was her captor, Hollie opted for volume over anything.

"*Help!*" she screamed.

"Jesus Christ, shut up!" The muffled protest sounded through the door.

A scrape from a lock sounded and the door opened to reveal a shadowy silhouette, the backdrop nearly as dark as the room she huddled in.

Hollie threw herself toward the exit, but the bite of unrelenting hands grabbed her by the shoulders and shoved her back against the wall.

"What the hell?" she cried out.

The door closed again and a light came on. Hollie blinked against the overhead illuminated bars. Finally acclimating, she gaped at the stranger. Expecting it to be the baseball cap man, she was startled to behold a tall man impeccably dressed in a dark gray suit. He was older, maybe late fifties, early sixties, with stylish silver hair and a tan that looked like it came from a bottle.

His face was inscrutable, and his arms crossed over a chest that heaved a sigh. Hooded eyes under thick silver brows regarded her for a moment.

"Hello, Hollie," he said levelly.

Startled into silence, she regrouped and filled her lungs, prepared to shout.

A large hand rose to halt her. She caught the flash of golden rings and a shiny cufflink.

"Please, let's be civilized."

"Civilized," she repeated with a croak. "You sent some thug to my home to kidnap me at gunpoint. Is that *civilized*?"

"Considering the circumstances, it beats several alternatives."

The smug response incited her anger. The recollection of the threat to Todd and the ladies heightened that rage.

"What circumstances? Who are you? Why have you been threatening me?"

Thin lips stretched into a tolerant grin.

"Do you remember me?" His voice was as polished as his attire.

Hollie stared hard into eyes dark enough to mark no beginning or end to the pupils inside them. They stared down an aquiline nose, over lips that clamped in distaste.

There was the vaguest trigger of familiarity—not enough to congeal into an actual memory. Maybe she recognized him standing across the street from her office building. Odds were that it had been baseball cap man, though. This man didn't look like the type to lean against a car and make gun threats with his fingers.

There was a cold detachment in his gaze. A condescending aloofness. It was underlined by a simmering malevolence. As composed as the exterior was, she saw hate in the core of those hooded eyes.

"I don't know you," she vowed. "So, there must be some mistake. Just let me go and I won't mention any of this."

A baleful smile was slow to form.

"I remember *you*," he ignored her plea. "I met you once. You were very young."

Alarm bells started ringing in her head. Searching his face, she drilled down on that nagging recognition that rolled back the years on the wrinkles and white hair.

"The photo," she whispered aloud. "The brothers. You are one of the Mariani brothers."

A bushy eyebrow crept up.

"Indeed. So you *do* know who I am? Well that clarifies things for me."

"It doesn't clarify *anything* for me," she shouted. "What do you want?"

The man winced with disgust. "There's no need to yell. No one is going to hear you, and I could do without the drama."

Hollie tried to wrench her wrists apart and felt her flesh tear in the process. "I don't give a—"

"Uh-uh." He waved a pointer finger censoriously. "Why don't you tell me what motivated you to go to Pennsylvania?"

"I travel lots of places," she retorted. "That's my job."

"Your job," he wiped at a piece of lint on his jacket, "does not require you to visit a farmhouse in rural Bucks County."

Hollie frowned. "It was *you*. Or your damn puppet. You drove me off the road. You tried to kill me."

The man leveled cold eyes on her. "My dear, if I wanted you dead, we wouldn't be sitting here talking right now."

Her hands curled into fists regardless of the pain. "What do you want from me, then?"

"I believe I just stated that," he replied calmly. "I would like to know why, after all these years, you have gone to the farmhouse in Pennsylvania?"

Disturbed beyond belief, she still managed a poker face. "*None of your business* would be the first response to come to mind."

"Fair enough." The man started to turn around.

The temper had finally reached its boiling point. Hollie bent over and charged, ramming her shoulder into the man's abdomen. There was a grunt of surprise at impact, and a cloud of bourbon-laced breath puffed over her.

"Goddammit!"

It was the first break in his fine veneer. He shoved her back, succeeding only because her balance was off with her hands pinned.

The man pounded the door behind him and then tugged the cuffs of his shirt down, cracking his neck and raising his head in poise.

The door opened and baseball cap guy was standing there.

"Keep an eye on her. She's very disrespectful."

Hollie didn't bother curbing the profanity that flowed from her lips.

The man snarled in disgust.

"See that she has the necessities," he instructed baseball cap. "Plug that damn refrigerator back in. And if she messes with anything again, tie her to the shelves."

As the man turned to leave, Hollie cried out, "Which one are you? Richard or Joseph?"

Sloped shoulders stiffened. He pivoted slowly.

"Funny how your memory isn't as meager as you'd portray." He paused. "Richard Mariani at your service. My brother is dead." He bowed somewhat and moved toward the door as the man in the baseball cap stepped out of his way.

"Dammit, you can't just leave me here. What do you want from me?"

Richard stood sideways in the door, sneering at her. "I don't want anything from *you*."

Before she could protest he was gone, and baseball cap guy closed the door, locking himself inside with her. He shoved past her and stooped to plug in the refrigerator, reestablishing the unbearable drone. When he returned to the door, he stood with his back to it, his arms crossed, obscure eyes staring straight through her.

"That's it?" she demanded. "You're just going to stand there and make sure I don't unplug the fridge?"

Stone-faced under the red cap, the man remained silent. He was dressed in jeans and a white polo shirt with sleeves that stretched tight across ridiculous biceps. The steroided physique was meant to compensate for his diminished height, she was sure—or perhaps something else that was diminished.

"Don't you realize how absurd this is? Just let me go. You can tell Richard, or whoever he is, that I escaped."

A snort leaked from the flat nose before he re-secured his frown.

"Sit down and keep quiet," he ordered.

Now that the lights were on, Hollie could confirm that she was in a storage room, but the floor was not covered in rats or excrement like her lurid thoughts in the dark had portrayed.

It looked like a dank pantry with shelves lined with canned goods and bottles. If she could just get her hands loose, she would start using those cans as projectiles, and then bat him over the head with a bottle.

In the corner stood a stool with metal legs and a wooden seat. She obeyed, but only because she needed a moment to sit and think.

"And you're just going to stand there—" she repeated, "—like you're guarding the Tower of London? I hope he pays you well."

"Sit down and be quiet."

Hollie tipped her head back, examining the cement board walls and aluminum shelves. An exhaust fan sat high on the ceiling, and worn gray rubber flooring ran the length of the room. She leaned against the stool, rather than sitting full on it. It was hard to climb up with no hands for balance.

Taking a deep breath tainted with dust and cheap cologne, she saw that the man had secured his gun behind his back again. She studied the shelving near him, dismayed to discover the apparatus was bolted to the wall. Hefting away from the stool she began to pace the narrow stretch of the room.

"I said sit," the gravelly voice commanded.

"I am nervous. I pace when I'm nervous."

The motion offered her an opportunity to search every aspect of the chamber for some means to incapacitate him. On her third sweep she felt fingers bite into the flesh of her arm.

"Let go!" She wrenched uselessly.

With his free hand, baseball cap guy hauled out another zip tie and fastened it through the band already securing her hands, tying it to the sturdy corner rod supporting the shelves.

Without another word, he resumed his stance by the door.

"Well, that's just great," Hollie muttered, tugging uselessly. "I need the bathroom."

"Too bad."

"I am serious. I'm a nervous wreck. It's not going to be pretty if you don't let me get to the bathroom."

Emitting a quick snarl, baseball cap guy unlocked the door and poked his head out into the hallway. His hand groped the back pocket of his jeans where he retracted what looked like a switchblade. Opening it, he came at her.

"There is a toilet directly across the hall. I will be standing just outside the door." He smirked. "Don't get any cute ideas. There are no windows in there. Just a toilet and a sink."

In an approach that looked like he might gut her, he snapped the blade through the rigid plastic that bound her to the shelves. The impetus of the release nearly sent her toppling into the opposite wall. With her hands still fastened, her shoulder slammed painfully into the cinderblock.

Baseball cap guy grabbed her by the arm, and after another perusal of the hallway, hauled her through the door and into the shadowed portal directly opposite it. He flicked on a light switch and a bare bulb high up on the peeling ceiling illuminated. A white porcelain sink with dripping green stains was affixed to the tiled wall, and a toilet with a cracked seat sat opposite it.

"My hands." She wiggled her fingers behind her. "I can't do this without my hands."

Grunting in acknowledgement, baseball cap guy snapped her bindings and an epic battle of pain and relief ensued between her shoulder blades. The victory was short-lived as he retrieved another zip tie and grabbed her wrist, pulling it down level with the toilet where he bound her to the pipe running into the wall.

"I can't do this!" she cried.

"You have a free hand. If you have to go as bad as you claim, I'm sure you'll figure out a way." He backed out into the doorway and added, "The door is unlocked and I'll be standing right here. You have two minutes and I'll open the door again."

He glanced down at his watch as he hauled the wooden panel shut.

Hollie stood paralyzed, staring at her reflection in the tarnished mirror above the sink. Splotches of red glared against skin so white she barely recognized it. Under the garish bulb her dark eyes looked ghostly, a haunting likeness of her former self. Sparse patches of blood stained her blouse.

"One minute," the soulless voice threatened from behind the door.

The pipe resisted her tugging. She searched wildly for anything to use against the goon outside. A stack of toilet paper on top of the toilet certainly wasn't going to do the trick.

The door opened and she nearly shrieked.

"I told you two minutes." His eyes roved up and down her body and his lip curled up in scorn. "I see you didn't use them wisely.

The pocket knife was back, severing her bond to the toilet. It was replaced by the barrel of a handgun that ushered her out. Inside that brief three-foot span between the two rooms Hollie let loose a banshee-like scream.

A shove from behind sent her sprawling on the dirty rubber floor, her already sore wrists throbbing from the force of the landing. The hollow sound of the door slamming shut was followed by the rough arrest of her arms as they were yanked together and the plastic tie applied.

"No!" she yelled.

"Shut up, or I swear to God I'll whack you in the head with this." Baseball cap guy waved the gun at her.

Perspiration dripped down the side of his face as he drew her bound arms alongside the shelf and fastened her to it.

Hollie drew one conclusion from her outburst. Perhaps he would knock her out with the gun, but he had no real intention of shooting her. They wanted her for some reason. In that respect she didn't immediately fear for her life.

But there was plenty else to fear.

CHAPTER FIFTEEN

Todd washed his hands and looked up at the image in the mirror.

Who is this guy?

This guy is smiling.

Sure as hell can't be me. I don't smile.

Another perusal and, in fact, it was him in the mirror. Massaging the stubble on his jaw, he wished he had taken the time to shave this morning. It wouldn't have mattered—the shadow would have returned by this hour anyway.

He tried a bit of finger-combing to his tousled hair, but that just resulted in wayward spokes. His cotton button-down shirt bore those fresh-out-of-the-overnight-bag creases. Even his face showed evidence of similar wrinkles.

And yet, Hollie had kissed that stubbled cheek. She had looked into those eyes rimmed with creases, and she had smiled in a way that made him feel like the sexiest guy alive.

As much as he balked at going down that wormhole of comparison, his wife's eyes had never revealed that same glow. They had been in love. In the beginning there was no doubt of that. But they were young and didn't have the burden of life and responsibility yet. Once domestication settled in, the relationship altered. There was no definitive moment, and he bore the brunt of responsibility for its demise.

But meeting Hollie—one certainly could not claim that situation was carefree and without burden. And still, despite the inauspicious origins of their meeting—it didn't temper her kisses. They were real.

He stared at the man in the mirror. For three years the reflection had been clouded. Now, he saw clarity, and he had an eccentric sports publicist with a posse full of delightful seniors to thank for it.

Trying to temper his grin, Todd headed back out into the lobby. There was no sign of Hollie. She might have gone to the bathroom as well, or maybe she ran upstairs. He glanced at the ladies still congregated around the short man slicing cake. Maryann, Hollie's next-door neighbor, broke from the pack with a worried look on her pallid face.

"Todd," she said, grabbing both his hands in hers. "Hollie just left here wiz someone. A stranger. I zink she might have been trying to signal me—that somezing was wrong."

Todd squeezed her fingers gently, but with urgency. "Okay," he began, trying to sound composed when he felt like he'd been fileted. "Tell me what you saw."

"A man came in. I didn't zink anything of it at first. He was just bringing in his groceries. But he set his bags down, zere," she nodded at two Publix paper bags just outside next to a cement planter. "And then he came inside and walked up to her. Next zing I knew, she was leaving wiz him—but—" she hesitated.

"It's okay, Mrs. Baumann," he clasped his hands around her shoulders because she was trembling. "What happened?"

"It was just the way she looked at me. She just nodded. Like some zort of signal. She looked scared." The last word was desperate.

"Okay." Todd tried to soothe, already easing his hands off her, ready to bolt to the door. "How long?"

"A couple of minutes. I tried to interrupt the ladies—"

As if catching on that something was astir, the heads popped up from their clutch.

With a quick squeeze of Maryann's shoulders, he rushed toward the door, nearly slamming into the glass when it did not part fast enough. Searching the parking lot yielded no sign of Hollie. There were no vehicles pulling out. No motion.

"Hollie!" he shouted, jogging out into the middle of the lot.

Executing a 360, there was nothing amiss. Cars rumbled by on the adjacent street, but none exiting from Harbor Breeze. Hollie's car sat parked exactly where they left it.

Todd hauled out his cell phone and pressed redial on her number. It rang hollowly and kicked into voice mail. He left a hasty message, but the sense of futility ripped through his rib cage.

Sprinting around the building, he ran its perimeter with no sign of her. Sweat crept down his spine and clashed with the blast of air conditioning as he rushed back into the lobby. The ladies stood huddled together looking up at him with rounded eyes. The maintenance man was behind the counter, packing up the remainder of his cake, deferentially remaining quiet.

"Any sign?" Maryann asked anxiously.

"No." Todd shook his head and hit redial again. No answer.

"I'm calling the police," he announced.

"Oh dear." Francine dropped onto the loveseat, holding onto her walker with white knuckles. Clearly Maryann had clued them in on the development.

Flo wilted against the armrest beside her, staring plaintively toward the sliding glass doors. Maryann stood off to the side, hugging herself and looking distraught.

Todd waited listlessly for his call to be transferred and as soon as he got a human, the story rushed from his mouth in a surge of angst. None of that urgency carried over to the automaton on the other end. Instead, he listened to the recited message, *any person between the ages of 18-65 must wait 24-72 hours before filing a missing persons report*.

Pressing his thumb on the red X, he paced in thought, and reflexively dialed Hollie again.

Think!

"Hollie told me about the notes," Maryann mentioned, subdued.

"What notes?" Frank wiggled to the edge of the cushioned seat.

Reading his indecision, Maryann nodded. "It's okay. Zey know about the dreams—the hypnotist. The—" she held her breath, "zee reincarnation."

Flo sucked in a breath and crossed herself.

"Hollie told you about Nina?" he asked, surprised.

"Nina?" Maryann's thin eyebrows knitted.

Todd collapsed onto the opposite armrest, planting his hands on his knees. A dull pain throbbed at the base of his neck.

What did he have to lose? These were Hollie's most cherished friends. Maybe one of the ladies saw something—knew some minute detail—

Attempting a quick text to Hollie in hopes that she would respond, Todd stared at the status of *delivered*, but not *read*. Glancing up, he found the women watching him like a group of young soldiers, eager to please, but not comprehending the scope of their mission. Haltingly he relayed his introduction to Hollie and the events that ensued.

Maryann shook her head. "She should have shared more. We could have helped. We could have been looking for strangers in the parking lot."

Florence nodded, bobbing her white skunk line.

"You think Hollie is this Nina?" Frank crossed her arms over the handle of her walker. She gulped in a breath that shook her second chin. "Come back?"

Todd's smile was weary. "No," he hesitated. "I mean, there have to be more plausible theories."

"But, it *is* still a theory?" Flo asked.

He could only raise an eyebrow in response as his eyes volleyed between the phone and the front door of the lobby.

"I can't sit here," he vowed. "I can't sit here for 24 hours and wait until the police can do something."

Vaguely aware of Maryann's hand patting his back, his head dropped as Frank started talking about restaurants again.

"There's that restaurant on Bayshore," she said to Florence. "You know, the one with all those marble statues outside. It looks like a Greek temple or something."

"I know it. Too fancy for me," Flo replied. "I was in it once with Harriet. Remember her from the Seniors club?"

"Is she the one who had a crush on Martin? She used to give him her bingo prizes. Such a shame he passed away."

"Yeah, she didn't come to Seniors anymore after that."

Maryann's hand stilled on Todd's back, and he nearly smiled when he heard her whisper, "is there a point."

Francine must have heard her because she turned her head sharply and huffed.

"Well, it's just the name. Mariani. I think that restaurant is owned by a Mariani."

Fully alert, Todd climbed to his feet. "Where? Where is this restaurant?"

Frank leaned back and gaped up at him. "Well—" she looked to Florence for affirmation as if she suddenly lost all recollection of the place.

"Bayshore *boulevard*," Flo emphasized. "Near the university."

"What's the name of the restaurant?" he asked.

"Man—Man—" Flo snapped her fingers, trying to remember.

"Manfreds!" Frank shouted.

Manfreds. Todd was already typing it into his phone to search for the address.

"I'll get an Uber or something," he declared.

"No such thing." Frank was rummaging in her purse and extracted a flamingo keyring with enough keys on it to vie for janitor status. "Take my car. It's the silver Impala in the handicapped spot."

Todd looked at the robust woman extending her hand over the aluminum bar of the walker. A sense of urgency was stamped on her face. In that moment he understood Hollie's adoration for these sweet friends. He stooped over and placed his palms around those full cheeks and planted a kiss on a forehead that smelled of pressed powder and flowers.

"Thank you," he uttered thickly.

"Oh," Frank cupped her hand on top of his, pressing it to her cheek. "Oh, you are so welcome. But go!" She released him and made a shooing motion. "Go, find our girl."

Todd pulled up across the street from *Manfreds*. Gaudy would be the tamest of adjectives to describe the restaurant. Complete with roman gardens and marble pillars it looked like something off a Caesar movie set.

Once again he tried Hollie's phone.

Once again it went unanswered.

Getting out of the car, the scent of talcum powder and pastries escaped with him. He stared across the roof, surveying the street for any pedestrian traffic, but there was only a couple walking arm in arm through the restaurant's open gate. Even at a distance he could tell the woman's stature was too short to be Hollie.

It was highly unlikely for him to find anything here, but it beat driving blindly, waiting until he could file a report with the police.

Dodging behind a motorcycle, Todd jogged across the street and walked through the ornate gate and exotic garden to the stained glass double doors with the simple gold script reading, *Manfreds*.

Opening the door, the din of patrons drifted through a vaulted foyer with a marble fountain at its center. Todd passed by it, tempted to toss a coin, as that seemed the most credible way to locate Hollie.

A well-dressed woman carrying a tablet stood off to the side next to a polished wooden pedestal. Her bright red lips offered him a cordial smile.

"Do you have a reservation, or will you be visiting our bar?"

One arched doorway led into a formal dining room, where the din of voices and silverware clanging emanated. The other arched door revealed a softly lit mirror-backed bar.

"The bar, thanks," he said, nodding.

It was a Tuesday night after 7 PM—not exactly the Happy Hour crowd. Most people were well-attired and waiting to be seated. Todd nudged a leather swivel barstool back with his hip and watched the bartender busily serving others. His eyes searched the bistro tables along the wall, most occupied by couples, their faces shadowed in the faux candlelight.

Continuing to scan the bar, his gaze collided with the mirror behind it. His casual apparel and hand-frayed hair didn't quite chime with the clientele. Still, there were a few patrons in polo shirts that looked casual enough. Judging by the watch on the guy next to him, his *casual* shirt probably cost a small fortune.

"Can I get you something?" At least the smooth offer from the bartender did not sound judgmental.

The last thing he felt like doing was putting anything in his riotous stomach, but Todd muttered, "One of those." He nodded at the closest beer tap.

As the bartender poured, Todd took stock of him. Black pants, white shirt, and a black vest. The bartender was clean-shaven and wore his hair neatly cropped. Refined—just like everything else in this place.

A tall mug was set down before him. Rivulets of moisture ran down the sides.

"I've never been here before. Nice place," Todd remarked.

Reaching for a towel, the bartender swiped at a pool of water on the wooden counter.

"It's a landmark. Been here since before I was born."

Todd estimated the man to be in his late twenties— maybe thirties. Making a show of looking around, and acting duly impressed, he asked, "Do you know who owns it?"

"Mr. Mariani. You'll see him in here from time to time."

"Is he here this week?" Todd tried to sound casual, but his hand gripped the mug with enough zeal to nearly crack the glass.

"I haven't seen him."

Distracted by new patrons, the bartender prepared to move on. Todd acted quickly, hauling out his phone and typing in a hasty search of Hollie's publicity firm.

"I'm supposed to meet a blind date here," he confided with an awkward grin. "Did this woman come in yet?"

The bartender leaned over to examine the headshot of Hollie.

"Nope." He winked. "I would have remembered that one. Good luck."

"Thanks," Todd mumbled after the retreating figure.

Leaving the beer untouched, he placed money down on the bar and searched for a restroom. Following a short corridor off to the side of the bar, Todd hesitated outside the door marked, MEN. Immediately next to it was a mirrored door labeled WOMEN, but further down the hall was an unmarked exit with a panic bar across it.

A quick check over his shoulder confirmed he was alone as he moved purposefully toward that door, pressing against the bar, praying it wouldn't set off a fire alarm. It opened to the outside. A row of garbage bins that emitted a rank scent of decay sat at the base of a short staircase. He peered around, but all he could see was the concrete exterior of the building next door.

Closing the door, he exchanged an embarrassed look at a patron entering the men's room. The guy hesitated, checking the door he was about to go through, and Todd just shouldered past him.

Back at the bar, he put on a performance, checking his watch and angling his head toward the entryway as if in anticipation of his blind date. He caught the bartender give him an understanding shrug.

Todd made a whirling motion in the air with his finger to indicate he was going to go search for her. The bartender gave a brief nod.

Now armed with an excuse to amble around, Todd returned to the vaulted foyer, spotting another corridor splitting off just before the dining room entrance. This hallway was much wider and lined with mirrored sconces. Ornate double doors on each side were tagged with ballroom names. Beyond them were more restrooms and a seating area. And lastly, a barred door marked EXIT.

Feeling the futility of this search, he peered back toward the foyer, assuring he was alone, and slipped into one of the ballrooms. Only a few emergency lights illuminated the room with chairs stacked along the walls and empty tables congregated at its sides. A small stage lined one end of the auditorium, but Todd worked his way to the opposite side, where a string of unmarked exits attracted him.

Somewhere in this garish tribute to roman architecture there had to be an office. There had to be a lair for its pretentious owner. He would search the very bowels of this coliseum for the man—just to determine what correlation he had with Hollie.

Trying the doors one-by-one at the rear of the auditorium, he discovered that most led into the same galley-styled kitchen. As there was no event taking place in the ballroom, the kitchen was empty. Meandering down the aisle of stainless steel counters, he cringed when his hip hit the handle of a soup ladle resting in a sink. It fell, clanging into the aluminum basin.

Apprehensive, he scanned the recessed corners of the ceiling, suspecting security cameras might be up there. If they were, no one came running to put an end to his exploration.

Continuing past a bank of ovens, he narrowed in on a door with an illuminated red EXIT sign above it. Occasional bursts of muted conversation and clashing dinnerware could be heard through the walls. Todd hesitated a moment, looking back, and then pushed against the bar to open the door.

A stark hallway lacked any of the gaudy flare of the establishment. Utilitarian tiling lined the floor. Cardboard boxes of paper products and restaurant supplies were stacked sporadically against white, water-stained walls.

Here, the cameras mounted every ten feet were hard to ignore, and he knew he was pretty much screwed if somebody was behind them, watching. The need for such excessive video surveillance in this area of the restaurant was sketchy. But if he was about to be caught where he didn't belong, he damn well was going to make it worthwhile.

The first door he encountered yielded a laundry room—the next, a break room. By the third door things turned promising. It was an office. Sparsely furnished—he doubted it was somewhere the owner would hang out. Deciding not to dwell on it, he moved on, locating only one more doorway at the end of the hall. This one was wooden and looked aged in comparison, as if it was the vestige of a previous establishment.

It was unlocked, but the swollen wood needed a little coaxing. It opened to the top of a wooden staircase.

Great. A cellar.

In stark comparison to the brightly lit hall above, this passageway was sparingly illuminated by strung lightbulbs. His guess was that it probably led to the proverbial wine cellar.

Ahead of him a door cracked open as Todd shrank back into the shadows of the stairwell. A man emerged, the silhouette of his shoulders growing wider as he approached. As he passed under a lightbulb Todd saw that he was wearing a baseball cap. A *red* baseball cap. The only key detail Maryann Baumann could provide.

The fact that a man bearing such a description was here in an establishment owned by Richard Mariani was way too much of a coincidence.

Not wanting to miss this opportunity, Todd disregarded his internal warning bells and stepped out from under the staircase to confront the man.

The face was obscured by the brim of the cap, but a flash of white teeth was visible in the shadows. Also visible was the barrel of a handgun that rose to point at Todd's chest.

"Whoa," Todd uttered, hoisting his hands. "Dude, I'm just lost. My fiancé wanted me to check out the ballroom—we're getting married here in the spring."

"Shut up," the man in the cap ordered.

"Isn't a gun a tad excessive for restaurant security?"

"Isn't rummaging through an empty kitchen and opening every door in your path a tad excessive for wedding planning?"

The damn cameras.

When he first glimpsed them he had contrived the wedding-planning tale—just in case. He never figured it would escalate into a confrontation with a gun. As much as it was a pipedream to come to this restaurant, this encounter confirmed that the man in the baseball cap had to be the same man that kidnapped Hollie. Which meant that she was close.

"You haven't met my fiancé." He forced the joke.

Indifferent, the man waved the gun, motioning him to follow.

"Mr. Mariani knows who you are," he announced in a gruff, don't-waste-my-time voice.

For a moment Todd considered playing the ignorant card once more, but he was tired of games.

He wanted answers.

He wanted Hollie.

"Great." Todd dropped his hands. "Then take me to him. I've got a lot of questions for the man. The first that comes to mind is, *where the hell is Hollie*?"

For an awkwardly long spell, the gun-toting thug just stared at Todd, the weapon held fast.

"You can't seriously shoot me," Todd rationalized, trying to stay optimistic. "There's a restaurant full of people above us that will hear."

A smirk that might as well have been a scar across the black facial hair looked anything but congenial.

"You're below the empty ballroom, and there is enough noise in the main dining room to conceal a small bomb down here."

Right.

"Fine. Just do what you have to do, then."

The baseball cap man motioned again with the gun, directing Todd ahead of him down the narrow hallway. Todd glared as he stepped past, reminding himself that this goon was the only possible means to locate Hollie. That fact, more so than the weapon, kept him from cramming his fist down the guy's throat.

Trudging forward, aware of the crosshairs on his back, Todd's muscles cramped in anticipation. He was ready for an assault from behind, an assault from the front—wherever—he was ready. Why? Because he wanted to punch something. He wanted to hurt someone for kidnapping Hollie—for the threatening messages—for the dreams—for the secrets—for his own misgivings—for not being there when he should have—for a wife who didn't love him—for years of being under a microscope. The list went on, and as it did his anger mounted.

Last night he had slept with Hollie tucked in his arm and nestled against his chest, one soft palm resting against a pec. His lips were in her hair, smelling that cloud of citrus. At some point, the rise and fall of their chests had meshed and he had never felt more at peace.

There was no denying that he had loved his wife at one time—maybe even longer than she loved him. But that blanket of trust Hollie had splayed across him—it triggered an overwhelming desire to protect her—it activated a raw need that staggered him.

Channeling his rogue thoughts, Todd forced his focus on the surroundings. Closed doors flanked either side of the dimly-lit corridor, but the occasional grunts from behind urged him to continue past them. A trickle of water meandered down the wall from a sodden leak in one corner of the low ceiling. A staircase was visible on the opposite end, but the nudge of the barrel against his spine and a terse command, "stop", drew him to a halt at a doorway just before the stairwell.

As the man held the gun with his right hand and hauled keys out of his pocket with the left, Todd gauged his chances at taking him. Expecting this, the guy raised his head. A warning brimmed in the eyes that peered out from under the cap.

Satisfied that Todd was staying put, the man in the cap unlocked the door and tapped the gun against

Todd's arm to urge him inside. As soon as the door cracked open an inch, a high-pitched scream pierced the gap.

"Help! Help!"

"Hollie!" Todd yelled, rushing inside.

The baseball cap man slipped inside and slammed the door shut behind him.

"Quiet," he hissed, aiming his gun at Todd while raising the back of his hand, preparing to swing it across Hollie's face.

"No!" Todd shouted, launching and flinching in preparation of the ensuing gunshot.

Instead, he saw Hollie's foot launch in a stiff kick to the thug's groin. The man doubled over and Todd slammed the hand with the gun into a shelf sending the weapon spiraling across the floor. The baseball hat flew off as well.

A roar of protest welled from the doubled-over man, where a glistening bald patch was exposed on the back of his head. Todd launched after the gun which had slid under an aluminum shelf.

Behind him, the door slammed open and an imposing silhouette filled it.

"Enough!"

The command was uttered with enough husky gravity to make Todd pause for a second. In that span, he registered the barrel of the gun aimed at his chest.

"Jesus Christ, I have to take care of everything myself."

This rebuke was aimed at the hunched man who now struggled to stand erect while his hand clutched his groin and pain creased his face.

"Tie him up," he commanded.

Vigilant of the handgun, Todd nonetheless shifted toward Hollie, his arm slipping around her waist as his eyes swept over her in search of injury.

"How damned tender." The man near the door scoffed.

Todd tensed, ready to launch at the closest captor, but Hollie's grip prevented him. He met her eyes for the briefest second, and in that short respite he was seized by the injured man. Todd's wrists were caught and threaded around an aluminum bar. The man used a thick zip tie—the kind used to secure human beings—not to cinch the trash. He glared at the Todd.

Looking past him, Todd directed his words at the figure looming in the doorway like a slanted shadow under a street lamp.

"I've told people I was coming here. They will call for help if I don't return."

It was a bit of a lie, but so what. It soured some of the arrogance on the polished face.

"That's a shame." the man said. Todd recognized him from the photo. Richard Mariani. "I really had no beef with you. You've been keeping my farmhouse in good shape. Your neighbors have kept their eyes on you on my behalf."

Blood crept up Todd's neck. "That would be *my* farmhouse as the deed currently states. And I don't appreciate being under scrutiny from anyone."

"Well—too bad. It's all too bad. It's too bad that you shared where you were going today. Now we'll have to move you." He nodded at Hollie with disdain. "She's making too much noise, anyway."

"You son of a bitch," Hollie seethed. "What do you want? You can't just kidnap people."

Richard Mariani's slow grin revealed implant white teeth. "Do you hear that, Chauncey? I can't just kidnap people."

Chauncey managed to stand upright, although he winced when he stooped to retrieve his gun. Once he had it, though, composure returned.

"Never seen you kidnap anyone, sir." His thumb clicked the safety release, prepping the 9mm.

Todd caught the motion and moved in front of Hollie as much as his binding would permit.

"You brought this on yourself," Richard chastised Hollie, tucking his gun in a holster beneath his Italian suit jacket. "I haven't even thought of you for many years, but you started snooping around in Pennsylvania…and well, then, you gave me a brilliant idea."

"Which is?" She tried to wriggle her way around Todd's wide shoulder.

Backing out of the doorway, Richard gazed down the hallway before he stuck his head back in.

"Get some guys down here, and transport these two to the mansion." He gave a telling nod. "*Discreetly*."

The door hauled shut as Hollie cried out, "Wait!"

When the lock clicked she shouted, "You coward."

"Shut up," Chauncey hissed, seemingly quite pissed off by the kick she managed to get in on him. "If you want to get out of those ties you'll pretty much have to cut your hands off, in which case you will bleed out in about ten minutes. And—" He patted the door with a furry hand, "—that would be futile anyway because this will be locked, and I will be back in a few minutes. So, do us all a favor and shut the hell up until then."

With a tuck of his head, he backed out of the door, the muzzle of the gun the last thing to disappear through the closing portal.

"It would appear that you placed a chink in the icy veneer of our resident thug," Todd observed coolly, although every vein in his body was on fire.

"Todd." She gaped at him until he saw tears brim around the edges of those wide brown eyes.

"Dammit," he cursed, yanking against the plastic tie with enough force to slice his skin.

"How did you find me?" she whispered.

"Frank," he replied with a quirk of the lips.

Her bound hands reached for him and traveled as high as they could up his chest.

"You were safe." Her voice was hoarse. "You shouldn't have come for me. This is my problem."

Rounded eyes searched the remote corners of the storage room. "For whatever reason, it's my problem."

"Hollie—"

"No." Her fingers clenched against his shirt. "That guy. That Richard Mariani. He wants me for something. Bait, he said." Her gaze dropped and her heart-shaped chin quaked. "I have no idea why someone with connections to the mafia would want *me*. I have led a very sheltered life. I haven't even had a speeding ticket."

"Hey—"

"But, whatever it is. It's *my* problem, and I am so sorry that I showed up at your house—if that's the catalyst to this. I am *so* sorry. You came down to Florida because of me. You came to this restaurant because of me. And look—" she touched his wrist again, where a trickle of blood meandered across the top of his hand. "Look what it's gotten you. Oh God."

She snapped her hand back and turned her head to conceal her eyes. The string of self-loathing curses was audible, though.

"Are you through?"

With her back to him, she shook her head.

"I can't reach you." He kept his voice even. "Please come closer."

Turning at a sloth's pace, she inched toward him. In time she was close enough that he could lean in and rest his lips against that silken hair. It was into that soft fusion that he whispered, "This situation is a bit— *extreme*," he hesitated. "But I seem to be the master of extreme circumstances."

Her hair tickled his chin as she shook her head.

"Listen to me," he instructed. "As long as I am with you—that's what matters to me. If I had been stuck back in the lobby of your apartment—not knowing—going crazy with worry—" He took a steadying breath. "I'm touching you now. And God help me, I will do everything in my power to keep you safe."

She almost cracked his nose, lifting her head so quickly. Bleary but soulful eyes consumed him. She searched deep into his gaze—into his very soul.

"I don't want to be the woman you need to save because you feel you couldn't save your wife."

A tourniquet wound around his heart, choking off his blood flow.

Tears filled her eyes again but she blinked them back.

"That sounded hurtful," she uttered in a raw voice. "It was not meant that way. I meant—"

"No, no." He hushed her. "Your point is very valid. I have held nothing but bitter contempt for three years—hell, longer than that. So much so, that you were a shock to my system. It couldn't be. It just couldn't be that I was attracted to someone. I felt—I didn't deserve that—"

"Well, that's just asinine," she interrupted.

"Thanks for the vote of confidence."

Her smile was enough encouragement.

"Look," he said, "if I'm going to have this conversation, I'm gonna damn well have my hands on you when I do. We'll exchange self-condemnations later. Right now we have to figure out how to get out of this mess."

Hollie leaned forward enough to tuck her forehead into the crook of his neck. "Self-condemnations be damned." Her words were muffled by his shirt. "I want you, Todd Hewitt."

His head jerked back. "Whoa."

"Okay, yeah, there's that—" She tried to chuckle. "But I meant—"

"I know what you meant." He tipped forward so that their foreheads rested against each other.

For a moment he closed his eyes.

Life couldn't be so cruel as to give him a second chance at—

The word almost formed inside his head.

"If you were looking to motivate me to get us out of here," he uttered, "you've done it."

The curve of her smile dusted across his cheek before she pulled back. The smile was nothing more than the tickle of a memory now, replaced by hard lines around her mouth.

Somewhere above them an air conditioner must have kicked on, its steady hum quivering across the ceiling. But this room remained stagnant, with the warped smell of a thousand meals lodged in the porous concrete walls.

"What do I have to do with all of this?" she asked in frustration. "Did I see something that I shouldn't have when I was young?"

Using her hooked hands, she reached up to swipe her hair back from her perspired face.

"Clearly I've been to your house as a child, but I can't remember the circumstances behind it. And I don't think this Mariani guy is looking for the reincarnation of Nina." She hesitated and looked at him. "Is he?"

Before Todd could even respond to that, the click of the lock snapped their heads in the direction of the opening door.

Chauncey returned, the baseball cap gone, replaced with close-cropped black hair that glistened across the thinning scalp. Even worse than his cool detachment was the dull sense of purpose in the slate eyes of the behemoth behind him. A stocky man, over six feet tall, with the distinctive curves of a lifetime gym rat turned his wide shoulders to enter the door at an angle. His gaze fixed on no one, but when Chauncey barked an order, he stepped forward with a box cutter, slicing through Todd's plastic shackle.

Relief and sharp pain volleyed for dominance, but Todd ignored both sensations in favor of prepping his fist. A pale eyebrow hiked up as those soulless eyes stared down a bulbous nose with forewarning. The man caught Todd's wrist, grounding his thumb into the ripped skin. Todd matched that gaze without a flinch, though he fought against the harsh tug of his limbs behind his back. Only the gun in Chauncey's hand that was pointed at Hollie's temple forced him into compliance. Within seconds his arms were firmly secured behind his back.

"We're going out the loading bay," Chauncey said. "There's no need to gag you. You can yell all you want. We're just going to the end of the hall and up the stairs. A doorway will be open and the van is waiting. No one will hear you over that span." He raised his gun, which now sported an extended barrel. "No one will hear this either."

A quick knock sounded outside the door.

Chauncey pulled it open, admitting Richard Mariani who was smiling like a Cheshire cat. Silver hair infused with black streaks gleamed under the overhead bulb. That smug expression drew his eyelids back tight as if he'd seen a facelift or two.

"Well," he announced, clapping his jeweled hands together. "It appears my plan worked better—actually, *faster* than expected." A cold smile was aimed at Hollie. "You must be very special."

"I have no idea what your plan is, or what you think of me. But people will be here shortly to look for me."

"*Mmmm*." He pursed his lips. "So you've said. I knew you were being followed—not by him—" he tipped his head at Todd, "—but I didn't realize how lucky I was going to get."

"What are you talking about?" Hollie barked. "*You* have been stalking me. Your thugs have been stalking me."

Impatient with the conversation, Richard ducked his head near Chauncey's ear and ordered, "Load them into the van and wait. I'll have another passenger for you in a few minutes."

Resisting the blunt fingers wrapped around his biceps, Todd growled the moment Chauncey laid a hand on Hollie.

"Don't touch her."

Chauncey pulled back his lips in a mocking sneer, and instead jabbed his gun into the small of her back, "Move."

Before she took a step, Hollie met Todd's eyes. Hers brimmed with hopelessness and regret, along with a strong dose of wrath that would become a tidal wave should her captor give her an opportunity.

Helpless now, Todd knew there would come a time—an errant moment when these captors let their guard down. And when that chance came, he was going to make these mindless brutes regret their treatment of her.

Ushered down the hall, Todd saw a mop leaning in a doorway. He could not reach it with his hands behind his back, but as they trudged by at gunpoint, he scooped his foot out and kicked it. It hit the door and then ricocheted across the hall, smacking the other wall, and finally collapsed onto the floor with another small racket. Granted, he could have hollered a lot louder, but the droll look Chauncey bestowed on him gave him some slight satisfaction.

Hollie was more inclined to use the verbal assault.

"Where are you taking us?" she demanded in a shrill voice.

"Quiet," Chauncey poked her in the ribs with the gun. "Up these stairs."

She was in front, with Chauncey directly behind her, followed by Todd and the heavyweight wrestler lumbering up the rear. Hollie mounted the steps with legs seemingly anchored by concrete.

"Hurry up!" her shadow commanded.

Todd encouraged her sluggishness. As much as they were tucked away in a remote wing of the restaurant, it was still a public venue—where there were more opportunities for exposure than inside the back of a van, or whatever fate lie ahead of them.

Natural light filled the top of the stairwell, and with it came a blended scent of garbage and tar and an assault of humidity. A door was open just ahead as Todd crested the staircase. The light was narrowed to a slim casing as the harsh beeping of a utility vehicle in reverse filled the space.

Chauncey pushed Hollie into the rear of the van, where she stumbled into shadows, her hands bound and useless for balance. Staring into the small round shaft of the gun's barrel, Todd could see the spiral grooves, a design to offer the bullet its spinning motion once fired.

Raising his eyes from that dismal view, he clashed with the hooded gaze of their balding captor.

"Let me make something clear," Chauncey uttered. "Mr. Mariani has no use for you. He wants *her*." He tipped his head at the van. "You've seen too much, so we can't just let you go. The alternative—well—" His smirk was cold. "Just give me a reason—that's all I'm saying."

You've already given me one, Todd thought.

I will make you pay.

"For now," Chauncey nodded at the hulk standing behind Todd, "do us all a favor and get in the van."

As much as he wanted to resist—to ram his fist in this man's already blunt nose, Todd didn't want Hollie left alone with them. He would play by their rules for now. He would bide time.

Balking against the shove to his shoulder, Todd stepped over the gap between the loading bay and the fold-out rear of the vehicle. Hollie reached for his arm, with her snared hands. He moved in front of her, creating a barrier between her and the henchmen, but it also allowed him to touch her with his own hands secured behind his back. In defeat he felt her head drop forward to nestle between his shoulder blades. Obscured like that, she didn't notice when two more henchmen appeared, each holding the arm of a sluggish figure whose face was obscured behind tousled brown hair. Handcuffs locked thin wrists in place as Todd roiled at the rough treatment of what on closer inspection was clearly a female.

"Are handcuffs really necessary?" he retorted, noting that the woman offered little resistance. "Does that help make up for what's lacking in your pants?"

The behemoth snarled, but Chauncey nonchalantly shoved the docile figure into the back of the van, her slight frame crashing into Todd.

"Sorry," she might have mumbled, as if colliding with him was her fault.

Todd curbed her forward motion as best he could, while meeting Chauncey's shark eyes over her shoulder just as he flipped up the lower tailgate panel and swung the doors shut.

A few seconds later he felt the van dip followed by the sound of two doors shutting in the forward cabin. In this commercial vehicle, the driver's cabin was blocked off by a wall.

A swift stomp on the gas sent the three passengers careening back against the closed doors. Todd took the brunt of the fall, his shoulder and thigh catching Hollie's body, and the other woman grunted as she caromed into Hollie.

The paneled van offered only two small blacked-out windows high on the back doors. Their circumference was too tight to squeeze through, and if there was any hope of breaking the glass, the noise would certainly draw the attention of their captors.

Limited light breeched the laminated film offering only vague silhouettes. Hollie was pressed against his side, where he could feel her grasping the thick plastic zip tie behind his back, as if she could wrench it apart with her trembling fingers.

He could hear the other woman slide her back down the side of the van, where she crouched awkwardly. In the hazy light, he couldn't tell if she was looking at the floor or at them. All he saw was a shadowy form that lost its substance with the waning sun.

"Why are you here?" Hollie asked in a tight voice. "Are there more like us? Is there a reason for all these kidnappings in one day, or just bad luck?"

Whether the response was a groan or a laugh was up for debate.

"Are you hurt?" Hollie pressed.

Todd dragged his fingers along the interior panel. What did he hope to find? A door lock? Would the panels swing open and eject them somewhere in the middle of 285 for another car to run them over?

"I'm okay for now," the hoarse voice responded from the shadows.

The van shifted, changing lanes most likely. This time Todd locked his legs and pressed back against the wall for balance. Hollie must have fashioned a similar stance because her arm only grazed his. On the floor, though, he heard an ungainly slump.

"I don't think we're going far," the woman rasped as if she had recently crossed the Sahara. "He has a mansion on Davis Islands."

Hollie stepped on Todd's foot in an attempt to plant herself. "You think we're going to his mansion? But, why?"

A weary sigh hissed from the dark followed by a rustle of movement.

"Oh, Hermey, I wish I knew. I wish I could have stopped this."

Todd felt Hollie's body snap taut. A strangled gasp ripped through her chest as she swayed.

"Who are you?" she demanded with a hiss.

Clearing her throat, the woman's voice came out more refined. "I think you know."

There was a charged silence until Hollie emitted a sound halfway between a sob and a screech.

"*Mom?*"

CHAPTER SIXTEEN

It felt like a flock of angry Starlings were swarming around inside her skull. They converged…batting against one side of her head, and then herding laterally, in a chaotic pendulum.

Hollie reached out with her bound hands, connecting with hollow space. The jostling of the van only added to the unsteadiness.

It's not possible.

Richard Mariani is mentally torturing me.

But why?

"Oh, Hollie," the voice wept in the dark. "All I've ever wanted to do is keep you safe." The raw protest wrenched from the woman's throat. "And it has all backfired. If I had—If I had died on that boat, none of this would have happened to you."

The woeful voice sounded familiar. Enough so to incite tears. But disbelief festered in the dark.

"Who *are* you?" Hollie demanded again.

"It's a very long story," the woman sighed. "One I've been longing to tell you—"

The van rolled to a stop and the sound of the passenger-side door opening halted any conversation. Even though night had fallen, both a cellphone flashlight and an overhead floodlight poured through the expanding crack, temporarily blinding them as the back doors were hauled open.

Rough hands touched her skin, riling her into a frenetic attempt to resist their grip. Todd's reaction wasn't as chaotic. He head-butted the stocky man and earned a punch for it. The hard crack of fist against jaw snapped Hollie to attention.

"Todd," she cried, reaching awkwardly for him, but he was hauled from the back of the van on unsteady legs and thrust down a sidewalk, his frame disappearing under the veil of night.

Only a hundred yards away she could make out the glow of neighborhood docks and the moving lights of a boat making its way through a narrow channel. Beefy tentacles now reached for her, but she thrashed against them.

She had to see.

Just give me a moment in the light.
Just let me see her.

While she was being manhandled by another thug, Chauncey climbed into the van to usher the other captive out.

The woman was hunched over, watching her footing as Chauncey's shove from behind forced her to leap to the ground. As those sneakers made contact with concrete, she straightened and looked at Hollie.

The garage floodlights reflected off dark hair with silver strands and framed a thin face with high cheekbones and slightly sunken brown eyes. She tipped her head back, flicking the long bangs away from her face and Hollie would have fallen were it not for the human manacles around her biceps.

"Mom?" she croaked.

Before the woman could reply, Hollie was yanked away, hauled down the sidewalk with her feet dragging in an effort to dig in.

"No!" she screamed. "No. Dammit. Let me see her."

"Quiet," the captor hissed.

Wild eyes searched her environment absorbing the exquisitely manicured grounds visible at the base of a stately Mediterranean-style mansion. With waterfront real estate being such a precious commodity, bordering mansions were erected tightly. She was certain her screams could reach them.

"Help!" she wailed. "*Help!*"

Chauncey yanked his captive forward so that he could get into Hollie's face.

"Do you think these neighbors are going to answer your call?" He sneered. "Seriously?"

The Starlings in her head grew angry, their temperature rising so that she had a swarm of hot, pissed-off birds zinging around behind her eyes.

"I don't know what to think," she spat. "I don't know where we are. I don't know who you are." Her eyes sliced toward the familiar face. "I don't know who *she* is."

And I don't know who I am.

"Will you let me have a few minutes alone with her?" the raspy voice pleaded.

"And you're in a position to make requests?" Chauncey laughed. "You're the one who should be worried. You're the one this is all about. You could have saved your daughter this aggravation. Now, who knows what *Sally* will do with her."

Any conversation was obscured by the pounding pulse inside Hollie's ears.

Tugged into a garage, she absently noticing the matching black and red Ferraris parked there. Hauled up a short staircase, she emerged into an expansive kitchen with polished wooden cabinets and sparkling granite counters. Ahead, floor to ceiling windows revealed her reflection, the view beyond now voided by night. In that reflection she saw red welts slashed across her forearms. Shock numbed the muscles in her face, leaving her with slack lips and haunted eyes. The reflection of the woman behind her came into view and quickly blurred as water pooled in Hollie's gaze.

In an arrival fit for a monarch, Richard Mariani sauntered into the kitchen, looking as polished as a Zamboni-surfaced skating rink. His jacket had been discarded, and he wore a crisp white shirt, unbuttoned at the collar to reveal a tuft of pepper-colored hair. His shirt sleeves were rolled up to expose copper arms.

"Put her upstairs with the other one until I figure out what to do with them. But this one," he grinned past Hollie's shoulder, "leave her with me. Oh, and replace her handcuffs with plastic. You know I hate handcuffs. What were you thinking?" He sighed. "Oh—that's right. You *don't* think. If you were capable of thought, you would have just *followed* Hollie in Pennsylvania as you were instructed—not ram her off the road."

Chauncey winced at the criticism and hurriedly withdrew a keychain, unbolting the shackle, and just as dexterously fastening a plastic tie in its place. "The driveway was so steep," he mumbled in defense.

Hollie looked behind her, angling past Chauncey's beefy shoulder. In this well-lit kitchen there seemed little doubt that the woman was her mother. It had been almost twenty years since she had *died*, but that wasn't enough time to forget every little facet that could never be replicated or diminished over time. The angle of her front tooth, the point of her chin.

"*No*." The denial wrenched from Hollie's stomach—her heart—her very soul.

Tears boiled up in the woman's eyes as she jerked free of her captor's slack grip. Stumbling forward she reached for Hollie's hand, the effort revealing raw, bruised wrists. Hollie froze at the touch, and stared into hauntingly memorable eyes.

Tiny cups of coffee at the kitchen table on Sundays.
Staying up past bedtime for a really good movie.
Eating peanut butter and jelly sandwiches at the beach.

The matching beauty marks on the throat that Hollie used to tease was a vampire bite.

Familiar hands that held her hair back so many times when she was sick.

Placing a rose atop a closed coffin.

"Mom." It was a hoarse croak.

"Baby," she whimpered, and then shifted her eyes to Richard who stood, twisting a ring around his middle finger. She glared at him with a hatred that knew no bounds.

"Damn you to hell. You wanted me. You got me. But give me a few minutes with my daughter."

"Why?" He polished the pretentious gold against his sleeve. "I didn't get any time with my brother before they dragged him away."

"That's bullshit!"

Hollie snapped at the curse. Her mother had been more the bulldonkey type. But, of course, it was a childhood recollection.

"*Ginger*," Richard said, exaggerating Virginia Musgrave's nickname. "My brother is dead because of you. I have waited nearly twenty years to find you— because I knew—" he tapped the side of his head, "I *knew* that you didn't drown. I paid close attention to this one," he nudged his head at Hollie, "and to your husband, but it appeared that they legitimately believed you were dead."

Legitimately.

Hollie's heart slowed down to barely enough beats to sustain her.

"But, when your daughter took off for the farmhouse, I realized you've all duped me. And that—" He yanked his sleeves down and snapped the golden cufflinks, "—that vexes me."

"Hollie knows nothing," Ginger argued, her fingers still dusting the bare skin of Hollie's arm. Hollie focused on that connection as she tried to assimilate the conversation.

"I don't know why she went up to the farmhouse, but I have had no contact with her. God help me, as much as I've wanted to," Ginger pleaded, "I have had no contact. She is innocent. Let her go. You have me."

Graying eyebrows dipped into a frown as he regarded her from beneath that bushy awning. There was no sign of compromise in that steady gaze.

"If she's so innocent, why would she go to the farmhouse? Clearly she remembered something. Maybe she witnessed too much up there. One Musgrave woman took away my brother—maybe another was coming after *me*."

"Your life is filled with paranoia," Ginger challenged, leaning forward. "People without secrets are not paranoid. People who have committed no crimes are not paranoid."

"People who are dead should have remained dead."

"Please," Ginger splayed her fingers in appeal. "Give me a few minutes with my daughter."

An eerie calmness settled over Hollie. She felt empowered now that the shock was abating. Yes, she gaped at the woman beside her, torn between wanting to cry in her arms and condemn the evident lie that had shattered her and her father's world. But she was concerned with the here and now. Todd. Todd represented the present. Todd came here because of her.

"Where is Todd?" she demanded.

Having been locked in an ocular duel with her mother, Richard seemed startled by the outburst. His composure slid back into place as easily as donning a jacket.

With a subtle jerk of the head, he looked at Chauncey and commanded, "Take them upstairs. Give them ten minutes and then bring *her,"* he glared at the older woman, "back down here."

Before the goliath behind her could latch on, Hollie swirled, condemning him to a life of misery with her scowl. "I can walk without an escort."

Beefy lids framed subdued eyes. It was as if she had never spoken. He stared right through her as he wrapped a scarred fist around her bicep and jerked her forward. In the corner of her eye she saw her mother—*her mother!*—wrenched in tow.

Guided down a long corridor with mirrors and lavish light fixtures poking out of the almond-colored walls, Hollie tried counting doorways—anything to mark her path. The claw around her arm tugged her to a halt as a key was thrust into the closest door. In her home—in most houses—the doors did not lock from the outside. It certainly had to be a custom request.

She was shoved through the doorway and her mother collided with her, likewise heaved. Lurching off balance, she stumbled into a solid barricade, struggling against it until she glanced up.

"Todd!"

"Hollie."

He tucked his head down atop hers, the only means he could embrace her with his arms still pinned behind him. "Thank God you're safe."

Safe.

She could only imagine the alternatives that must have roiled through his mind as he was locked alone in this room.

As the door was drawn shut behind them, he rushed it, turning his back toward the doorknob, yanking futilely. "Son of a bitch." He kicked the panel.

Hollie stood in the center of a spacious guest suite. A mahogany four-poster bed seemed excessive with posts nearly as thick as trees. Golden brocade pillows and matching drapes added to the opulent flare. On the opposite side was an equally excessive marble fireplace, its innards uncharred.

An upholstered daybed stretched along one wall with a matching hardback chair adjacent to it. Her mother made it to that chair and dropped onto it, hunching over with her hands clasped between her knees.

Hollie felt Todd's eyes on her. Her mother's stare followed her as well. Being the subject of such scrutiny made her uncomfortable. The pervasive chill of the air conditioner triggered bumps all over her skin.

"Todd," she swallowed. "Meet Virginia Musgrave—my mother."

Each remained silent, aware of Hollie's discomfort.

"Hello, Todd," Ginger acknowledged softly. Sharp brown eyes slid between Todd and Hollie. "I'm sorry you have been drawn into this, but I thank you so much for looking out for Hollie."

"*Sorry*," Hollie recited. "It will take a lot more than sorry to explain how you could destroy your husband and daughter."

As familiar as the face was, it now bore lines etched at the corners of downturned eyes, and scores carving lips that had always smiled. Silver strands wove through dark hair layered above her shoulders. The heart-shaped chin so similar to Hollie's quivered. From the eyes of youth there was no judging weight, but Hollie always remembered her mother as a normal-sized woman. Now Ginger seemed reed-thin, and the passing years had given Hollie a few inches in height on her.

"You can hate me," Ginger rasped. "I understand that. But everything I have done, I've done to protect you."

Pain and yearning took turns wrenching at Hollie's heart. She paced the confines of the guest room, pausing to gaze out a pair of French doors that led out onto a balcony. A quick glimpse down revealed an exterior light three stories below.

"Tell me," she strained.

Ginger ground her bound palms against her eyes, sniffed, and then straightened her spine. Deep lines of pain faded into resolve.

"You remember the restaurant I managed?"

Oh, she remembered it, all right. Any time work took her past that mausoleum she thought of her mother. She and her father refused to ever eat there because of the memories.

"Manfreds?"

"Yes. Did you recognize it just now?"

"Recognize it?" Hollie frowned. "That's where they took me? I sensed I was in a restaurant or club, but I was in a van with no windows, and then just shoved inside a door, down a hall, and then locked in a storage room. It's all I saw." She stopped her pacing and dropped down onto the foot of the king-sized bed.

"Why did they take me there? Please don't tell me you've been working there all this time."

If only Dad and I had gone in.

"No, no." Ginger shook her head forlornly. "But Manfreds is owned by Richard Mariani. The man you just met. The man who owns this mansion."

"I wouldn't call it, *just met*. Abduction is the word that comes to mind."

"Yes, yes. Please don't misunderstand. Richard— they call him *Sally* for his middle name—he is evil. Extremely dangerous. He will go to any lengths to take revenge on anyone who has wronged him. And when I say, wronged, that could mean you look at him crossly."

"And you worked for him?" Hollie gripped the edge of the mattress. "Why?"

Ginger's glance fled to the French doors, where she winced at her own reflection.

"I was hired by a panel of people, and I was one of several managers at Manfreds. I didn't come to know the owner until I had been working there for a year. The owner at the time was Joseph. Richard's brother."

Hollie met Todd's eyes.

"An equally upstanding citizen." Hollie smirked.

The hostility was a defense mechanism. It was clear the zingers hurt her mother, but this was the only way Hollie knew how to control her emotion. Focusing on the pain was the only way to cope.

"So, what happened?" she asked, dreading the answer. "Did you—did you *work* work for them?"

"We have less than ten minutes." Ginger surged to her feet. "And he will hold us to that. Let me tell it all. Let it all be said before he takes me away."

"Takes you away!"

Hollie rushed toward her, any hint of anger giving way to fear.

Ginger stepped forward and laced the fingers of her bound hands through Hollie's. The sensation charged from Hollie's fingertips up through her arms with an electrifying jolt to her heart. Silent sobs jarred the slim frame that leaned against her, and at some point, she suspected that her grip alone kept her mother standing. Tears spilled from Hollie's eyes, the moisture pooling atop her cheekbones. It was so hard to uphold the resentment of betrayal when she felt her mother's touch.

Gradually, Ginger tried to extract herself, staggering backwards onto the loveseat, her touch guiding Hollie down beside her. Still clutching Hollie's hands as if they were on a trapeze above a hundred-foot netless drop, she wiped her face against her shoulder, blotting some of the moisture from red-rimmed eyes.

"I had been working at Manfreds for over a year when I finally met Joseph."

Ginger struggled, but straightened her spine. Withdrawing, she clamped her hands atop her knee with enough force to turn her fingertips alabaster. "He was polite, but aloof. I could tell he was all business and didn't really have time for conversation of any sort. I appreciated that. That was how I worked. There was so much involved in managing that place. Weddings. Conventions. High-profile guests. Just dealing with the select alcohol supplier list was time-consuming. I found it odd that we were just using one distributor, but the rest of the management team explained that Joseph Mariani had ties with the supplier." Ginger's pale lips twisted into a smirk.

"I just thought that meant he had relatives or friendly ties," she considered.

Hollie felt a clench in her stomach and noticed Todd casing the perimeter of the room, pausing to test the French doors leading out onto the balcony. His eyes met hers in the reflection of the glass and he shook his head.

"Somehow I became the go-to person for this distributor. I don't know. They liked to work with me. They found me professional. No-nonsense, they said. And their feedback eventually made its way to Joseph," Ginger explained in a barren tone.

"He was handsome. He was rich." Her face pinched at Hollie's raised eyebrows. "It wasn't that I was attracted to him, but I did feel like doing a little fist pump when I started gaining his approval. Most of the employees at Manfred's were jealous because the boss never associated with the staff, regardless of their position. Usually requests and orders were communicated through handwritten correspondence, or word-of-mouth directions from one of his many *assistants*."

An image of a tall man in a suit handing her a bowl of ice cream briefly passed through Hollie's mind.

"I think I remember something—" Hollie said, concentrating on the image. "A big kitchen. All steel. A man bending down to hand me ice cream. It had sprinkles on it."

A haunted smile played across Ginger's lips.

"Yes. It had sprinkles. I brought you into Manfred's kitchen a few times when you were young. You met Joseph. He—" she hesitated, "—adored you."

It was hard to correlate the smiling man with ice cream with the defiled feeling that currently made her want to scratch at her arms.

Glancing nervously at the gilt metal mantle clock, Ginger pressed on. "One time I walked in on a meeting being held in one of the downstairs conference rooms. Joseph looked irritated, but still smiled patiently at me, and quickly escorted me from the room. It was the reaction of the others seated at the table that was troubling. I didn't recognize these men from any of Manfred's business dealings. They were all in suits, smoking cigars. Before Joseph got me to the door, one of them stood up and blocked our path. His jacket fell open and I saw a gun strapped beneath his arm."

"Son of a bitch," Todd muttered, but Ginger's head was down, still locked in her tale.

Hollie dipped her head, attempting to catch a glimpse of her mother's eyes. "What happened?"

"Joseph put both of his hands on my shoulders and ushered me out of the room, and left me standing out there as he stepped back in and closed the door behind him. I heard him arguing. Loudly. I heard the words, *she saw us*."

Ginger hooked her pointer finger around the plastic tie between Hollie's hands and fresh tears brightened her eyes. She shook her head in anguish.

"To make a long story short," she rasped, "I evidently saw something I shouldn't have. No doubt you've gathered by now that the Marianis are involved with the Mafia."

"Yes." Hollie didn't recognize her own thick voice. "Todd and I have done some research—"

Ginger nodded absently. "Well, I didn't know what the mob was. I mean, aside from movies, and maybe some history tales. But that's just it. I was naïve. I thought the Mafia was all something from a bygone era. And if I was to even consider it still existing, I certainly wouldn't expect it to be in Tampa. Anyway, apparently Joseph's assurances inside that room didn't go over well. He came out of there and quickly escorted me out of the building and into his car."

A bitter smile was followed by a roll of misty eyes. "I am not a shallow person, but I was still reeling with the fact that Joseph Mariani, a man I considered larger than life, had his arm around me, and that I was getting into his *Rolls*."

A faint pulse of empathy beat dully beneath Hollie's skin. It weakened back into lassitude.

"Always so stoic and composed, it was the first time I had seen Joseph sweat. He had one hand fisted around the steering wheel and the other around the back of his neck as he kept searching the rearview mirror. He pulled out of that parking lot and didn't speak for a long time, no matter how many times I asked, *what is going on*?"

Ginger gazed sightlessly into the dark beyond the French doors.

"He finally pulled into a parking lot, and to my horror, he pulled a gun out of the glove compartment."

"Oh, Mom—"

"Yeah. I reached for the door handle and couldn't get it open, so I started really panicking. He just said, *Virginia, stop. I'm not going to hurt you. This is to protect you*."

Ginger's slim shoulders squared in resolve. "He sat there and explained that his family had many unsavory ties, many of which he wasn't proud of, but that had been handed down to him. Basically, finally, he revealed they were Mafia ties. I looked at him like, *this has to be a joke*, but I'd just seen two handguns in less than an hour, when prior to that I'd never seen one in my life. Denial wasn't going to get me anywhere. So, I just asked him, *what now*? I barely remembered their faces. But that wasn't good enough, right?"

Hollie heard Todd's shoulder pop as he righted himself. He shook his head at her concerned look, and shrugged to show he was okay.

"Joseph said that I needed to get out of town for a few days, until the *summit*—his word—ended. I said that was absurd, and that if necessary I'd call the police instead. Hollie—" Ginger's eyes widened, "—the look he gave me when I said that. It was cold. Emotionless. It was very much like what you've experienced with Sally."

Sally. Such an innocuous name.

"He said that I didn't understand. That these men would have no issue with killing me just for having seen them together. I freaked, of course. I hollered at him, *well, if it's that dangerous for them to be seen together, what were they doing in a public restaurant?*"

Hollie silently cheered on her mother in that scene from the past.

"It was his restaurant. His private locked conference room, and his staff, which had been ordered to leave the conference room unattended. He didn't share that order with me beforehand. I think I was supposed to be off that day, but I was looking for him because I had a question about a shipment of wine—" Ginger looked at the clock and her eyes slid edgily to the bedroom door.

"He told me that police were out of the question. It seemed a topic that wasn't up for debate while the man held a gun. He said that although he has *operations*—again, his word—in Tampa, that his work is based in the northeast, which probably explained why I rarely saw him in the restaurant. He said that he worked mostly in New York and New Jersey, but had a farmhouse in Pennsylvania. It was safe. It was a good place to ride out the storm, so to speak."

Ginger's voice had grown hoarse, but she pushed on.

"Naturally I told him I wasn't going anywhere. He explained that I didn't understand the gravity of the situation—and that I had others to consider. My husband. My daughter." She choked on the last word.

"Now I was in horrified disbelief. I tried again at the door handle. I was ready to run out into the street and wave my arms at any police car I could find. His car phone rang, startling me. He answered it and looked somber, just nodding, never saying a word to the person on the other end. When he hung up he stared straight at me."

"You have to leave with me right now. There is a hit on you."

"A hit? Are you serious?" Ginger tried to make light of it. After all, it was completely surreal.

"Listen to me." he leaned forward, his perfectly manicured black hair beginning to curl at the bottom from the perspiration on his neck. "The alcohol distributor that we use—that always demands to work with you—well, they—the shipments come to us without being taxed."

"Tax evasion," she surmised out loud. "I should have seen that with the numbers, but I was juggling too many things—too concerned with meeting quotas and deadlines."

Joseph managed a rare smile. "It was why they, and I, trust you. Your concern was always for the restaurant and its clientele. You have no idea how much I've valued your work."

The thought made her ill. She had willingly been working with a mob-related distributor—ignorant, but actively participating in tax evasion.

"Mom, you couldn't have known."

"I didn't know because I had my head up my ass."

Hollie flinched at her mother's assessment.

"I didn't know what to do," Ginger explained. "All I could think about was you and Stuart. That was all that mattered. Joseph said that by me witnessing that group of men, I could associate them with the corrupt distributor. Granted, it was one of the Marianis many illegal facets as I later came to learn, but at the time I was dealing with one disaster at a time. He explained that my immediate concern was that several of the men in that room wanted to silence me."

Hollie drew in a swift breath.

"I should have talked to your father. I should have explained everything, but instead I panicked. I believed Joseph when he said he was going to make everything alright by me. He came across as very sincere."

Ginger laughed bitterly at her own assessment.

"He said if Stuart remained naïve, he felt he should be safe."

"Should be," Hollie snorted.

"And, of course, you were barely four. You would be safe unless—"

"Unless?"

"Well, like Stuart, he thought that they could use you against me." Ginger clutched her fingers, the horror mirrored in similar deep chocolate eyes.

"Ladies," Todd broke in softly. "The clock."

Ginger's head sprang up. "Oh no," she cried. "I need more time." She caved forward, resting her head on Hollie's shoulder.

Rising awkwardly, Todd lurched, and took a step to right himself. Hollie reached for him, torn with the quandary of prying herself from her mother's grasp in order to assist him.

Todd's keen eyes scanned the room and settled on the bedroom door.

"I have an idea," he uttered quietly. "It's a longshot, but—"

"But, it beats doing nothing," Hollie finished, anxious for any strategy that offered them a fighting chance.

CHAPTER SEVENTEEN

There was a loud crash—the jarring clatter of broken glass echoed by Ginger Musgrave's piercing shriek.

The bedroom door banged open with Chauncey's stocky frame slamming through, followed by the bulky profile of his colleague.

"What the f—" Chauncey shouted, taking in the chaotic tableau.

Hollie lie inert on the carpet while Ginger hovered over her, caught in an earsplitting blend of screams and sobs.

As Chauncey aimed his gun in a 180 degree pan, he nodded at the hulk to search the room. Wasting no time, Chauncey brought the muzzle down next to Ginger's head as she rocked over her inert daughter.

"Shut up and explain this or I shoot your daughter."

That threat muffled Ginger's outburst immediately.

"We need a doctor," she whimpered. "My daughter—"

"Where is the guy?" Chauncey interrupted.

The hulk returned from searching the closets and bathroom, shaking his head.

Chauncey tipped his head toward the broken French doors as his cohort jogged over there with his gun extended.

Pressing his Glock into Ginger's hair, Chauncey repeated, "Where is he?"

Ginger's hands shook, one settling on Hollie's neck, checking for a pulse.

"He—he—just kicked it, and then he—jumped," she cried. "He thought he could escape and save us, but the fall—" Ginger's voice faded into a fresh bout of tears.

The hulk returned from the open French doors and shook his head. "No sign of him from up here."

"Get down there and find him," Chauncey barked. "And what about her?" He waved his gun at Hollie's prone form.

"What the hell do you think happened?" Ginger growled, stooping to place her ear against Hollie's lips. "She just found out that her mother is alive after twenty-some years, and then her boyfriend leaps out a third-story window—and we don't know if he survived. She passed the hell out. Probably the best thing for her."

Chauncey kept the gun on her and hefted his phone to his mouth, barking into the speaker. "Anything?"

An out-of-breath report that the grounds below the balcony were empty made Chauncey bare his teeth. "Find him!"

He took the pistol out of Ginger's hair and stooped down alongside her to give Hollie's cheek a smack with the back of his hand. His head nearly snapped off his neck as Todd's foot connected with it.

"Hurry," Ginger urged, crawling toward an unconscious Chauncey, and prying the gun from his fingers with a grimace. She aimed it at him, but her hands shook slightly.

Hollie sat up, her arms tucked between her knees.

"Are you okay?" she asked Todd.

"Yeah," he smirked and then winced when he stood straight. "Amazing how flexible your body can become with a little incentive."

Glancing at the ornate fireplace screen knocked ajar, she marveled at how Todd's long frame was able to climb into the narrow space.

"Do you know how to shoot that?" she asked her mother.

"Given the circumstances," her mother muttered, "I thought it was wise to teach myself."

"We need to cut these ties," Todd said, searching the room. "And secure him."

The phone that had flown out of Chauncey's hand barked from several feet away. "Chawnz? Chawnz, there's no one down here."

The trio stared at the cell phone, paralyzed until Todd disappeared into the bathroom.

"There's an iron in here." He popped his head out and looked at Ginger. "If you could plug it in, maybe we can melt these things off."

Ginger handed the gun off to her daughter who held it awkwardly in her bound grip. Ginger tripped on Chauncey's unfurled arm and stumbled through the doorframe. A few seconds later she stood in the doorway with an iron in her hand. "Okay, let's try this."

Todd turned his back to her.

"Try to hold your wrists as far apart as you can," she instructed. "If I burn you, I'm so sorry."

"Don't worry about burning me."

Hollie kept the gun trained on Chauncey in case he woke. She smelled the tangy heat of burning plastic and heard Todd suck in a breath as the plate must have touched flesh. One quick wrench and his groan of relief gave her a boost of confidence. Maybe they were going to pull this off.

"Hollie," her mother called.

Hollie held her hands out before her, clutching the gun with a single finger looped through the trigger guard. Once the zip tie melted enough, she jerked her wrists apart and secured her hold of the weapon. Todd moved in to grab the iron and maneuvered it to release her mother.

"Chaunz, you there?" The phone barked. "I'm coming up."

"Hurry," Ginger encouraged, grabbing Hollie's shoulder and urging her toward the balcony. "Do you think it's safe?"

"I got a peek when I kicked it in," Todd remarked. "It won't be smooth, but there's a way down. Let's go."

Ginger didn't budge, which stopped Hollie in her tracks. "What are you doing? Come on, let's go."

Tears formed in Ginger's dark eyes, but she blinked them away. "You have to go. They want me, not you. You were just bait."

"So I've been told."

Ginger grabbed her shoulders. "Get out and find special agent Kyle Bjornson. Tell him what happened here. He will know what to do."

"Mom—" Hollie pleaded.

"Hurry!" Ginger commanded.

"No!"

If there was ever a time that she was resolved, this was it. There were a lifetime of questions—a generation taken from her. She would not lose her mother again. "Todd, get out of here. Get help if you can."

"Son of a bitch," Todd muttered, circling back to reach for an arm of each woman. "From what I saw, it looked like Spanish roof tiles, so it's not going to be a solid landing when we jump, but the first tier wasn't that far down."

They were out on the curved terrace, leaning against a wrought iron railing. A humid breeze rolled in off the water. The moon had popped out of the clouds—

enough to reveal the short, angled rooftop down to the next level. What couldn't be determined in the dark was what existed after that. Another gable? A cascade of tiled layers? Or a sudden drop to a merciless concrete driveway?

"I will go first," Todd whispered. "If I don't call for you to follow me, then assume the drop was worse than we expected."

He reached for Hollie's face, curving his palm around her cheek. "And if that happens, stay here. Trust that you'll find another way to escape."

"Todd." She grabbed his arm.

A glint of moonlight clipped his eyes, revealing a sad smile in them.

"I thought I was coming down here for a vacation," he murmured. "Maybe a little fishing—maybe something more." He stooped and pressed his lips to her forehead. "This is definitely something more."

With a gentle squeeze of her shoulder, he turned and hefted one leg over the railing, sitting atop the thin bannister so that he could swing his other over. Without looking back he executed a cautious leap into obscurity.

Hollie surged toward the rail, searching the few orange tiles illuminated by the moon. She heard motion below, but the acoustics distorted their proximity. A hand on her elbow alarmed her until she felt her mother press in close.

The sound of traffic from the highway in the distance mingled with the rustle of the palms below.

"Okay," a hushed command beckoned from the dark. "Climb over like I did, and you can slide down on your butt."

Hollie started at the sound of the door to the guest room opening. There was no time to dwell. She and her mother scrambled over the railing side-by-side, clutching the wrought iron behind them.

"Go!" she whispered.

Feeling her mother's eyes on her, Hollie was relieved when she obeyed the command and squatted down, sliding down the Spanish tiles.

"Hollie, now!" Todd's urgent plea came to her just as she heard a raucous outburst behind her.

Relaxing her grip on the balustrade, Hollie dropped into the night, landing with a jarring halt six or eight feet below. Her hand smacked against the hard clay, knocking Chauncey's gun from her grasp and spiraling it into the abyss.

Todd's fingers caught her shoulders preventing her from following that bleak swan dive.

Cursing her inept grip on the gun, she tried to search the ground for it. At least fifteen or twenty feet down an oval-shaped pool was illuminated by bulbs embedded in the blue cement frame. That light fluttered under the rippling water.

She sucked in a breath and checked to make sure her mother was beside her. A few inches away a white hand clamped around the roof's edge.

"Are we going to jump into that?" Hollie asked.

Todd looked up at the activity on the balcony above. Hollie turned just in time to see the outline of a handgun aimed into the dark.

"No," he managed. "Quick, follow me, and be careful or you *will* end up in there."

Cosseted in the deep shadows of the second floor roof, they were temporarily concealed from the audience above. From that elevated perspective, all that was visible was the pool and the landscaped grounds below.

Scaling the roof's edge like three nimble squirrels, they stopped at the command of Todd's upheld hand. They were tucked in a nook of another wing of the house. From this spot they paused to see Chauncey's balding head leaning across the balcony, eclipsed then by the meaty shoulders of his partner.

Hollie held her breath as Chauncey slammed the rail with his fist and then backed away.

Warm breath fanned her ear as Todd leaned in.

"We'll follow along the roof as far as we can. They should be looking for us on the ground. As soon as there's a place—an opportunity—we'll drop down."

Futility choked off any further insight. Hollie felt water creep behind her eyes. This man had put his life on the line for a near stranger. For what? They'd shared a few kisses—some long nights of conversation. And for *that* he had been held at gunpoint and now was perilously perched on a rooftop, waiting to be shot at any given moment.

She reached out, balancing on one palm, using the other to claw at the collar of his shirt. "When this is over, we're going to have a huge frozen pizza together."

The puff of air from his soundless laugh ruffled her hair. "What more temptation to escape can I possibly have than that?"

Boots scuffing concrete below arrested their attention. To Hollie's horror, their captors were swinging flashlights across the grounds, piercing the sculpted bushes with the beams, and creating arcs of light in their hasty pursuit. Some of those haphazard arcs climbed the wall just below them. Another few feet and the beam would expose them perched like a trio of terrified gargoyles.

As the wayward beams hooked back toward the pool, Todd whispered, "Let's move."

Hollie felt a pat of support on her back from her mother.

So many questions.

She had so many questions for her.

They crawled along the edge of the tiles, the portion that flattened out, scarcely a foot wide. Hollie's knee missed its mark causing her left leg to dangle into open space. She gasped and forced all her weight onto her right side until she was able to tuck the limb back up under her.

So intent on making progress, she bleated in alarm when Todd halted abruptly. His arm swung back like a steel barrier, locking her in place.

Dipping his head, his voice came to her through the gap between his arm and the roof. "These mansions are built on top of each other. Prime real estate. There is a corner of the roof that seems to jut out over the next property's fence. If we're lucky, the neighbors have lots of palm trees."

Hollie's first fear was for her mother. She would be fifty-six now. She never forgot her birthday—always managing to have some treat in her honor. Every memory of her mother involved the woman enjoying sweets of one kind or another.

But what would a fall at this height do to her? Could she leap onto a tree? The alternative was whether she could survive a gun shot or not.

There was no time to dwell, and no answer that bode well. They reached the sharp corner of the roof that jutted out over a thick concrete barricade.

Todd stopped and leaned his head again. "I would imagine a guy like this has sensors around the property walls. Too much of a risk to actually land on the wall itself. We have to jump past it."

She nodded her agreement, and heard her mother whisper, "absolutely."

Perched on the narrow projection, Todd stooped as far as he could. There was little effective light at this end of the property and the moon was locked behind a thick bank of clouds. It would literally be a leap of faith from their second story position.

"Okay," Todd said. "It looks like there is a pretty sturdy oak up ahead. A thick branch is only a foot away from the roof. It won't be easy in the dark—"

"We'll make it," she assured, just anxious to get off the property.

Todd stretched his leg out, testing the distance, and then hooked his ankle around the limb before reaching with his hand. Shifting his full weight onto the limb, the aged oak seemed to withstand the pressure with little more than a slight tremor of the limb. Soon she could barely distinguish his gangly silhouette inching hand over hand across the branch until he reached the trunk where she lost sight of him.

A few seconds later she heard his hushed call from below.

"Okay, you next. If you fall, I'll try my best to catch you."

What more could she ask for?

She turned back toward her mother. "Are you sure you can do this?"

"That's why I'm going last—so that I have two people down there to catch me." A flash of her white teeth was all that revealed her smile.

That smile, and the ever-present optimism, nearly brought Hollie to tears. God, how she'd missed it. But now was not the time to cry. She gave a nod that she realized went unnoticed and turned back to the outstretched tree limb. Once her weight was on it, she paused to link her legs tighter and then began the meticulous process of inching toward its core. Reaching her hand out for the next increment, she latched onto a dangling patch of Spanish moss rather than solid oak. Suspended by one arm and an ankle, she quickly grappled back into position. The grade of the long limb angled down so that once she reached the trunk, the ground was a manageable jump away. Todd's shadowy profile stood at its base with anxious arms stretched out in summons. One quick leap and she landed with a jarring pain in her ankles, but secure in his embrace.

"I think we need to go try out for one of those warrior reality shows," he murmured into her ear.

Still shaking from adrenaline, she fisted her fingers in his shirt. "I'm ready."

Todd's hands dropped to her hips and he set her back a step to trace the movement above.

The lithe form of Ginger Musgrave crept along the branch until her legs slipped loose and she hung precariously suspended by her hands. Her legs scissored in the air, a sneakered foot trying to reach for purchase of the branch again. The efforts loosened her grip.

"Mom!" Hollie swallowed down a shriek.

Ginger dropped with a curse, but Todd took the brunt of her fall, collapsing onto his back with a *humph* as the woman bounced against his abdomen and then rolled off him like a SEAL in training.

"Are you all right?" She scrambled on her knees to examine his face.

Todd coughed and accepted Hollie's assistance to stand.

"I'm fine. What about you?"

"I had a soft fall." Ginger flashed a rare grin.

Searching the six foot wall for any signs of Richard's men, Hollie paced nervously.

"What now? We can't just go up to the neighbor's front door."

"No," Todd agreed. "If *my* neighbors were enlisted by Richard, I can certainly imagine that *his* neighbors are equally as corrupt."

The house was twenty feet away. Stately, but not near the grandeur of the mansion beside it. They dodged open spaces, hugging a perimeter of tall junipers. These bushes were like Greek pillars under a now traitorous moon.

Nearing the street, the signs of activity next door became evident. A trio of black SUV's pulled through the gate, and even worse, two men were marching down the sidewalk toward the neighbor's house— and they didn't look like they were bringing over cookies.

"They took your phones too?" Ginger whispered as they congregated behind a wall of vegetation.

"Yes."

"We need to get to a phone," she proclaimed. "I can call the FBI. They'll be here in a heartbeat."

Hollie's jaw slackened. "Seriously? You must have some pull."

Her mother's face was obscured in shadow, but the brief puff of air from her nose revealed her grimace.

"One thing I have learned is that if you tell the FBI you have dirt on the mob—they'll come. And they'll come fast."

"Okay—so, we have to find a phone," Hollie acknowledged, searching the lack of possibilities.

"It's all residential out here," Todd remarked, risking a step closer to the circular driveway.

This property did not have a gated entrance, but the driveway exit was well lit, and the lot across the street appeared to be empty—or a black hole. No one wanted to build across the street from the water.

"There." Todd pointed down the road.

Hollie put her hand on him and stood on the tips of her toes to see over his shoulder. "I can't tell what it is."

"It's a construction zone. The road is closed off— as in this convoy of theirs can't follow us through it."

A streetlight a block away confirmed his assessment. The shadows of cones blocked off the side street, and the mammoth profile of a tractor lurked in the moonlight like a dormant dinosaur.

"If we cut through that site, the next road over should have more commercial options. I don't trust knocking on anyone's door on this street."

"Todd's right," Ginger said. "Don't trust anyone."

Hollie couldn't see either of their faces, but these were two people who had tackled their share of drama and had earned their cagey perspective on life. If she made it through this situation, she would become a crown member of their cynical club.

"So," Hollie surmised bleakly, "it will be a foot race. I mean, if they see us, we better pray there is somewhere safe on the other side of this construction site."

"At this point, I think prayer is all we've got," Ginger muttered.

Hollie rubbed her wrist, wincing at the bruises. "Let's do it. Let's do it now before more men on foot come over here."

The two men in dark attire had now reached the front door of the neighbor's house. The exchange at the entryway was the perfect distraction and opportunity to make their move. As soon as the door opened, Todd motioned them down the driveway, jogging with their shoulders hunched. Once they reached the road, they sprinted, avoiding all streetlights until they slipped between the cones and ducked behind the oversized tires of the tractor.

Hollie's chest heaved from more than the exertion. For a moment she thought she might be sick. But once she realized that they had escaped without being noticed, her breathing started to regulate.

"Okay, come on," Todd encouraged.

It was a treacherous surface of sand, roots, and chunks of broken concrete that they traversed across under minimal light. In the distance, the large green 7-Eleven sign might as well have represented the gates of Oz.

Out of breath, and constantly looking over their shoulders, they reached the mini-mart, but feared how exposed they would be in its parking lot. Under all those lights, they found a pay phone mounted to the exterior of the building.

"I didn't even know they still had payphones."

"Pay phones will take 9-1-1. That's all that matters."

"I have a number I can dial that doesn't require coins," Ginger stepped in between them. "I've had it memorized for many years in case of circumstances like this."

Hollie stared at her, recognizing the shadow of the woman she had known, but admiring the strength in the woman she had become.

"Mother, you've got a lot of explaining to do."

Ginger nodded. "That I do. But for now, you two stay here. If I get caught at the phone, remember, I'm the one they want. Get away and call Special Agent Bjornson."

Hollie wanted to protest, but Todd recognized that this was the best option.

"We'll be right here. Make it as quick as you can."

Drawing in a deep breath, Ginger squared her shoulders and jogged over to the payphone.

Every second dragged for Hollie as she watched the lithe figure in jeans and a hoodie stand crowded against the half-enclosure, trying to minimize her appearance as much as possible.

In a matter of moments she was darting back to join them, trembling, and clutching her jacket tight about her, even though the temperature had to be in the high seventies.

"Someone is on their way," she assured.

"It's just a matter of time before Richard's men expand their search." Hollie sank back into the shadow of a thick oak trunk.

Watching her mother shrouded in the hoodie, she felt chilled as well. Relief came in the form of Todd's arm slipping around her. If not for her mother's presence, she would curl into that embrace and soak up the heat and strength his chest provided. What this man had done—been subjected to, at her expense—and to still want to hold her. She looked up at him and wished he could read her eyes. Maybe he interpreted her gaze. Assuring lips touched her forehead.

In her periphery she caught a discreet smile on her mother's lips.

A vehicle pulled into the parking lot. A black SUV. Ginger squinted at it and the dread on her face said it all.

"I was given the license plate of the vehicle that was coming for us," she whispered, stepping back.

There was no need to elaborate that this plate didn't match.

CHAPTER EIGHTEEN

Two men emerged from the utility vehicle. One bore the distinctive husky profile of Chauncey's sidekick.

Slinking deeper into the trees, the trio watched as the brutes paced the perimeter of the parking lot, at one point standing only ten feet away.

Cloistered like paralyzed deer, they waited until the men circled back and entered the 7-Eleven.

Hollie swallowed, but there was no saliva in her throat.

"The guy behind the counter might have seen Mom on the phone."

Giving credence to her fears was the quick exit of the two figures, and their synchronized split to span the perimeter of the store. Executing a full border patrol, the hulk stood under an overhead light and spoke on his cellphone. Slapping it into his back pocket he gave a summoning wave toward the SUV.

Headlights approached from the opposite direction as a dark sedan pulled into the parking lot.

"Oh my," Ginger muttered. "That's the license plate."

The sedan pulled up to the gas pumps and a man stepped out, casually surveying the lot and then slinking around the back end of the car to put his credit card into the console. Under the illuminated bars of the short pump roof, Hollie studied the figure in dark pants with a white long-sleeved shirt rolled up below the elbows.

As casual as he portrayed, she could tell by the slight tilt of his head that he was studying the men standing just outside their SUV. They, on the other hand, weren't so casual in their scrutiny. In fact, one appeared to take a step in confrontation, but the hulk grabbed the guy's forearm and leaned in to say something. Whatever the conversation was, it ended with both climbing back into the SUV.

Sitting in idle, the vehicle's white reverse lights finally switched on, and the SUV pulled out of the lot. Hollie saw her mother reach out to the tree beside her, holding on for stability. Placing an arm around her shoulder, she squeezed encouragingly, but all of them were focused intently on the man at the pump.

Casting a glimpse at his watch, the man proceeded to place the pump in the car's gas tank, and then leaned his hip indolently against the vehicle with his arms crossed, staring out into the darkness.

"What now?" Hollie asked.

"I go out," Ginger declared.

"But, Mom—"

"I have to trust this—but if anything looks off—"

"I know. We should run," Hollie finished bitterly.

Ginger gave her a quick grin and nodded at Todd and then walked hastily across the parking lot.

The man noticed her, but finished up his task, mounting the pump back in place with no apparent rush. As Ginger approached him, Hollie saw the man's gaze search the parking lot, lingering on the entrance. After a brief exchange, his sharp gaze penetrated the shadows at the far end of the lot. Ginger turned and made a slight beckoning motion.

"Do we go?" Hollie asked Todd quietly.

"One more second," he cautioned. Every facet of his body appeared on alert, his hands clenching and unclenching in preparation.

A tip of Ginger's head and another emphatic wave and Todd reached for Hollie's arm.

"Let's do this," he announced in a subdued tone. "No rushing."

"Got it."

She stepped out of the trees alongside him feeling as exposed as a fawn in a lion's den. But they walked purposefully forward just as Ginger slipped into the front passenger seat. The man held open the rear door and gave a curt nod to Todd, a silent command to get in. Todd hesitated for a moment but caught Ginger's assuring bob from the front seat.

With his hand on the small of Hollie's back, he urged her inside and then slid in next to her, hauling the door shut behind him.

"It's okay," Ginger assured. "This is Tom Harper. He works for Kyle."

Nonplussed, Hollie anxiously waited for the ignition to turn.

"Do you have some sort of ID?"

Okay, she felt the question was something straight out of a bad movie, but her mother always told her—*don't get in a car with strangers.*

The man leaned forward against the steering wheel to extract a wallet from his back pocket, and flipped the trifold open to reveal his badge and ID. Only the diffused light from the gas pump canopy filled the car, making it hard to read, but she did see the words SPECIAL AGENT.

"It's alright," he affirmed. "Here—" He picked up the phone that was resting against his thigh, and pressed a button. When a male voice barked on the other end, he handed the device over to Ginger.

"Kyle?"

Her profile softened with relief. She nodded at the driver and said, "Let's get out of here."

Special Agent Harper put the car in reverse as Ginger wrapped up her conversation.

"Where are we going?" Hollie asked, her hand curved around the car seat in front of her.

"A safe house," Ginger answered for Agent Harper.

"A safe house?"

It was all so much. The abduction. The sudden revelation that her mother was still alive. The escape. The yawning chasm of the unknown. She was too tired to weep. Too spent to protest. She was numb. They could poke needles all over her body and she wouldn't feel the sensation.

Something warm stirred at her side.

She felt that.

Long, masculine fingers reached for hers, and she latched onto them like the proverbial life preserver. It wasn't the venue to say the things she wanted to convey to this man.

Remorse.

Gratitude.

Feelings that ran deep and foreign.

Instead, all she could do was lean into him and rest her head against his strong shoulder.

"Why is it only you?" Todd asked the back of the short-cropped head driving.

"I was the closest. Special Agent Bjornson wanted you out fast. It would have taken too long for him to get here. He'll be waiting at the safe house, though."

"And what happens to Richard Mariani?"

"There is a team heading to his mansion now. I'll let SA Bjornson fill you in."

Outside, streetlights provided a strobe effect. Inside, Todd's arm was rigid with barely contained tension. The silhouette of a childhood idol rested against the seat in front of her. All she had to do was reach out and touch it.

"Dammit, Ginger."

A man in his late fifties, possibly sixties, paced the narrow living room of the fourth-floor condominium they had been escorted to.

"I'm literally three weeks away from retirement, and you pull this."

Hollie looked at her mother who seemed unaffected by the berating. In fact, it looked like a debate that had occurred many times before.

Special Agent Kyle Bjornson was a fit man for his age, but anything to be gained in the well-maintained physique was traded in a weathered face that bore deep ruts around the mouth and eyes. Gray eyebrows knit together as the man kneaded his forehead with his fingertips.

"Kyle, he kidnapped my daughter."

"Yes." He paused to glare at the woman seated on the arm of a guest chair. "And how did you know that exactly? Richard didn't call you up and say, *hey, I just kidnapped your daughter*. No, he didn't do that because he had no idea where you were."

Ginger tucked her chin, acknowledging the point, but hefted it again in protest.

"What if it was Gracie?"

Agent Bjornson threw his hands into the air. "Don't start, Virginia."

From an outside observer it seemed a conversation of two people extremely familiar with each other—even intimate. Could it be? Agent Bjornson was handsome in a rough way. But wait, he was wearing a wedding ring, and for that fact, so was her mother. *Still*. Hollie recognized the Celtic band with intertwined gold ribbons. It was an heirloom passed down in her father's family that she had always fussed over as a child.

"You were following your daughter," Agent Bjornson accused. "Long before Richard kidnapped her. Why? You were safely tucked away in Iowa. I knew the moment you came back to Tampa. Did you think I wouldn't?"

"Did you think I would care?" Ginger challenged, rising to her feet so that she could pace as well.

The duo were doing laps around the living room like a couple of boxers gauging when to throw the first punch.

"You kept tabs on me," she said. "I kept tabs on Hollie." Her eyes swept guiltily in Hollie's direction. "I couldn't help it. She was my baby girl. I always found a way to see what she was up to. The internet became my best friend. I had alerts set up every time her name appeared. Graduation from college. Her first job. The talented publicist she's become. I followed every event her firm was hired for. Yes. I stalked. She was—*is* my girl."

Something twisted inside Hollie's heart. She was tempted to rush to her mother and wrap her arms around her, something she had yet to do since finding out she was alive, but the questions were far too numerous to ignore.

"And yes," Ginger conceded, "I followed Stuart online. He needs to learn more about privacy settings on his social media." A faint grin toyed with her pale lips, but it quickly evaporated as she added, "And yes, my stalking extended to Sally Mariani as well. As long as he was alive and free, I never felt my family was safe. If he was in New York or Pennsylvania, I would breathe a little easier. But any time I caught posts of him hosting events at Manfreds—" Her fingers trembled nervously over the zipper of her jacket.

"And then—" She strolled toward the window, but shied away from it—a sign of a clandestine life. "—then Hollie posted a comment that she was heading to Pennsylvania."

I did?

Immediately Hollie tried to retrace her digital steps, and recalled one comment response to an office party invitation that came via social media.

Thanks, but I'll be in Pennsylvania and New York for the next few days.

"I panicked," Ginger hugged herself. "I knew all of the places she generally traveled to for work, and Pennsylvania was not one of them. Of course, it could be innocent. I don't know all her friends." She cast a quick glimpse at Todd. "But I had some time off from work. I have plenty of money because I have no one to spend it on. So I booked a flight to Philadelphia, and I drove to the farmhouse…just in case…just in case she somehow remembered it."

"And I did," Hollie's voice was hoarse. "Those dreams, Mom. The one's you played off as *remembering a former life*—they came back."

Ginger's head dropped forward in defeat. When she looked up, tears moistened her dark eyes. "I thought you were too young to remember. It is what I told Joseph. It is what I argued with Kyle all those years ago. You were too young to remember that trip to Pennsylvania. You were only four. And Stuart knew nothing about the Marianis. You were both innocent. You didn't need to have your lives upended because of me. And you—" she turned to Agent Bjornson, "—you worked miracles to keep them out of it. To let them continue as if—"

"As if you had died," Hollie finished.

A raw pain chewed at her stomach—like a set of chomping teeth working their way up her esophagus.

"Hermey." Ginger sagged off the fluffy arm of the chair and down onto the seat cushion.

A subtle nod from Special Agent Bjornson prompted Tom Harper to amble toward the door.

"I'm going next door." Tom nodded at his supervisor. "I'll let you know if I hear any updates."

Once he was gone, Kyle Bjornson pulled back a dining table chair and squatted down onto it. The condominium had a kitchen connected to a dining room and living room via a serving bar. A hallway presumably led toward the bedroom.

"The FBI rents several condos in this building," Agent Bjornson explained, sensing her scrutiny. "They're usually for out-of-state agents, but in rare instances they are used as temporary safe houses. Every unit on this floor is currently occupied by an agent of the Bureau," he added.

Hollie heard the assurance, but her focus was on her mother sitting across from her.

"Tell me."

It was a guttural command that might as well have been wrenched from her bowels.

Ginger winced, and then she glanced up at Agent Bjornson.

"What? *Now* you want my advice?" He paced in the opposite direction, yanking his phone up for a preview before finally turning back and sighing dramatically. "Go ahead," he said. "Evidently, the time for discretion has long passed."

Knotting her fingers together nervously on her lap, Ginger directed her words at that tangled mess, keeping her eyes down.

"I didn't go to Pennsylvania with him. With Joseph." She picked up where she had left off with her story. "Up until the meeting that I had stumbled upon, I had no reason to even suspect Joseph of any wrongdoings. Joseph drove me home and told me to take a few days off."

"When I returned a few days later, it seemed like everything was normal. I was busy as heck. There was no sign of the men I had witnessed in that conference room. I started to convince myself that it had all been a fluke—that I exaggerated what I saw."

Peering up at the FBI agent, Ginger hesitated until he gave a perfunctory nod.

"Then the men from the meeting returned."

Hollie felt her stomach clench—not so much from the statement—but from the quiet dread in the voice that delivered it.

"They were in the bar, having drinks and chatting like any other patrons, but when I strode through the room, I saw them—and I froze right in the middle of the tables. They must have been surprised to see me. I think Joseph might have convinced them that I quit. The man who had threatened me—the one I saw with the gun, he got up and approached me. He grabbed my arm and escorted me downstairs—to the very same conference room I had first encountered him in. He—he threatened me. I mean—he tried to—"

Hollie squeezed her arms around her sides in a tight hug. "It's okay, Mom," she assured thickly, "I understand."

Ginger nodded, a lump passing down her throat as she swallowed.

"I fought against him, but he drew his gun and held it to my head. I didn't know what to do." Her hand flapped helplessly. "And then, there was a sound—a whoosh, and a startling pop right near my head. I snapped away from the noise and watched the man slump to the ground. A second later blood started to pool on the carpet."

She drew in a long breath. "I stumbled backwards, looking down at my clothes, half expecting to find blood there as well. Then I saw him."

As if locked in that moment, Ginger's head tilted, looking up at the juncture of the wall and ceiling.

"It was Joseph," she rasped. "He held a gun—still pointed where the man had stood before he dropped." Her head shook in disbelief. "He had this snarky smile as he said, *I never liked that guy much.*"

Beside her, Hollie felt Todd lean forward, his hands fisted between his knees, his elbow poking her thigh.

"Needless to say, that moment changed my life. Men appeared out of nowhere to attend to the body. I was escorted out into the hall." She hesitated. "And then Joseph finally joined me. He was his usual charming self. Like nothing had happened. But he was adamant that I had to get away now. I told him I wanted to go to the police, but he just gave me a *you know you can't do that* expression. A thousand protests came to mind. I reminded him that he killed the man to protect me. There was no need to be afraid of the police. It was all self-defense."

She paused. "All of those arguments fell flat from the cold look in his eyes. Reality, which I had been fighting, finally hit hard. The men might have whisked away that body, but the pool of blood was beginning to ebb into the grout of the tiled dance floor. Shock was setting in. Irrationally, I was worried about calling the staff down to clean it."

Causeway traffic could be heard in the distance. No matter the hour, cars were always buzzing along that thin ribbon over the bay.

"Joseph took me by the shoulders and said that he had to get out of town for a few days—until the mess was cleaned up. Cleaned up. Like it was a matter of mopping that blood out of the grout." Ginger's head swung in disbelief. "He said that I had to go with him. That I was in danger—from his associates—from the law. He said that he only wanted to protect me. Deep down, I'd known all along that Joseph had some feelings for me. They were never reciprocated. I never led him on or anything. He knew I was happily married. I don't think he cared. Still, he was a gentleman, so to speak."

Hollie held her tongue. She leaned over her clenched arms but hung onto her mother's every word.

"I didn't know what to do. Again, I wanted to tell Stuart what happened, but I was afraid to. Joseph had played with my mind to the point that I truly felt culpable in the matter. So—" she drew in a deep breath, "—so, I went home and told Stuart that Grandma Rose had fallen ill, and no one was around to take care of her. And I told Joseph that if I was going anywhere, that you were coming with me. I couldn't leave you. Even for a few days as he claimed it would be."

This time when she lifted her head, her eyes were red and the corners of her mouth tugged like they had been latched onto by fish hooks. She cleared her throat and tried to straighten her shoulders.

"Tell me what happened up there," Hollie demanded, but her voice lacked verve, knowing her nagging dream was about to come to life. "In Pennsylvania."

Ginger stole a deep breath.

"Well, this was when my web of lies first started. I called my mother and told her I had to go away for a few days, and that if Stuart phoned her to just tell him I'd stepped out and would call him back later. Which is what I did so that he was never any wiser. Back then, he could only use a land line. He could not trace where I was. To this day it kills me that your grandmother assumed I was having an affair."

To some extent you were.

You were leaving my father to go spend time with another man.

Hollie withheld the accusation. Let the story play out.

"Joe adored you, Hollie. He played with you the whole flight up. Had toys waiting for you on the plane—"

Resisting the urge to scratch at her arms, Hollie averted her eyes, focusing on the gray, textured carpet.

"A man who just murdered someone before your very eyes was giving me toys—Mom—" she didn't even know how to finish the thought.

Ginger's almond eyes looked bleak.

"Hollie, I've had nothing but time to beat myself up over everything. All I can hope is that, in the end, I did the right thing."

To this, she looked toward Kyle who wrapped a hand around his chin, nearly concealing his nod.

"Let me finish," Ginger uttered. "Then—then you can—" She too fumbled to complete her sentence.

"When we got to the farm you played outside while Joseph and I talked. He kept watching you out the window, and he said that the safest thing was for me to leave my husband, and that you and I would become his family. Joseph said he would protect us. He would take care of us, and raise you as his own—" her voice caught.

"I ran out of the house because I just needed to hold you. I felt violated. I wanted to get away. I'd made a huge mistake in trusting him." Ginger's head shook in despair. "But he beat me outside—he literally slammed the door in my face. You—you saw that and you ran up the steps to get to me, but he caught you before you could reach the door, and he held you by both arms as I came out."

Tears now fell unchecked down Ginger's cheeks. Hollie felt those tears on her own cheeks. She blinked in frustration to clear her view of her mother.

"I've never been so scared in my entire life as I was seeing you there with Joseph's hands on you," Ginger rasped. "And then—then he told me about his daughter. How he had lost her so young. It was filed as an accident, but he said it had been a deliberate attack by a *zip* from an opposing family."

"A zip?" Todd inquired quietly.

"Italian slang," Kyle provided. "Usually someone brought over from the homeland to do the dirty work."

Hollie vaguely heard the segue. Her mind drifted.

Back.

Back.

The man came down the porch stairs toward her. He had been nice. He had given her a stuffed lion.

But something was wrong. He didn't look nice now. He looked angry. And inside she heard her mother cry out.

"Mommy!"

She ran past him and reached for the railing and climbed as quick as she could. Her other hand curled into a fist as she prepared to pound on the door.

She never reached it.

He grabbed her from behind, pulling her back. Back.

Back.

Hollie snapped back to the present. The haunting dream was just that now. A distant memory.

Her mother was here. She was not locked behind that door. And this time when Hollie reached for her, their hands touched—and they did not let go.

Hollie was up off the couch and curled up at her mother's feet, their hands clasped tight.

"I knew I had to tread carefully," Ginger continued, releasing Hollie's hand long enough to swipe at a tear, and then quickly returned to grab it. "So I switched gears and played along. I pretended that it might be an option, but I told him we had to move slowly. My only goal was to get us back home. He seemed appeased, but cautious. I made us dinner. We carried on like everything was alright. He was a gentleman in that he didn't try anything with me. And with some sort of an Oscar-winning performance, I managed to get him to schedule his plane to return to Tampa the following morning."

Hollie clutched onto those fingers, thin, but strong. She soaked up the scent of her mother—some sort of floral lotion, applied long ago, but still lingering upon close inspection. It wasn't the scent she remembered. She remembered the smell of pecan pie—a pie that she would not eat to this day because she had witnessed it *breathing* on the kitchen counter. Despite any assurances by her mother, she was convinced the pie was alive.

"I don't remember the inside of the farmhouse," she observed hollowly.

"You did go inside, but you were exhausted. You slept until it was time for us to leave," Ginger explained. "I told Joseph I needed to go home and portray like everything was normal—and that if I was missing from work, that would draw more attention. People would wonder where I was when I was such a workaholic. Thank God he saw credence in that. Meanwhile, I kept telling you that we met your Uncle Dave, my mother's brother, in case you accidentally said something to your father. I must have said it so many times that you told Stuart Uncle Dave gave you a lion."

Even now she took a deep breath of relief at her child's naivete.

"And then, when I was finally alone, I made my first call to the FBI. I had no idea how to do it. I looked up a phone number in the phone book, and after being transferred several times, I ended up being put through to a young agent. And that was when I met Kyle. He wasn't as cordial as Joseph, but he was on the correct side of the law. It wasn't until the whole WITSEC endeavor that I truly gained appreciation for Special Agent Bjornson." She looked up and smiled tearfully at Kyle.

Special Agent Bjornson cleared his throat and shifted uncomfortably. "Yup," he said. "And in case I hadn't mentioned it, I am three weeks away from retirement."

Somewhere in the background Hollie heard Todd snort.

"Long story short, I began working with the FBI to mount evidence against Joseph, while simultaneously maintaining my restaurant duties and keeping Joseph at arm's length. Somehow I assured him that I was someone to be trusted."

Ginger released Hollie's hand so as to clutch her stomach. It looked like she was going to be ill.

"It was like walking on a tightrope of dental floss," she uttered. "I was so wrapped up in lies and secrets that I lost myself. It took years to reach the point where we could go to trial—"

"We had to make sure it was going to stick," Kyle defended. "Virginia was adamant that you and Stuart were going to be safe if she testified. And if she testified," he hesitated, "she knew she was a dead woman."

"So you entered witness protection," Hollie finished quietly. "You faked your death."

Ginger wrenched her gaze away from Hollie. "It was the only way you would both be safe. It was at the trial that I first saw Richard Mariani." A tremor went through her. "If he could murder me on the witness stand, he would have. If I remained alive, he would use whatever it took to get back at me. He would have used you—your father." Her voice caught. "And then, you started having the dreams. I never imagined you would remember that incident at the farm. I always thought I had convinced you that we were at Grandma's. I tried to play off your dreams as—"

"Reincarnation," Hollie observed.

In the background she heard Kyle grunt.

"Everything had reached a critical level," Ginger acknowledged. "Kyle, the rest of the agents—they arranged the boating accident—they were out there in the water to retrieve me."

"That last day—that last day with you—I—"
Ginger shook her head, unable to go on.

Hollie reached for her mother, wrapping her arms
around her to try and still the quaking body. She
murmured assurances even as she reeled at the tale.

"The pain I have caused," Ginger whispered into
the crook of her neck. "Guilt consumes me every day.
Not just for you and your father. There is a small part of
me that feels guilt for Joseph. He shot a man to save my
life, and I testified against him. I sent him to prison—a
place that clearly was not safe for him."

She wiped at her eyes again and glanced up at
Special Agent Bjornson. "Kyle assures me that I have
probably saved many lives by my actions, but I can't
help to think about how I should have handled
everything. I should have called someone after that first
meeting I stumbled across. I was just so shocked.
Overwhelmed. And look what I've done. I did not
save—I destroyed lives. It's why I always had to keep
an eye on you. I needed to know you were okay. That
you grew up to be a wonderful woman. I just—I just
dread the fact that you hate me."

"I don't hate you," Hollie managed hoarsely. "I
love you." She gave one last squeeze and settled back
on her heels. "But I am hurting. Twenty years have
been taken from me. High school. College. All the
times that I wanted to talk to you. Lean on you."

Ginger settled back as well and a steely look of
resolve replaced some of the tears.

"I'm done with WITSEC." She slashed a look at
Kyle, daring him to retaliate. "The FBI is on their way
to take Sally Mariani in. I can testify against him for
kidnapping as well as arson—" again she stole a glance
at Kyle who nodded bluntly.

"Arson?" Hollie asked.

"There was a restaurant that burned to the ground along Bayshore. It was a big event back when I was working at Manfreds. That restaurant had been considered competition. On the flight to Pennsylvania, Joseph told me that Richard was responsible. I think he was trying to tell me things to make me feel that I was part of the family." She hugged herself. "Anyway, I am assured that we have enough to put Richard away for a long time."

"There will be a period of caution," Kyle interrupted. "We'll have security around you all—unless you prefer WITSEC. In this day and age it's getting harder to maintain the program. Social media and digital imprints have cost some people their lives. Your mother has not been an exemplary participant." His droll look brought the first hint of a smile to Ginger's lips. "So, if we can keep you all out of it, it's in everyone's best interest."

"Amen," Hollie confirmed.

Ginger suddenly turned her gaze to Todd. She rose and hesitantly held her hand out.

Todd's eyes shot up in surprise. He accepted her handshake with cautious curiosity. Then, to his astonishment the woman stooped over and looped her arms around his shoulders, hugging him.

"Thank you," she wrenched. "Thank you for taking such good care of my daughter."

Floundering for a response, Todd met Hollie's eyes over her mother's shoulders. She smiled and nodded at him.

"I'm so sorry you had to be exposed to all of this," she apologized. "I know my daughter is worth it, but now you've put yourself into a position where you need guarding."

To her surprise Todd chuckled.

"Mrs. Musgrave, I've been guarding myself for too long. Since I've met your daughter, it's the first time I don't feel so caged."

In that instant, Hollie knew she had found the man she wanted to spend the rest of her life with. But would he be willing to put up with all the baggage she evidently came with? That was probably doubtful.

Her brimming eyes met his and something shifted in his gaze—shadows dissipated—ghosts receded—what was left were raw feelings—sincerity—and hope.

A cell phone went off and was abruptly silenced.

"Well—" Special Agent Bjornson rose with a groan. "As illuminating as this conversation has been, and as pleasant as it has been to meet you—" he bowed his head at Hollie, "—my wife will have my head if I'm not home in time for dinner. Furthermore, she'll have other parts as well if I don't retire in three weeks." He cast an amused glance at Ginger.

Before she could respond, he added. "You're to stay here for the night—until we receive word that Richard and his men are in custody. Last text I got, the teams had the mansion surrounded. No one will get out."

Only a slight hint of relief emerged in Ginger Musgrave's dark eyes. She hugged herself and nodded.

"Thank you, Kyle. Give Bonnie and Gracie my love. Thank them for—"

"I know, I know. Their patience. How many times are you going to fall on the sword, lady?"

"Until I finally rest in peace."

The words caused the air conditioning to bleed deep into Hollie's skin as if her natural shields could not deflect the cold.

A knock on the door made everyone jump. It was Agent Harper holding two pizza boxes and a grocery bag.

Seeing their agitation, he grinned defensively. "Since you're stuck here I had some food delivered. I'll be outside—" he nodded toward the corridor, "—if you need anything. My replacement should be here around ten."

"Please take some of the pizza," Ginger offered. "You got us too much."

"Already had some, ma'am." He smiled and winked before stepping back out of the condo.

"Are we being protected, or are we prisoners?" Hollie asked. She didn't mean for it to sound bitter. It was a sincere question. What was in store for them?

"You want to go, no one is going to stop you," Special Agent Bjornson said. "But if you go and something happens to you, we'll lose our whole case against Mariani. Humor me. Please wait until tomorrow when the dust has settled and we can escort you back home. There are supplies in the rooms. You should have most anything you need, but if you're missing something, just ask Agent Harper."

Ginger walked Kyle to the door and after he left, her back collapsed against the closed panel as anchors of fatigue tugged at her limbs.

"Mom?" Hollie stood in the center of the room— adrift—dizzy with revelation.

Their eyes locked. Eyes that were so similar. Warm, brown, curious gateways for epic imaginations. Mischievous and capable of ferocious love.

Ginger planted her palms on the door and hefted off of it, launching at Hollie until they collided in an embrace so fierce it brought them to their knees. Sobbing, Hollie held on tight—not saying a word—not capable of it. Instead she soaked up lost time with touch and smell, like a babe still in the womb, bonding through presence alone.

Finally drawing back to look at each other through bleary eyes, Ginger smiled, running her fingers through Hollie's hair. "Hermey, you're so beautiful." The shrewd dark eyes shifted, catching movement. "Don't go, Todd." She caught the motion of him discreetly leaving the room.

"Please don't go," she pleaded quietly. "Let's all sit down and eat." Surveying the items on the dining room table, she smiled at the six-pack of beer. "Or drink."

Hollie's stomach let out an unseemly growl. When had they eaten last? They were with the ladies.

The ladies!

Hollie rushed to the front door of the condo and tested the doorknob. It opened. They truly weren't locked in. She poked her head out and saw Agent Harper sitting on a dining room chair tipped back on two legs against the wall. It snapped to the ground and he sprung up at the sight of her.

"Special Agent Harper, I don't see a phone in the condo."

"No ma'am. Honestly, it has nothing to do with safety. It's budget. Everyone has cell phones. They cut out land lines in the condos."

"Can I borrow your phone, or can you place a call for me? I want to call my friends back home. They have to be worried sick."

"Of course," he replied, and then cautioned, "but not too many details. You understand."

Hollie placed the call as swiftly as possible to Maryann, who assured her that she had not been awakened by the call. Even as she spoke, Hollie could hear that the ladies had spent the night in Maryann's condo and were now clawing their way at the phone, talking over each other.

It did Hollie's heart good to hear them, and finally, after several assurances, she hung up the phone with a lighter heart. Todd caught her smile and raised his eyebrows. "And?"

"They're okay. They're sleeping together tonight because they were worried about us."

It was obvious in the warmth of his amber eyes that he was touched. He nodded approvingly and then swept his arm toward the dining room table in invitation.

Hollie dropped down on the chair he pulled out for her. Ginger was already seated across the table and gnawing on a slice of pizza.

"Sorry," she blushed. "I am suddenly famished. More so than I've been in a long time."

They ate, and the conversation fluctuated like the most tumultuous of oceans. Ginger talked of Stuart, and how much she loved him, but knew it was impossible for them to be together after everything that transpired. Hollie wasn't sure how her father would receive this news. He had never married again—never even had a girlfriend. But he was happy. More social than ever in his community. It was all going to take time.

"So, I have a question," Todd inserted, leaning back in his chair, the signs of fatigue only maturing an already handsome face. "Why do you call Hollie, *Hermey*?"

Hollie exchanged a collusive grin with her mother.

"Well—" Ginger wiped some sauce from her lip with the napkin, "—that would be Hermey, the elf, from Rudolph the Red-nosed Reindeer. My daughter was extremely *independent*," she mimicked the elf's voice, "when she was young."

Todd chuckled, his eyes alighting on Hollie with a brief smoldering effect that made her tremble with recollection of what his kisses had felt like.

"She refused help with anything. If I tried to cut her food for her, her little hands would ball up into fists and she would pump them in frustration," Ginger explained, oblivious of the heated exchange of glances. "She'd pretty much earned the name Hermey by the time she was three."

"I guess I can't call her that anymore," Ginger sighed. "She's a beautiful woman now."

"Still independent and headstrong," Todd stated. "The name definitely suits her."

Hollie's face burned. "Dad still calls me that."

The notion seemed to sit well with Ginger as she smiled to herself and spun the bottle of beer between her fingers, not sipping from it.

"What did you do all this time, Mom?" Hollie asked. "Where have you been living?"

Ginger's eyebrows snapped, broken from her reverie. "Well, now that my cover is completely shot, I guess there's no harm in talking about it. I lived in Iowa. Des Moines." Looking up at their incredulous expressions, she chuckled. "Okay, slightly different than the Gulf Coast, but it was nice. It was safe. I started out with administrative tasks. I preferred to work from home—and not be seen. Eventually I became a web designer."

She laughed at Hollie's gaping mouth.

"Seriously. I mean, heck, I spent enough time on the internet, trolling—why not work on it for a living?"

"And no—" Hollie found it awkward to get the question out, "—no male friends along the way?"

The frivolity drained from Ginger's face, leaving it stone cold for a moment. "No. I didn't want to mix with people in public. It became awkward dissuading any sort of advances so I avoided putting myself in any situation like that."

They ate and drank and Ginger took the opportunity to apologize to Todd for leaving the note on his doorstep.

"I knew Hollie was in trouble the moment she pulled into your driveway," she said. "I had to sneak onto your porch under the cover of darkness because I knew Hollie was being followed—I mean, besides by me."

Hollie shook her head. How clueless she had been.

"But, what I didn't know," Ginger continued, "was that she was in such good hands with you."

As inadvertent as the observation was, Hollie's eyes strayed toward Todd's hands splayed flat on the table as he shared the tale of her storming down the side of the road. They were strong hands, doused with a sprinkle of copper hair, and notched with a scar across the middle finger. A ring of bruises surrounded his wrists, and she flinched at the thought of what she'd put him through, yet here he sat, laughing with her mother.

Ginger caught her looking at him and smiled. She slumped back in her chair and swiped her hands over her face, rubbing at the corners of her eyes.

"There's simply too much to talk about for one night, but—" she dropped her hands, "—this time there will be a tomorrow. I'm not losing you again."

Hollie reached across the table and clasped her fingers, running the tip of her pointer over her mother's wedding band.

"I'm going to turn in," Ginger announced over a yawn.

Todd's chair scraped against the carpet as he backed from the table. "I think they said there were two bedrooms. I'll take the couch."

A mirthful snort escaped Ginger's nose.

"I'd like—" Hollie felt conflicted. "I'd like to come with you, Mom." She looked apologetically at Todd, but he blinked the regret away. In the dusky nuance of his glance he conveyed understanding.

How she wanted to wrap her arms around him, and hold him so tight—grateful for his safety—grateful for his support. Yeah, those were noble sentiments, but a flame had been lit between them, and it had been forced to smolder for a prolonged time. Would it ignite into a full blaze or would this stretch make it fade into ash?

CHAPTER NINETEEN

Resting against the pillow, Todd's arms were crooked behind his head. He lie prone, staring up at the wedge of light on the ceiling that pierced a gap in the drapes. 2:30 AM, the digital clock read.

So much had transpired in such a short time. They had only retired to their rooms a half-hour ago, but it was impossible to switch off the adrenaline. He tried to close his eyes, but every time he did, he saw Hollie with her arms bound and her dark eyes rounded with fear.

His eyes flew open again. The wedge of light was more placid than what lurked under closed lids.

Were they sleeping now? The Musgrave women? Even his eyes had blurred at the sight of them launching together in the middle of the living room in a flurry of anger, love, and loss. It was an emotional reunion to clog the throat of even the most stoic of bystanders.

And that's what he was. A bystander. The proverbial third wheel. But by virtue of proximity he was ingrained in the fallout. It didn't matter, though. He wanted to be here for Hollie. Even if it just meant an arm across the shoulder. Words of encouragement. Protection at any future trials.

There had been no one to stir up such senses—no one to want to comfort—no one to want to protect—no one to want to hold, and he wasn't going to surrender those desires easily.

The click of the bedroom door had him bolting upright as a slim shadow passed through the doorway.

The lights of the adjacent hotel poked through the gap in the drapes to reveal half of the stealth figure.

"Hollie," he whispered anxiously. "Is everything okay?"

Her profile nodded and to his surprise he felt her climb onto the bed and slide alongside him, propping her head up on an elbow.

"In the lobby this afternoon—when you went to the bathroom—" she started in a hushed voice. "If you could have seen my face. I had the most ridiculous smile on. I stared at the closed door, and just couldn't wait for you to return."

A rustle of air stirred inside his lungs, a pent-up reciprocal notion.

"All I wanted to do was get upstairs and kiss you," she continued. "In a way that the ladies shouldn't see."

Another pent-up portion of his body stirred.

"Your mom," he cleared his throat. "She needs you right now."

"Yes."

He could see the outline of a pert nose tipped up in thought.

"My mom and I have a long path ahead of us. It can't be tackled tonight. Tonight, I wanted to crawl in bed with the woman I lost when I was ten years old. Instead, I held an older, compellingly familiar version of that woman. We held each other…and then she fell asleep. She is exhausted. I'll go back before she wakes. She won't even know I've left."

"I'd know if you left me," Todd murmured.

He had been aware of every shift of her body as they lied on the couch in her condo.

Had that been only yesterday?

The thought was interrupted by the softest sensation. A feathery brush of fingers on the bare skin of his forearm.

"I am *so* sorry." The words were torn from her chest—wrenched with a rawness that scraped her throat.

"For God's sake, Hollie." His voice was just as rough. "Why?"

"*Why*?" she echoed loudly, and then swallowed her outburst, mindful of the silence.

"Look what I've done to you. I nearly got you killed. And now you're trapped in here—"

Her fingers bit into his arm.

"Last I checked," he said. "I make my own decisions. When you were taken—" the recollection still caused his pulse to jump, "—I could have said, *Oh, hey, this is trouble, I'm going back home*."

In the soft light he caught a flash of her teeth as she smiled at his impression. His own lips quirked in response.

"But it was too late for me. You talk about when I went into that bathroom. If you had seen the idiot smiling at himself in the mirror in there."

His arm slipped around her. "Life is complicated. I mean, look at both of us. We've both seen too much drama. We've both experienced loss."

"And you wanted to push me away because of what you've experienced. Everyone in general—you wanted nothing to do with anyone."

"Yeah," he conceded. "But, you're damn cute."

Caught off guard, Hollie snorted into his shoulder. Her palm landed on his chest and lingered there, slowly drifting up, gently tracing the curve between his neck and shoulder with her fingertips.

"I like—" she hesitated. "I like to touch you." Her fingers continued to roam, across his collarbone and down his sternum, their trek leaving a path of electrical charges.

"I like when you touch me," he murmured huskily.

They were splayed out on the bed, Hollie stretched out beside him. Her hip prodded against him, and one of her long legs slipped atop his. Shifting his angle, that leg dropped in between his thighs as he swallowed a groan.

"Hold me, Todd. Hold me so tight that I can't even breathe."

Her arms linked around his neck and her hip nudged closer, winding her leg in like a python until every inch of her was plied against him in a way that took intimacy to a whole new level.

Mercy.

"I've got you, Hol," he whispered into silky hair that smelled musty from the restaurant. "I'm not letting go."

She nestled closer, seemingly intent on burrowing into him. He clutched her tight, kissing that hair and whispering incoherent assurances.

Certain that she wanted comfort and support he was startled when the glossy haven shifted and he felt the ethereal trace of lips climb his throat. What were initially tentative caresses turned into long, sweeping passes, one of which he felt the moist tip of a tongue brush his hot skin. Pumping the muscles in his neck in an attempt to check himself, he growled in defeat and dipped his chin to catch her mouth in a hungry kiss. Her lips parted in welcome as tiny whimpers of need crept from the bottom of her throat.

The kiss became wanton and his hands slipped down her back, cupping the precious curves of her rear. In one fluid move, she straddled his lap and he latched onto her hips, hauling her tight against him.

"Hollie," the word rumbled from his chest.

A glossy veil of hair ringed his face and stroked his neck as she gripped his shirt with tight fists and unconsciously began to nudge him with her hips.

Todd reached up and cupped her face in his palms, reluctantly drawing the seductive lips away.

"Baby, you have no idea how much I want you." He averted his head and whispered into her ear. "But I don't want our first time to be like this. Quiet, because your mother and 52 FBI agents are nearby."

"I want you to make all the noise you need to when the time comes," he said, feeling her body quiver. "And I don't think there's any way in hell I'm going to be quiet if I make love to you."

Hollie sat back, still fastened across his lap. The wedge of light dissected half of her face, revealing half of a grin, and one sleepy and seductive eye.

"Was I too aggressive?" she teased, but there seemed a trace of naïve sincerity to her plea.

Todd sat up, his arms locked around her hips preventing her from climbing off. He found that blue half of her mouth and brushed his lips against it, tasting her until she opened for him.

"Save some of that aggression for when I'm not exhausted."

She budged ever so slightly.

"You're not *that* tired," she observed wryly.

"Ummm, that much is true."

With a sensitive amount of friction, Hollie slowly slid off of him. She nestled alongside his body, disregarding her pillow by tucking her head into the crook of his shoulder as he wrapped his arm around her. Her arm looped across his chest.

"This will be the second time we have slept together," she murmured sleepily into his shirt.

"Next time we'll make it stick," he teased.

Hollie sucked in her breath and then let it out in a pleasing string of giggles.

"All right. If not here, tell me where," she commanded dreamily. "Take my mind away from this and tell me where."

Todd smiled against her hair.

"The beach," he answered softly. "Your condo. My farmhouse. The couch in your lobby."

"Todd!" She protested with a chuckle.

"Anywhere. Everywhere, Hollie."

Drawing patterns on his chest with the tip of her finger she asked quietly, "What if I'm not very good?"

Todd reached for that spiraling finger and clasped it in his hand. "There's no good or bad. It's what *we* make of it. It's ours."

For a moment she remained silent, and then he heard her soft whisper.

"You're tempting me to fall in love with you."

An unusual smile worked at his lips—a motion that went so much deeper than a reflexive muscle gesture.

"Am I, now?"

Effects of the past 24 hours nagged at him. Burning pain around his wrists. Aches in his shoulder blades. A sore jaw. Anxiety at the close proximity to near death.

Holding Hollie tight against him as sleep claimed them, his last conscious thought was that she wasn't the only one being tempted.

Pounding at the door jolted them awake.

Hollie's skull cracked against Todd's chin as she leapt from the bed, standing at its side with her head swiveling in an attempt to orient herself.

Todd rose and approached the door, motioning her back—more for protection than decorum.

A dour-looking Special Agent Bjornson stood there with one hand up high on the doorframe, the other locked around his cell phone, taking his eyes from it only after he realized the door was open.

"We have an issue," was all he said.

Todd felt Hollie's fingers latch onto his arm as she moved in beside him.

"The teams that surrounded Mariani's mansion last night—" Kyle started, his attention still divided by the cell phone "—well, they were successful in rounding up all his men. They got the man you call Chauncey, and the other guy who looked like a mountain."

Todd glimpsed beyond Special Agent Bjornson into the living room where Ginger sat with her hands clasped between her knees, her expression tense as she spoke to Special Agent Harper, who looked like he'd had little sleep.

"What happened?" Todd demanded.

Kyle Bjornson finally settled the cellphone against his thigh and met Todd's eyes. The older agent's eyes were bloodshot.

"Mariani got away."

"Of course he did," Hollie muttered in alarm.

"Hollie."

Seeing her daughter, Ginger rose from her chair with plaintive eyes ringed by shadows. Hollie gave Todd's arm a quick squeeze and then slipped through the doorway to join her mother on the couch.

When he was alone with Agent Bjornson, Todd leaned in and spoke abruptly.

"What does this mean? How are you going to protect them?"

Both men angled their heads to gaze at the women consumed in anxious conversation.

"You're going to have to stay in here longer. We will bring clothes and any essentials you need. I've called Agent Harper back in to stay with you."

"What's he had, three hours of sleep?" Todd mused, noticing the weary stance inside the front door.

"About the same as me," Kyle replied. "Look, we have our men on it. You'll be safe here. The airports are covered, including private planes."

Kyle stepped back as Todd edged past him, offering a quick nod at Agent Harper. He placed his hand on Hollie's shoulder, feeling the tension there. Beside her, her mother refused to look up.

"All my fault," she moaned. "You're both in jeopardy and it's all my fault."

"No one is in jeopardy," Kyle refuted. "We have this under control."

No one believed him, as evidenced by the skeptical look on Agent Harper's unshaven face.

"I'm heading out now," Kyle continued, either unaware, or purposely ignoring their reactions. "I'll call Agent Harper as soon as I have more information."

Dressed in the same black suit pants and white button-down short-sleeved shirt he had on when he left yesterday, Kyle Bjornson walked past everyone without a glance, only flinching at the doorway when he heard Ginger whisper, "three weeks."

Hollie kept her arm around her mother, consoling her, while Todd walked toward the window.

"Uh—better not do that," Agent Harper warned.

The cautionary note made Todd pause and reevaluate the casement window. They were on the fourth floor, but there was an eight-story hotel directly across from them. Sunrise reflected off the glass architecture, making him see spots.

"I made coffee," Harper stated, reaching for the pot to top-off his half-filled mug.

Todd walked into the galley-styled kitchen and grabbed two mugs hanging from hooks above the sink. He poured a cup for Hollie, feeling a pleasant satisfaction that he knew how she liked her coffee.

"I'm worried about them," he said to Harper. "How long can you keep them in here?"

"Keep *all* of you, you mean? Not long. You'll have to be moved to a safer location."

"I thought this was supposed to be safe."

Harper leaned his hip against the counter. "It is. It is. But a good number of our agents are out looking for Mariani now. Kyle doesn't like you being in Tampa."

"So, what?" Todd frowned. "Are you shipping us off to Iowa as well?"

Staring down into his coffee, the agent shrugged.

"Not my call. Let's just get the guy."

Todd raised his mug in salute. "How'd he get away? I mean, you had the mansion surrounded. You caught everyone else."

"By boat."

Todd and Harper jerked at Ginger's interruption.

"That would be my guess," she said.

Hollie came into the narrow kitchen and wrapped her hands around the mug on the counter, offering Todd a quick smile of thanks. Her eyes returned to him and he saw a trace of longing for the hours they had shared last night.

"There would have been agents on the dock," Harper argued.

"Did you lose anyone last night?"

It was odd to hear such a petite woman, Hollie's mother, so casually inquire about loss of life. He could see that Hollie was startled by it as well. But to imagine what Ginger Musgrave had witnessed in her life—the sacrifices she made—these facets earned her the right to be callous.

"I'm not at liberty to say."

It wasn't necessary. The guarded eyes and sloped shoulders revealed that all hadn't gone as planned in the FBI's raid last night.

"I've got to get in touch with work," Hollie declared. "I was supposed to be on site today. That's all you need is my firm filing a missing person report." She shook her head. "And they'd do it. I never miss a job."

Agent Harper sighed and hauled his cell phone out of his pants pocket. His thumb scrolled through texts as he blatantly ignored her complaint—or, so it would seem. He then grabbed the device in both hands and typed a quick message. After a brief delay he nodded at the screen.

"You can make a quick call from this phone," he said. "Brief, and no details."

Hollie perked up. "Great. All I need is my voice mail. I don't have to speak to anyone."

Some of the tension left Harper's face. He handed over the phone.

"I have work commitments that need to be addressed too," Todd mentioned while Hollie walked out of the kitchen for some privacy.

"Hey!" Harper called after her, beckoning her back with his hand. "Sorry." He didn't look contrite. "But I have to hear."

She wrinkled her nose and hunched over the outside of the service bar.

"Look," Harper turned his attention to Todd. "Just be patient. I'm sure Special Agent Bjornson will move you by the end of the day."

"When did you come back here?" Todd asked conversationally.

"It was around 3 in the morning when we all got the confirmation that Mariani had escaped, and yes—" he looked at Ginger, "—his boat is gone. Which is a good thing. Easier to track than wheels."

Ginger shook her head, unimpressed, and Todd echoed her lack of enthusiasm. Harper was giving them false assurances. His pained expression confirmed it.

"*No!*"

Hollie disappeared from the other side of the bar as Todd sprang around the counter to find her crouched down, clutching the phone to her ear, her breath escaping in rapid successive bursts.

"Hol." He stooped down beside her, clutching her arms. "What is it?"

Powerless, she pressed a button on the keypad and handed the phone to him.

Todd hefted the device to his ear and heard, "You have one new message…"

"Hollie? It's Maryann." A lengthy pause with an unidentifiable rustle in the background. *"Zere iz a man here. He—he has a gun. He wants you to come to us. He says you and your mother. Your mother?"* Maryann's voice trilled, and Todd felt his stomach clutch in panic. *"He is wiz me and Frank and Flo. He says to come—"* a brief pause, and she hastened, *"—but don't listen, Hollie. Stay safe. Don't—"*

The message ended and Todd couldn't see the phone before his eyes. Bursts of red anger blinded him.

The ladies.

No.

Hell no.

This bastard was not going to mess with the ladies.

"What?" Harper demanded, yanking the phone out of Todd's hand.

Hollie haltingly relayed the message as the agent got on the phone, listening to her in one ear and barking at someone on the other end.

It was pandemonium from that point on.

Special Agent Bjornson arrived, trying to assure a distraught Hollie that agents were on their way to Harbor Breeze. He was still in the same suit pants and white shirt, but the shirt was now tarnished by the trail of a hasty breakfast behind the steering wheel.

Ginger was busy arguing that she needed to go, as she was the person Richard was really after. Kyle refused to listen.

"Look, I'm just here as a courtesy to check on you," he said, already edging toward the door, "but I have to get over there."

At the doorway he stopped and addressed Agent Harper. "They are not to leave. No phone calls. We will address Hollie's messages here on out in case he tries to make further contact—which I'm sure he will—arrogant bastard."

Hollie and Ginger crammed forward, still firing off demands, but Kyle simply held up his hand in dismissal.

"It's going to be okay," were his parting words as he hustled out.

Agent Harper now filled the doorway, his face dour, his arms crossed in deterrence. "Go sit down. There's nothing you can do, but wait."

"I'm tired of waiting," Hollie countered.

Harper glared at her. "I'm tired too. Your chance of survival is much better here."

Some of Hollie's ire was tempered, but Todd saw her fists still curled up as she paced back and forth across the living room floor. Ginger's weary eyes followed the human metronome.

Harper's phone rang, as everyone's eyes alighted on him. His half of the conversation consisted of one-syllable answers. Finally he hung up and met the expectant faces. Wiping a hand across his bristled jaw he closed his eyes and said, "Richard has them held in a unit on the third floor. Kyle says it's the unit next to yours." Harper looked at Hollie.

Hollie crumbled down onto the couch and Todd wrapped his hands around her shoulders for support.

"Our team has been able to confirm that all three women are alive," he assured.

The shoulders in Todd's grip quaked.

"Thank God," Hollie whispered.

"The unit is surrounded, Miss Musgrave," Harper stated. "The negotiation team will work on him. This is all positive news."

"Positive?" Hollie gripped the edge of the couch and gaped at him.

"Yes," he argued feebly. "At least the man is contained."

Feeling as if the muscles beneath his palms were about to snap, Todd leaned over and said, "Come with me into the other room. You need a change of scenery."

The last statement was uttered with a frank glare in Harper's direction. He didn't blame the guy. He was just doing his job. But frustration levels were off the charts, including his own.

Looking at him incredulously out of the corner of her eye, Hollie followed him down the hall, rounding on him as soon as the bedroom door was shut.

"I can't do this. Those ladies are my family. They are always there for me. If anything happens to them—" Her lips quivered and her voice faded.

"I know," he assured quietly. "There's no way in hell I want to put you in harm's way, so I will represent you. I'm going to find a way out of here and get to Harbor Breeze. If the ladies hear a familiar voice, it may give them some comfort. I'm sure they're terrified being pinned in on all sides by unfamiliar people."

Hollie stared at him like he'd grown three heads.

"No," was all she said.

"Richard Mariani could care less about me. I will be fine." *Unless I get shot.*

"No," she repeated. "And how would you get past our guard dog? Do you think that front door is still unlocked?"

"Doubt it, but there's always the fainting trick."

"No way will that work. And no way am I allowing it. Unless—"

"Unless?"

"Unless I'm going with you."

Before the denial could fall from his mouth her hands were on her hips and her lips were clamped in a non-negotiable line.

"Todd, they're my family."

It was the raw desperation in her voice that did him in. He understood. He didn't approve, but he understood. And as long as he was there with her...

She read his acquiescence before he said anything and lunged forward to wrap her arms around his neck.

"This has been a nightmare," she murmured against his ear, "but this nightmare brought me to you."

Todd's arms slipped around her back. "Gee, that makes me feel awesome."

Hollie pulled back, her smile dropping with each centimeter of retreat.

"Okay," she said. "Now send my mother in here and tell her how *distraught* I am."

His eyebrow inched up in collusion. "You're a piece of work, Hollie Musgrave."

"Is that a compliment?" she asked just inside the doorway.

With his hand on the knob he stopped and touched his lips to her forehead. "Oh, it is. It definitely is."

Out in the living room, Todd found Ginger snapping through television stations, barely spending enough time to register what was on each. Finally reaching the group of news channels, she slowed down to scan each headline before moving on. He leaned over the back of the couch and muttered, "Your daughter asked for you. She's—" he didn't want to alarm the woman, but he quoted, "she's distraught."

Harper looked up from his seat at the dining room table, unfazed by this revelation.

Worried, Ginger rose hastily, but caught a glimpse of Todd's eyebrows hefting and recognized it as a signal of some sort. She hastened into the bedroom and closed the door behind her.

Leaning against the back of the couch, Todd watched the current news program, but there was nothing about mobsters holding little old ladies hostage. He glanced over at Harper who was staring at his phone in a near trance, waiting for it to do something.

"Hey, is there any more coffee left?"

Without looking up, Agent Harper nodded.

Todd moved past him, eyeing the front door in the tight foyer. If it was unlocked he could reach it and be out before Harper could dislodge his legs from under the table. But how far would he get?

A blood-curdling scream sounded from the other room as Agent Harper knocked over the dining room chair and launched down the hall.

Hollie stuck her head out the door, her face white and panicked.

"She's trying to climb out the window!"

The delivery was so genuine, Todd nearly sprinted after him, but there was a slight negative shake of Hollie's head as Harper pushed her aside and ran into the room. The door slammed shut behind him and Hollie was sprinting toward the front door, summoning Todd with a wave of her hand.

Vaguely aware of shouting behind him, Todd joined Hollie and they reached the front door simultaneously, testing the knob. It was locked. With a bleat of frustration, Hollie tried the bolts and her efforts worked. The door opened and they were out in the long corridor, sprinting in the opposite direction of the elevators. Instead, they launched toward an EXIT sign where a concrete staircase zigzagged its way to the ground floor.

On the second floor, Todd heard the door slam open above them and Agent Harper's command to stop echoed through the stairwell. This only spurred Hollie on as she leapt down four steps to hit the ground floor. Todd caught up as they crashed through an emergency exit into the bright Florida sunshine. There was no time for blinding disorientation, though. Todd took the lead and prompted Hollie into the parking lot, tugging her down behind a car only a few spots from the door.

Agent Harper barreled through the exit a moment later, pausing to look left and right. To his left was a grass division and then the parking lot for the hotel next door. On his right was a sidewalk leading around the condominium complex, and eventually to the street. He launched to his right, yelling into his cellphone as he ran with his head twisting like an owl. As soon as he reached the far corner of the building, Todd and Hollie darted in the opposite direction, making their way toward the hotel.

Closing in on the high rise, Hollie said, "We can find public transportation in there. All I want is to get to Harbor Breeze."

Todd threw a look over his shoulder and nearly snapped a femur as he ground to a halt and pivoted around in an attempt to shield her.

"Run, Hollie!" he cried without looking back. "Get inside!"

Standing in the middle of the parking lot was a lanky man in suit pants and a satin shirt stained dark with perspiration. Silver hair hung in gelled curls about his ears, and even at this distance Todd could see the steely resentment in the man's eyes. He also saw the revolver in his hand, the gun pointed at Agent Harper who stood with his chest pounding and his hands slightly raised.

"No!"

The cry came from directly behind Todd.

Dammit, Hollie. Run!

She had enough headway that she could reach the hotel doorway. It was only a back entrance, with no foot traffic to speak of, or any audience like the lobby, but she would be inside. Safe.

"Come here, Hollie," Richard Mariani beckoned in a polished voice that carried over the plane taking off from the nearby airport. Warring gulls squawked overhead as they staked claim over one of the hotel's dumpsters.

To Todd's dismay he heard Hollie's tread angle in beside him.

"Why didn't you run?" he demanded under his breath.

"My battle," she whispered in response. "Not yours. Not Agent Harper's."

"Dammit, Hollie."

"That's a good girl, Hollie," Richard commended in a near sing-song voice. "A simple exchange. This fine representative of the Federal Bureau for you. And, also the promise that your boyfriend will be safe." He shrugged casually. "Seems fair, no?"

"My friends," she pressed, slightly breathless.

Agent Harper leaned to his right—a nearly imperceptible motion, as if the wind had tugged at his short-sleeved shirt.

"Eh," Mariani counselled, reaching out to grab the man's arm, while thrusting the gun tight up against the side of his rib cage. "In due time, Mr. Federal Agent," he chided.

Ignoring the jibe, Agent Harper growled, "Don't go with him, Miss Musgrave."

Hollie stood rigid at Todd's side.

"Step back, Hol," he rasped. "Fairness. Safe. You know those aren't words in this guy's vocabulary."

Another plane rumbled overhead, drowning out any rebuttal from the man holding the gun. As soon as it had passed, Richard raised a graying eyebrow in anticipation.

"I'm not moving until you tell me what happened to my friends."

Richard shrugged, perspiration beading up on his forehead.

"I have no idea. I was never there. I sent over one of the few men I could trust after this guy's team raided my home." He jabbed the barrel into Harper's shirt making the agent flinch and cough. "You all just assumed it was me. "And you think I don't know every safe house the FBI has in Tampa? This building was my second try. Imagine how pleased I was to see you come storming out of the building. It saved me the elevator trip."

His grin was forced, his patience and veneer both wilting in the heat.

"Get over here, Hollie," he ordered. "You and I are going to go get your mother. I understand from this fine agent that she is confined upstairs. How convenient."

"Don't," Todd warned her. "It's a no-win scenario. Don't give him what he wants."

Sunlight glinted off of the stony eyes that latched onto him. The barrel of the gun swung with those eyes, and in that split-second Todd caught a glimpse of Richard Mariani's inner-self—as if the flesh and blood melted to reveal the savage lurking beneath.

"I *am* going to move," Hollie rasped. "*Now!*"

They lurched apart, Hollie tripping and falling to the tar as Todd rocked to his left, jolted by the sound of the gunshot. For a moment it felt like there was no sound. No distant traffic. No airport activity. No seagulls. No breathing. Just a lethal hush.

Todd searched for Hollie and found her nearby, rolling onto her backside and propping herself up with her arms behind her. His hands grappled down his own body, taking a quick assessment.

And in all that time, Richard Mariani stood still. The man's eyes rolled up into his head like the shark that he was, and he collapsed in slow motion as if each bone in his lower extremities was broken one by one. Once he hit the ground, Todd could see Ginger standing ten feet behind him, her arms still extended, their grip locked around a revolver.

"Son of a—" Harper grunted, nearly tackling her to regain control of the weapon.

Todd launched at the crumpled form of Richard Mariani, prying the gun from inflexible fingers, wary of the black eyes that reflected the sky above them.

Despite the growing pool of blood that extended into the cracks of the parking lot, Todd walked backwards with his aim fixed on the inert figure as he reached out with one hand to haul Hollie off the ground. She came up alongside him, her arms wrapping around his waist and her nose lodging into his chest.

"I thought he shot you," she moaned.

He squeezed her with one arm, dropping his head into her hair.

"Hollie!" Ginger cried, breaking away from Agent Harper and charging toward them.

She hesitated when she reached Richard, staring down at him. She clutched her arms around her stomach and doubled over, trembling from dry heaves.

"Mom!"

Hollie ran to her mother who was still hunched over.

Agent Harper approached, and muttered, "Give me that."

Todd handed him Richard's gun, but kept a wary eye on Mariani even though the man's eyes were locked open, glaring in condemnation at the gates of Hell.

CHAPTER TWENTY

They stood in the crowded receiving area at Tampa International, waiting for the arrival of flight 165 from Phoenix. Ginger Musgrave wrapped her fingers around the hanging rope barricade as if she needed the support. Hollie knew it was to conceal the quake of her fingers. She placed an arm around her mother's shoulder and squeezed encouragingly.

Even Hollie felt a twinge of nerves as a new wave of arrivals exited the shuttle tram. Her parents had already spoken on the phone—several times. Each call was followed up with a private conversation between Hollie and her father—a debriefing of sorts—a buffer to allow Stuart Musgrave to vent—to acclimate. By the third call he was booking a flight to Tampa and Hollie knew it was going to be okay.

Neither of her parents had ever remarried. So much ended that day on the bay when Virginia Musgrave *fell* off the chartered boat. It was going to take a long time to reconcile that. But they were taking the first step.

Another tram arrived, the doors sliding open and a new set of tourists, businessmen, and family poured out. Hollie recognized her father's white hair a minute or two before her mother, despite her mother having seen recent pictures. He was a tall man, but time had narrowed the gap between his shoulders and the rest of the world.

The snowy hair clashed with the healthy Arizona tan. Shrewd blue eyes scanned the crowd, settling on

Hollie with a bright smile. Then that eager gaze dropped to the woman beside her. Hollie felt the moment her mother made the connection. A jolt snapped through the limb next to her and she heard her mother whisper, "I'm scared."

"There's no rush, Mom. Just say hello."

It was doubtful her mother heard her over the joyous reunions going on around them. Someone had brought balloons, and one bobbed in front of Hollie's face.

When the string was pulled taut, and the balloon gone, Stuart Musgrave stood before them. He wore jeans and a pale blue polo shirt, with a travelling bag hanging from his shoulder.

"Hermey," he said, pulling her into his arms. "You keep getting more beautiful. Am I going to meet this man of yours?"

Hollie beamed. "Yep. He's waiting for you back at the condo."

Todd knew that the ladies needed to make this trip alone. But his parting kiss, and promise to be waiting, was all the encouragement Hollie needed. She couldn't wait to get back to him.

But her mother—well, looking at her now—Hollie realized the encouragement she had provided was floundering.

This morning Hollie had taken her mother to the salon where they put highlights in her hair, auburn streaks that warmed the dark brown shoulder-length tresses. The dress was new as well. A violet wraparound that revealed a slim figure sorely in need of some ice cream and TV nights.

"Ginger?" Stuart's voice cracked as he hesitated before her.

"Stu," she replied, nodding with brimming eyes.

It was an awkward silence, as if they were stuck in a transparent capsule inside this boisterous throng. Several seconds passed and then the blue gaze misted.

"You look beautiful too," he murmured.

Determined to be stoic, Ginger took a step as Stuart took one too. One more stride and they were joined in a self-conscious embrace that soon lost its inhibition.

Hollie could only stand back and watch with a cautious smile that blossomed as she witnessed her parents together.

It was a party.

Granted, it was one night off before a long road of healing and legalities. In the government's eyes, Hollie's mother was still Gina Horvath. Her father's answer to that had been to get married...*again*.

Special Agent Bjornson warned that Richard Mariani's death did remove the threat, but they were to remain cautious. And there were interrogations and paperwork still outstanding.

When the FBI arrived at the scene, they discovered Special Agent Harper standing over Richard Mariani's body. It was confirmed that his weapon was responsible. In the chaos of those initial moments, Harper had neglected to draw attention to the fact that he had not properly secured his witnesses. Nor did he dispute the initial observation that he had shot Mariani.

"No, no." Todd sat beside Hollie on the lobby couch, rubbing his stomach and waving off Francine's advances. "Please. I can't."

The weapon of choice was a box of Baklava from the Greek bakery down the street.

"You're too skinny," she chided with a plump-cheeked smile.

"Not after tonight," he defended, spreading his arm out to indicate the buffet of goodies across the coffee table and entrance bar.

At that bar, Hollie's mother and father stood, each holding a plastic cup of punch. Ginger laughed at something he said as Tony Maillis reached over and topped off each of their cups.

Flo and Maryann chatted on the adjacent loveseat, Maryann catching Hollie's glance and rolling her eyes and clapping her fingers like a bird's beak. It was a party. For once, Florence would not shut up.

Hollie felt Todd's arm slip around her and she leaned into his side, reaching up to place a soft kiss on his cheek. His head turned into hers so that their lips could meet.

"It's the Greek food," Francine pronounced, hanging over her walker. "An aphrodisiac, I tell you."

"Frank," Maryann called out. "Can you help me pack up zese croissants?"

As Francine ambled over, Maryann leaned back and winked at Hollie.

"I think that's our cue," Todd whispered against her ear, causing a pleasant eruption of goosebumps.

"Oh?"

"Mmm. Come—" he rose and held his hand out, "—let's take a walk."

Hollie snatched that hand with a smile and climbed up next to him, steadying herself against his chest. It was just an opportunity to touch it. He looked so attractive in the white button-down shirt with the sleeves rolled up, showing off strong forearms. His tawny hair was dark with moisture from a recent swim in the Harbor Breeze pool, which had probably been a designed excuse to get her into a bikini.

Todd guided her toward the rear of the lobby, passing by her parents with a quick grin. As soon as he was past them her parents gave her a thumbs-up behind his back.

The poolside veranda was lit with outdated tiki torches casting light on palm fronds that fluttered in the breeze. Round bulbs inside the pool made the blue depths shimmer.

"You know—" he took both of her hands, searching her face, "—I'm going to have to go back. I've got work—"

Her smile fell and her eyes dropped to the cement. "I know. Of course you do."

A finger caught the bottom of her chin and lifted it. "I don't want to leave you."

Hope blossomed in her chest, but she kept it in check.

"I don't want you to go," she whispered.

The flames from the torches danced in his eyes.

"What if I sold it?" he asked. "That farmhouse is a bad omen. I can sell it. I can move—my work—it's not at a desk. It can travel with me."

Hollie finally wrenched her gaze away from his. The lights of the causeway painted a fanciful trail across the waterway, and in the distance the towers of the Clearwater Beach hotels dotted the horizon.

"The farmhouse," she said. "It will always be inside me. Maybe the dreams are coming to an end— and with them, the memories." She looked through the glass, into the lobby where her parents were leaning in close together and still smiling. "But, I have new memories there." She looked back at Todd. "I met you there. We braved the cellar together."

"We ate pizza and drank beer."

She laughed. "Do you know how much I would like to be there right now, eating pizza and drinking beer with you?"

"No." He smiled. "Tell me."

"Besides the obvious that I want to be with you— there is a peace to that place. No traffic. No lights."

"Quiet it is, but tell me more about how much you want to be with me."

Hollie reached up and looped her arms around his neck. "I'd rather show you."

"Mmm."

Wide hands scooped her bottom and pressed her tight against him.

"I always wanted to be a snowbird," he murmured against her lips. "We can compromise for a while until we decide where we'll live."

"Where *we'll* live," she repeated with a smile.

"Damn woman, if you haven't guessed by now that I'm ridiculously in love with you—"

Hollie reached up and shushed him with her fingertips.

"Snowbirds we'll be. For now. Until we settle down with five dogs." She replaced her fingers with her lips. "Because I love you too."

Thank you for taking time to read DISTANT MEMORY. If you enjoyed it, please consider telling your friends or posting a short review. Word of mouth is an author's best friend and earns you hugs!

Sincerely,
Maureen A. Miller

ABOUT THE AUTHOR

USA TODAY bestselling author, Maureen A. Miller worked in the software industry for fifteen years. She crawled around plant floors in a hard hat and safety glasses hooking up computers to behemoth manufacturing machines. The job required extensive travel. The best form of escapism during those lengthy airport layovers became writing.

Maureen's first novel, WIDOW'S TALE, earned her a Golden Heart nomination in Romantic Suspense. After that she became hooked to the genre. However, recently, Maureen branched out into the Young Adult market with the popular BEYOND and BENEATH Series. To her it was still Romantic Suspense…just in different worlds!

Find more about Maureen at
www.MaureenAMiller.com